Fracking Justice

To Sue:
Enjoy this and
remember it's
fiction for
least so,
All the best,
Fitzgerald
ne lo true
(even if
distant!)

6-2-15

FRACKING JUSTICE

BY THE AUTHOR OF *THE FRACKING WAR*

MICHAEL J. FITZGERALD

MILL CITY PRESS, MINNEAPOLIS

Copyright © 2015 by Michael Fitzgerald

Mill City Press, Inc.
322 First Avenue N, 5th floor
Minneapolis, MN 55401
612.455.2293
www.millcitypublishing.com

This is a work of fiction. Names, characters, brands, media, and incidents are either the product of the author's imagination or are used fictitiously. Any references to historical events, real people, or real locales are used fictitiously. Other names, characters, places, and incidents are the product of the author's imagination and any resemblance to actual events or locales or persons, living or dead, is coincidental. The author acknowledges the trademarked status and trademark owners of various products referenced in this work of fiction, which have been used without permission. The publication/use of these trademarks is not authorized, associated with, or sponsored by the trademark owners.

All rights to republication of this work are reserved. No part of this publication may be reproduced, stored in or introduced into a retrieval system, or transmitted, in any form, or by any means (electronic, mechanical, photocopying, recording, or otherwise) without the prior written permission of the copyright owner. For permission or information on foreign, audio, or other rights, contact the author at authormichaeljfitzgerald.com.

ISBN-13: 978-1-63413-555-9
LCCN: 2015907728

Cover design by Amy E. Colburn
Typeset by MK Ross

Printed in the United States of America

For Joseph and Yvonne

Acknowledgments

Writing a novel for me is solitary business.
I rarely discuss specific aspects of what I am writing with anyone.

But when my novel manuscript is completed, it takes a literary village to bring it into readers' hands.

Fracking Justice was no exception.

This book – like its predecessor *The Fracking War* – would not have made it into print or e-book form if it wasn't for the unwavering support and encouragement of my editor, best friend and wife, Sylvia Fox.

Through the drafts and redrafts, she kept me on track and moving forward, even as the sometimes-dark portions of this novel threatened to overcome me with angst. Her willingness to let me rant about the justice and injustice-related issues I researched in the course of this novel made it possible for me to write every day – but without my head exploding.

She also was amazingly patient in dealing with her husband-writer-husband, who like all writers sees their words as precious gems, not wanting to discard a single one.

Special thanks also goes to the five beta readers of this novel – Sylvia, Peter Mantius, Billy Pylypciw, Wrexie

Bardaglio and Sjoukje Schipstra – each of whom contributed their time and energy reading the first drafts to help me polish the manuscript.

Each offered thoughtful suggestions for strengthening parts of the novel and encouraged me to get the book into readers' hands as soon as possible.

Thanks also to professional book editor Darlene Bordwell, who was kind enough to lend her talents, too, giving the book a close read.

I would be remiss if I didn't thank the Finger Lakes wineries for making the finest Reisling wines anywhere in the world, a wine that helped at the end of many a long day of writing.

And lastly, I would like to thank my four children, Jason, Anne, Dustin and Dylan and my many friends who encouraged me to take this sequel from idea to fruition.

I leave it to them and readers if there is real justice in *Fracking Justice*.

Watkins Glen, New York
February 2015

Preface

The idea for writing Fracking Justice rolled around in my head even as I was finishing the manuscript for its predecessor novel, *The Fracking War*.

In researching *The Fracking War*, I ran across many instances where it seemed that people objecting to the use of hydrofracking technology to extract natural gas and oil were being targeted by the oil and gas industry as enemies – way out of proportion to reasonable protests taking place.

Some strains of that over-the-top industry reaction to protests can be seen in chapters of *The Fracking War*, too.

But evidence that law enforcement agencies at all levels are increasingly siding with industry – well beyond simply protecting private property rights – helped prompt me to write this book.

The rapid, almost out-of-control spread of hydrofracking technology has encouraged an amazing culture of corporate greed. It has also spawned an attitude that anyone who challenges a company's desire to drill, extract (or dump at will) should be quashed, not listened to.

The civil rights of protesters be damned, it seems, if they conflict with corporate goals.

In the months *Fracking Justice* was taking shape, a

frightening militarization of police forces across the U.S. – some of it funded by the federal government, some of it by the gas and oil industry – became a public issue as police began dealing with legal, relatively benign protest activities in ways more common to military dictatorships than democracies.

In the Finger Lakes area of New York – where a regional anti-fracking, anti-gas storage movement has been building for years – it has become common for supporters of hydrofracking and the storing liquid propane gas (and natural gas) in unlined salt caverns to label protesters as *eco-terrorists*.

Fracking Justice was set in small towns in Pennsylvania and New York because, at the local level, the influences of industry, examples of corruption and displays of heroics play out closer to the surface than trying to delve into the byzantine corridors of our nation's capital.

It's at the local level where justice – or the lack of it – touches the most people in the most powerful of ways.

Much of the inspiration for writing this book came from the non-fiction book by Will Potter, *Green is the New Red*, which is as terrifying and compelling a story as any fictional account of the attacks on environmentalists that I could have ever imagined or written.

Inspiration also came from filmmaker Josh Fox's *Gasland II*, a movie that dramatically shows how the oil and gas companies promoting hydrofracking technology have twisted legal and regulatory systems into a tangle of knots.

I hope *Fracking Justice* can help cut those knots away and let people get a glimpse into an energy industry whose focus does not include the safety of our communities or our environment.

Ulysses Returns

Chapter 1

ROCKWELL VALLEY, Pennsylvania – Tyrone Arthur Garber sat in his Central Pennsylvania Railroad pickup truck eyeballing the single-track, 400-foot steel and wood train trestle that spanned Rockwell Valley State Park gorge, 200 feet above Rockwell Valley Creek.

He cursed that he had forgotten to swallow two of his wife's anti-anxiety pills before he left the house.

The work order was straightforward: "State Park trestle inspection. Check top and bottom of entire structure. Two hikers on the state park creek trail reported something below the tracks mid-span."

Just another day on the railroad for Tyrone – known as Tag to friends and railroad employees. Except during the last six months, 45-year-old Tag had developed a case of acrophobia – fear of heights – that this morning had him in a literal panic.

He had been waking up with night sweats after having bad dreams about falling from buildings, waterfalls, trees, and into wells. Then just two nights before, he dreamed of taking a header off a railroad trestle.

Just like the trestle he was looking at.

Tag opened the truck door, a blast of freezing January wind hitting him hard. He could feel his hands sweating inside his heavy wool gloves. He left the company truck running to keep the cab warm.

He saw that the trestle was mostly clear but had some snow pushed up in a few spots. The 9:05 freight wasn't due for another hour, plenty of time for him to carefully pick his way out across the bridge, inspect it, and get back to the warm truck.

Tag had parked as close as he could below the bridge, using his field glasses to get a peek at whatever the hikers had seen. But he couldn't make out what it was other than it was the size of shoebox. He thought maybe it was a dead animal of some kind.

As he gingerly stepped in the center of the first railroad tie, he wished for the second time that morning he had his wife's anxiety pills.

When he inspected a trestle over a state highway a month before – a bridge barely 50 feet off the ground – the pills took enough of the edge off that he didn't have any problem.

Tag stopped to put on his sunglasses, fumbling with his gloves. Then he slowly started making progress across the span, the roaring creek clearly visible between the railroad ties. He didn't feel any vertigo in the middle of the tracks as long as he kept looking straight ahead. But he needed to get to the edge with a mirror on an extendable pole to check whatever was lodged underneath the bridge.

His cell phone suddenly started to ring, startling him so much he slipped down onto all fours. He froze in that position, quietly cursing until the phone went to voicemail.

Tag saw he was about mid-span on the bridge, perhaps even right above the object beneath the trestle. He stayed kneeling and slid the mirror down through the space between the railroad ties, twisting it slowly to get a look.

The cold fogged the mirror just enough that it took him a moment to realize he was seeing a half-dozen slender red tubes just ahead of where he was kneeling.

Holy shit, he thought. *Dynamite?*

Tag forgot all about his acrophobia as he crabbed his way sideways on his knees to his right, right up to the edge of the trestle where he could slide the mirror over and get a better look.

Still on his knees, he focused on the reflection in the mirror and tried not to let his eyes wander down to the rocks and swirling water.

He thought he could see a small curling wire sticking out. *A fuse?* he thought.

He reached into his jacket pocket for his phone, fumbling with his stuck glove. He leaned back slightly to shake the glove loose, moving his right leg a fraction of an inch too close to the edge of the icy trestle, feeling a sudden rush of cooler air on his knee.

He pancaked his body on the edge of the trestle a moment too late as he felt his right leg go over the edge.

Tag valiantly hung on for about 10 seconds, half on the bridge, half off, his head below the span, one hand clawing at the tracks. He stayed that way just long enough to read the word "*Wolverines!*" written across several of the tubes.

When his grip gave way, Tyrone Arthur Garber screamed

once as he plunged off the railroad trestle. Then he passed out, dropping silently the rest of the way down.

A Rockwell Valley State Park ranger found Tag's shattered body at the bottom of the gorge later that morning after the engineer of the 9:05 freight train alerted the main Central Pennsylvania Railroad office that there was a company track inspection truck with its engine running at the top of the Rockwell Valley State Park gorge, but no one was around.

Chapter 2

Rockwell Valley Police Chief Melvin "Bobo" Caprino poked his No. 2 lead pencil at the package of red cylinders on his desk, a six-inch piece of fuse-like material sticking out of the middle.

He rolled it over, looking at the lettering that said "Wolverines!" then back over to the other side, where the outside tubes were clearly marked as standard issue roadside safety flares.

"Some stunt, huh chief?"

Caprino looked up to see his second-in-command, Lieutenant Del Dewitt, leaning in the doorway, his ever-present coffee mug in front of him. Dewitt's nickname among the other members of the force was Dim Wit, a clever label – but inaccurate.

Dewitt was the only one on Caprino's police force who had gone to college, coming home with a degree in forensic science.

"What do you make of this, other than the obvious?" Caprino asked. "It's a stunt for sure. But it killed Tag, even if it was an accident."

Dewitt came into the office and picked up the road flares with his free hand. "We've already checked this for any prints. Don't worry," he said. "Whoever did it did a nice job to make it look like explosives to someone who didn't know about them."

For the first few hours after Tag's body was discovered, the Rockwell Valley Police Department treated it as a simple slip-and-fall accident. Tragic, but such accidents were not unknown in a town that had seen a spike in industrial mishaps in recent years, most linked to the natural gas well drilling in the area, part of the boom of a gas extraction technology known as hydrofracking.

Then Dewitt found Tag's clipboard stuck between two rocks 100 feet away. It had a notation about a suspicious item lodged underneath the train trestle, which the park ranger confirmed had been reported by the park office to the railroad.

"Thank God we've kept the media away from this," Caprino said. "They'd be having a field day."

Because of the foul weather, only a financially starved local alternative monthly newspaper showed up to the scene, no doubt alerted by listening to the police scanner. The Rockwell Valley PD used cell phones to avoid being tracked in their patrols. But the local ambulance service and the park rangers chatted like magpies on their radios.

The editor-reporter-owner of the *Rockwell Valley Tribune* shot a few pictures of Tag's body covered by a sheet and had left by the time Lt. Dewitt had dispatched a couple of officers with ropes to climb under the trestle and see what Tag had been searching for.

"Good thing it wasn't really an explosive," Dewitt said.

"They just yanked it out from under the bridge. A real terrorist would probably paint the explosives to look like road flares to throw us all off."

Dewitt put the package down carefully on the desk, then laughed.

"Gotcha chief... These *are* road flares. And the numbers under the tape says they are long expired. No worries. It was a prank. Pretty good one, too. Sorry about Tag, though."

Caprino watched Dewitt head back out of his office, no doubt to the coffee pot in the squad room. *He must have a bladder the size of an elephant*, Caprino thought.

Caprino *was* worried – but not about the road flares.

He had just gotten two phone calls in quick succession before Dewitt meandered in.

The first call was from Rockwell Valley's newly elected mayor, a 39-year-old transplant from Missouri who had moved to Rockwell Valley six years before, right at the start of the natural gas-hydrofracking boom that had brought a modest amount of financial prosperity to the town and a boatload of environmental and social headaches along with it.

Mayor Will Pennisen was also the local manager with Grand Energy Services of Flathead, Missouri, working on the installation of infrastructure to get ready for salt cavern propane and natural gas storage in some abandoned salt mines at the north end of Rockwell Valley Lake.

He was also lobbying hard for a pipeline from the natural gas wells to the west to the proposed gas storage site and another pipeline to the east to send gas to the coast for export.

"Bobo, I heard about the package under the bridge,"

Pennisen had said on the phone. "This is terrorism pure and simple. No other way to look at it. I want you to have your officers investigate this as eco-terrorism. We don't need any more of that Wolverine bullshit here. I bet that old crone Alice McCallis had something to do with this, too."

Caprino knew that Pennisen's call had probably been prompted by Pennisen receiving a phone call from GES headquarters – maybe even right from the desk of GES president and CEO Luther Burnside himself. From what Caprino was hearing and reading, Burnside was living up to his in-house, company nickname of Luca Brasi, the name of a ruthless strongman-hit man in a 1969 novel about the Mafia.

GES and other gas companies had started ramping up a coordinated counter-offensive against protesters in the last year, filing lawsuits, calling anyone with an anti-hydrofracking sign an "eco-terrorist" and launching a campaign of dirty tricks against environmental groups.

GES had also quietly donated enough money to Rockwell Valley police so that Caprino's 14-officer department was equipped with amazing new weaponry, body armor, full riot gear and a closet full of sophisticated surveillance equipment, including a small helicopter drone.

The drone was under lock and key after Caprino caught an officer using it to spy on a woman sunbathing in her backyard.

That equipment came in addition to the crates of U.S. Department of Defense surplus gear that had been given to the department.

The DOD had offered an armored assault vehicle, but Caprino turned it down, thinking it was overkill.

Caprino had a hard time imagining that Alice McCallis – a nearly 80-year-old retired chemistry and biology teacher from Rockwell Valley High School – would have scaled the trestle to put the highway flares up there.

And as a big a pain in the ass as she could be, McCallis was unlikely to take part in any kind of covert actions, he thought. Alice McCallis came at people straight on.

The year before she had been arrested at a natural gas well protest when she refused to move to let GES trucks pass through. She even served a week in jail when she refused to pay a fine.

Still, Caprino knew that unless he sent his officers scrambling in that direction chasing the specter of terrorists, Pennisen would be telling the town council that Caprino was soft and not up to the job of being police chief. Or maybe even being a cop on the force at all.

And a couple of the double-digit-I.Q. bumpkins on the town council would probably go along with pushing Caprino out the door so fast he would barely have time to grab his personal gear.

I just have to hang on for two more years for early retirement, Caprino thought, looking at his desk calendar underneath the still-bound road flares. *Hell, not even two years. Just 22 months.*

Caprino was used to rolling with the political punches after nearly 30 years with the Rockwell Valley Police Department. His nickname "Bobo" had come from when he was a young teenager and got into fights with older boys. They would knock him down, only to see him spring back up, like the popular sand-filled punching bag toy called Bobo the Clown.

He was mentally recovering from the mayor's phone call when the second call rocked him back.

The phone call was from a cop friend in Horseheads, New York, just across the Pennsylvania-New York border.

The friend said he had read in that morning's *Horseheads Clarion* newspaper that Jack Stafford, the newspaper's investigative columnist and publisher on a leave of absence for the last two years, was coming back to take over the publication's helm.

Stafford had published scathing columns before he left, claiming that Rockwell Valley's public officials were nothing but company shills for Grand Energy Services, doing the corporation's bidding to the detriment of everyone except for themselves, GES shareholders and gas company executives.

After he hung up, Caprino reached into his desk drawer to get a slug of milky medicine for his increasingly upset stomach, getting more upset as the day went along.

But the growing uncomfortable gas bubble in Melvin "Bobo" Caprino's stomach was also there because sitting in a holding cell in the back of the Rockwell Valley Police Station was Eli Gupta, the current editor of the twice-a-week *Horseheads Clarion,* who had been remanded into police custody just a few hours before by a local judge. Gupta and the court bailiff got into some kind of courtroom altercation over a camera Gupta had brought into the courtroom.

Stafford will have a field day with all of us over this, Caprino thought.

He took a slug of the medicine and was about to toss the road flare package back into the evidence sack on his desk. Then he noticed the road flare in the center of the package *seemed* to be of a slightly smaller diameter. It looked like it had a few beads of condensation on the outside of it as if it might be sweating.

"DEWITT, DEWITT! – GET-IN-HERE-NOW," Caprino screamed.

"NOW!"

Chapter 3

The inter-island prop plane with 28 passengers aboard swung over tiny Lata Island, dipping its right wing so passengers could get a good view of the land, its protective, encircling coral reef and a smattering of small resort buildings.

Jack Stafford had arranged with the pilots to make the diversion from the normal flight path nearly two months before when he had expected to be leaving the Vava'u Island group of the Kingdom of Tonga to fly back to the United States.

Today he sat on the opposite side of the plane, alone, unable to look at the island he had called home for nearly two years with his wife Devon, his three-year-old-son Noah and a Tongan friend named Gideon, who had saved Noah's life.

Noah sat in the window seat watching his home below. His aunt Cassandra held him around the waist, whispering in his ear as the plane made a quick circle of the small island before heading south to the Tongan island of Tongatapu, where they would connect with flights to Fiji and then the U.S.

Cassandra – who liked to be called Cass – had flown in a week after the boating accident that killed her older sister,

Jack's wife Devon, thinking she would stay just long enough to help Jack get things under control.

She had only met Jack once before, at Devon and Jack's wedding in the offices of the *Horseheads Clarion* a few months before Noah was born.

Looking out the window of the plane with Noah, she remembered the happy scene with what seemed like hundreds of people crammed into the small newspaper offices. She also remembered the twinge of envy at her sister's glowing happiness.

Cass's own love life had been a series of disappointments, brought on in part by her vocation of acting, writing and directing stage plays. The men she dated were all from the theatrical world. *A shallow pool of raging narcissists*, she had thought at the wedding. She had met a friend of Jack and Devon's named Oscar, a winery owner and big bear of a guy who was so gracious and so polite and so courteous, she couldn't believe he had never been married. But then *neither* had she. And now she was staring down 40.

"Jack. Jack!" Cass called across the aisle. "You sure you don't want to look at this side, even for a moment?"

A dark look passed over Jack's eyes. She returned the look with a reprimanding scowl, then softly smiled.

"I'd rather sit here, Cass. Really," Jack said. "I'm okay. Really. Okay."

Cass kept looking at him until he looked back out his window at the vast Pacific Ocean.

Okay my ass. This is killing *you*, she thought.

When she had arrived on the nearby Tongan island of Neiafu after the accident, local residents warned her that Jack was wild with grief. He had holed up on Lata Island with Gideon, Noah and several members of Gideon's extended Tongan family. Devon had been buried there, counter to local custom, and had caused a stir among the various church leaders.

The woman who ran a Neiafu restaurant called Café Pa'alangi told Cassie she heard that Jack hadn't drawn a sober breath since the funeral. The whole community was mourning Devon, too.

Cass hugged Noah as he turned away from the window, ready to find something else to look at. He often seemed confused when he looked at Cass. He knew she wasn't his mother, but the resemblance to Devon was remarkable. Cass was thinner than Devon had been and had more reddish hair. But when she smiled she had the same dimples in exactly the same spots on her cheeks. Cass's mother had described them to her three daughters as "Walsh family beauty spots."

Cass's eldest sister, Anne, couldn't join them in Tonga but was waiting for them on Vashon Island near Seattle at the estate she, Cass and their late sister had inherited from their parents years before.

Cass pulled out a coloring book for Noah, who grabbed some crayons from the seat back and who was quickly engrossed with the sea creature images in front of him. She unbuckled her seat belt and slid across the aisle to sit next to Jack.

"Remember what we talked about? About breathing? About thinking about Noah?" Cass asked. "I can see what you can see. I'm sorry, Jack. But breathe. Please."

Jack leaned back and closed his eyes, reaching for Cass's hand.

"I forget you are a *true* Cassandra," he said. "Good thing

for me. It's just that living in a Greek tragedy is different than reading about one."

They sat quietly for a few minutes, with Cass glancing over at the very industrious Noah.

Since Devon drowned and Noah nearly died, too, Noah hadn't uttered a single word, or if he had, no one had heard it. Efforts to get him to speak only made him burst into tears or throw a ferocious temper tantrum.

"It's still best for both of you to go back to the U.S. We agreed on that, Jack. Even as hard as this is," Cass said. "Staying on that island isn't going to help. You can go back eventually."

Cass had rescued Jack as best she could. Her own grief over losing her sister was overwhelming, too. But pulling Jack back from the brink kept her distracted enough to forget how much she missed her older sister.

Two weeks after she arrived on the island Jack was still getting roaring drunk every day – barely sober even first thing in the morning, sometimes fortifying his coffee mug at breakfast with cheap rum.

Then one night she awoke to the sound of Tokanga, Jack's dog, barking wildly at the ocean. She checked Noah's bed, afraid that he had wandered outside.

But Noah was sound asleep.

By the time she got outside Gideon was already waist deep in the surf and pulling Jack out of the water, with Tokanga barking and circling the men as they got to shore.

The next morning, Jack confessed that he had drunkenly decided to swim across the two-mile channel to the next island. "I guess I thought I would give the ocean a chance to take me, too," Jack said. He glanced over at Noah, then at Cass, tears in his eyes. "That little guy got me swimming back."

Cass looked out the plane window past Jack at the vast Pacific Ocean.

"You know there are some pretty good Greek plays that are *not* tragedies, Jack," Cass said. "Your whole newspaper crusade against the hydrofracking? Before you moved to Tonga to write that book? That was heroic stuff. Right out of the Iliad. Remember, all real heroes have terrible trials, terrible things. But they triumph. Like you will."

She put her arm around Jack and gave him a gentle hug.

Jack smiled, the first one Cass had seen since they got on the plane hours before.

"You're right, Cass. Devon and I did some great work. And I am going home. Maybe like Ulysses went home. Maybe I will clean house."

Cass took his hand and waited for him to look her in the eye. "Okay. But use your sword wisely. Don't let your anger overwhelm you. Remember *him*," she said, gesturing towards Noah.

"And plan on staying on Vashon Island for awhile. I want Noah's Aunt Anne to meet him. And you need a *full* medical checkup with some real doctors, not those clinic trainees. You were in shock for weeks, Jack. I mean it."

Across the aisle, Noah kept coloring but watched Cass and Jack out of the corner of his eye while the plane coasted over the small islands separating Vava'u from the other islands in the South Pacific chain that made up the nation of Tonga.

He wondered why when people moved their lips, he couldn't see the words in his head anymore.

Chapter 4

Jack Stafford to return as Clarion publisher

Jack Stafford, publisher of the *Horseheads Clarion,* will resume his duties as publisher this spring.

Managing editor Eli Gupta said Stafford had completed his book, *An Endless Quest for Hope and Solutions*, and will be returning to take the helm of the newspaper after his leave of absence.

"The staff is excited to have our publisher back," Gupta said. "And he has agreed to resume writing his "Column One" feature every Friday."

Stafford left the newspaper to take a writing sabbatical. He and his late wife Devon lived in Tonga with their now 3-year-old son, Noah.

Devon Walsh Stafford – who had been a writer and consultant to the *Clarion* – died in a boating accident late last year in that island nation.

Stafford is a Horseheads native and began his career at the *Clarion* as a sports writer under the tutelage of the late Walter Nagle, the former publisher of the *Clarion*.

He also worked in California as a journalist and investigative reporter.

"I'm looking forward to coming home to resume my column and work with the *Clarion* staff," Stafford said. "Horseheads is a my home and is a great place to raise my son."

Stafford said he and his son Noah will move back into their family home in Horseheads.

Chapter 5

Luther Burnside, CEO of Grand Energy Services, had never really liked his nickname of "Luca Brasi" much when he was growing up.

He liked that the gangster from the novel *The Godfather* was greatly feared. But Luther hated that the Brasi character was portrayed as basically a stupid lug who got himself murdered through sloppiness.

Even so, the nickname had been an asset, mostly because people thought Luther was ruthless and willing to strong-arm anyone who was in his way. As he moved up through the corporate ranks, he watched a movie version of the book and learned to imitate the facial expression: a menacing mask.

Now at Grand Energy Services headquarters in Flathead, Missouri, that reputation helped keep subordinates from challenging his decisions. And even in the natural gas industry, other CEOs often acted a little uneasy if Luther showed signs of unhappiness.

And today Luther was unhappy, but he was unsure exactly what his next move should be.

A huge toxic chemical spill in West Virginia had poisoned the water quite thoroughly for nearly 300,000 people. And even though the spill had nothing to do with the ongoing pollution woes of the natural gas industry or hydrofracking, it had drawn unwelcome attention to the old pollution stories about GES and other gas companies.

A summary of gas industry-related stories compiled daily for Luther by GES vice president Rod Mayenlyn showed dozens of daily newspapers around the country and television news reports comparing the West Virginia spill to a years-old tale about how GES had been dumping all manner of toxic chemicals into wells as part of their hydrofracking drilling cocktail.

The trouble was that he knew the toxic chemicals were unneeded for the gas drilling. GES and other companies were just maximizing their federally approved exemptions to clean air and clean water laws to run a toxic waste disposal business on the side, one that was very successful financially but a public relations disaster when the public found out.

That scandal and others had forced out former CEO Grayson Oliver Delacroix, who died in a mysterious natural gas explosion at his Flathead, Missouri home right after he was fired.

Luther heard whispers that *he* was somehow responsible for that blast – whispers he didn't try to quash.

It all helped Luther Burnside with his Luca Brasi gangster image.

Luther was also unhappy because tucked in among the West Virginia stories was a copy of a story from the *Horseheads Clarion*, a weekly newspaper from Horseheads, New York, that had emerged as a leading media voice against hydrofracking during the past several years.

Its publisher, Jack Stafford, was due back from a leave of absence and would be resuming his once-a-week column and running the newspaper. Luther remembered breathing a sigh of relief when Stafford left for the South Pacific to write a book, leaving some young Indian reporter named Eli Gupta in charge as editor-in-chief.

Stafford's occasional columns from the tropics lacked the punch of his "Column One" reports when he worked in Horseheads harrying the gas industry nearly every week.

Luther reread the brief story, then buzzed the intercom for Rod Mayenlyn to come in.

Luther decided that today he would be more like the character Don Corleone from *The Godfather*.

Don Corleone was a much more ruthless bastard than Luca Brasi.

And he was smarter. He needed to be if he was going to neutralize Jack Stafford.

Chapter 6

> From *The Horseheads Clarion*
>
> Column One
> *The Horseheads Clarion*

A clear and present danger

By Jack Stafford

The late Walter Nagle, the greatly admired publisher of this newspaper for many years, used to say, "The more things change, the more they stay the same."

He didn't make that up. A French novelist named Alphonse Karr did.

But it rang through my head this past week as I returned after my two-year leave of absence from the *Clarion*.

When I left to write a book titled *An Endless Quest for Hope and Solutions,* I was hopeful that the natural gas industry and its many political allies were willing to clean up their respective acts, be responsible for the industrial and social messes they have created across the nation and become responsible corporate citizens.

Instead I returned to see the same poisoning of groundwater, people getting sick from polluted air and wells and increasingly aggressive legal tactics to silence critics.

The *Horseheads Clarion* fully expects those aggressive legal tactics to be used against this newspaper.

If so, we will continue to use these pages to remind Grand Energy Services and other firms that the First Amendment to the United States Constitution provides a pretty good shield against bullies.

All that falls pretty much into the category of "the more things stay the same."

But I also returned to find that our Pennsylvania neighbors in Rockwell Valley face a new threat - a clear and present danger - from an ill-thought-out plan to store propane and natural gas in salt caverns abandoned nearly 30 years ago at the north end of Rockwell Valley Lake, just 10 miles away from the town of 5,000 people.

Storage of these gases in salt caverns is a recipe for disaster. It has drawn criticism from many members of the community.

Complicating all this, Rockwell Valley's municipal government is clearly under the thumb of Grand Energy Services, the Flathead, Missouri-based company that is doing most of the hydrofracking in the surrounding countryside.

Rockwell Valley`s new mayor is also employed as the general manager of the Rockwell Valley GES organization and tasked with getting the salt cavern project approved as soon as possible – which is also tied in with a proposed natural gas pipeline project that is also drawing howls of protest.

But those protestors are being muted, too, thanks to some GES-friendly judges who are quick to issue restraining orders against protesters at the encouragement of equally GES-friendly prosecutors.

The proposed salt-cavern storage is not a done deal. But GES has started construction on the site, including upgrading the railroad tracks that run through Rockwell Valley State Park and up the west side of the lake to the old salt mines area.

If it does win approval, local activists – the ones not *already* gagged by some legal order or other threats

— say Rockwell Valley will be neighbor to a potential bomb with explosive power sufficient to flatten the town.

That`s not hyperbole. It`s all in a report by an independent consulting firm of geologists.

If you haven`t read about that report until this moment, that`s because GES attorneys were able to legally seal the documents from public access.

But the *Clarion* has some bad news for GES and good news for the people of Rockwell Valley.

The *Clarion* came into possession of a copy of that consulting firm`s report prior to a judge slapping the gag order on the geologists.

And the title on that document is the same as the headline of today`s column: *A Clear and Present Danger*.

No wonder GES wants it kept secret.

Jack Stafford is the publisher of the Horseheads Clarion *and publishes Column One every Friday. He can be reached at JJStafford@HorseheadsClarion.com.*

Chapter 7

Eli Gupta sat nervously in Jack's office.

Since Jack had returned and taken back the reins of the newspaper, Eli thought Jack was acting recklessly in his news decisions, overriding many of Eli's ideas about what stories to run and when.

I wish Devon was still here, Eli thought. *They made such a good team.*

"So Eli, you look worried," Jack said. "Was it my column today? I was just stirring the pot. We need to get after these bastards again with a little more punch. Right?"

Eli shifted uneasily in his chair. He had idolized Jack and Devon when they took the *Horseheads Clarion* from a sleepy twice-a-week newspaper to near-national prominence with hard-hitting pieces on hydrofracking. Walter – and then Jack – had given Eli the go-ahead to punch up the website, which had become not only profitable but respected across the nation as a source of hydrofracking news.

He had been a part of that shift and loved the excitement of breaking stories about the gas companies and their illegal dumping of fracking fluids and other schemes.

When Devon drowned in Tonga, Eli was devastated. And today he wondered how much of Jack's kinetic energy was aimed at simply keeping busy so he wouldn't think about his late wife.

"Jack, your column was great," Eli said. "Anybody who might have doubted you would pick right up again chasing the gas companies understands. But Jack, we don't have that consulting firm report. I don't get why you said we did."

And Devon would have kept you from saying it, Eli thought.

Jack leaned back in his chair and studied Eli for a full 10 seconds before he replied. Jack had promoted Eli to editor-in-chief when he, Devon and baby Noah went to Tonga.

"Eli, you've done a great job. And you and Shania are well liked in the community. We were so happy when you two decided to get married. And if I have been stepping your editorial toes, I don't mean to. But I've come back to a community that's as bad off – maybe worse – from hydrofracking and all that goes with it. That's not your fault. You ran plenty of stories and kept the news alive. But we need to hit them harder. That's my job. That's why Walter brought me in, remember?"

Eli was glad to hear the praise. They were the first really kind words out of Jack's mouth since returning the week before, blowing through the *Horseheads Clarion* office late one afternoon, barely saying more than a hello to anyone after more than two years had passed. It was like he was just coming back from lunch.

Eli expected Jack to call a general staff meeting right away. But Jack said that could wait.

"I said we had that consulting report because I want GES to react with some half-assed legal maneuver that will give us the news peg to keep writing about what we *know* is in that report. I'm picking a fight and I know it."

Eli was grateful when the phone rang on Jack's desk and Jack answered it, waving Eli out of the office.

The Jack Stafford that Eli remembered from before would never have told a deliberate lie in a column or news story.

Never. Not even as a device to flush someone out.

Whatever was going on, Eli was now worried not just about *his* job as editor, but the *Horseheads Clarion* itself.

Chapter 8

Cass and Noah watched Jack thread his way up the slippery walkway to his front door.

The February snow was piled up around the house, the house he had inherited from his father just before he moved back to New York from California. It was also the house in which he and Devon had lived before they headed to the South Pacific.

Cass could see he was talking to himself as he walked, deep in thought and having a conversation in his mind with someone.

Since they had returned from Tonga, Cass was struggling with what she should do.

She hadn't signed on to be a long-term nanny to her nephew, as darling as he was. But at the same time, Noah had bonded with her so fast it was dizzying.

And Jack?

Jack vacillated between showing great appreciation for her help and being so obtuse Cass felt like a piece of furniture in the big house, less than a mile from the *Horseheads Clarion* newspaper office.

Noah put his finger on the window, pointing to his father heading up the front steps. If he was excited, it didn't show. And when Cass talked to Noah he gave her a blank stare.

"Oh Lucy! I'm home," Jack said in his best Desi Arnaz

accent as he opened the front door. "I hope you guys had as good a day as I had."

Cass closed the door behind Jack and took his coat to hang it up.

My God, she thought, *I'm acting like an English maid.*

Jack picked Noah up in his arms, but Noah squirmed and Jack put him down. Noah ran over to Cass, putting his arms up for her to pick him up.

"Jack, we need to talk about some things," Cass said.

Jack smiled and out of habit walked towards the cupboard where he and Devon had kept their wine glasses next to a small wine rack. His ritual after a day at the newspaper was to grab a glass of wine as soon as he got home.

He stopped midway to the cupboard, remembering the agreement he made with Cass that there would be no alcohol in the house for now.

Jack's late-night drunken swimming excursion in Tonga had sufficiently frightened her – and him – that she made the no-alcohol-in-the-home rule a condition of her staying around.

And Jack agreed, reluctantly.

"I was talking with a friend – a pediatrician in Seattle – who said we need to get Noah's ears tested by a specialist," Cass said. "It could be that he has hearing loss from the accident. But she also said it could be that when he tries to speak, his throat might be painful for him. Maybe that's why he won't talk."

Jack plunked down on the sofa, his mood obviously dampened by the combination of medical news and craving a glass of wine so much he considered heading out to one of the local bars.

"Of course. Let's get his little ears tested. It makes sense. The doctors on Vava'u were mostly worried about water in his lungs after the boat flipped and …"

Jack's voice trailed off.

"That's fine, Jack," Cass said. "But *you* will need to do this. I'm an aunt, not a mother. And I don't really have the legal right to get him medical care, even as casual as people are around here."

Jack smiled, thinking about how the small-town approach to things in Horseheads made life less *by-the-rules* and more personal. The downside of that was everyone in town knew within a day of arriving that Jack's sister-in-law had moved in with him and was taking care of Noah. And a lot of them knew the details of the boating accident that claimed Devon's life or that Noah had nearly drowned, too.

Cass watched Jack's eyes ease their focus as he sat staring out the window. She kept thinking about the expression "the thousand-yard stare" usually associated with battle weary soldiers. But anyone traumatized the way Jack had been when Devon, Noah and their Tongan friend Gideon had flipped their boat in a squall had earned that label.

"Jack. Are you okay?" Cass asked. "A few minutes ago you came in like Ricky Ricardo from *I Love Lucy*. And now you look like you're ready for bed."

Jack's eyes refocused on Cass, still standing and holding Noah, who was clutching her around the neck, studying his father on the couch.

"Sure. Well, sort of," Jack said. "I had to do something at work today I hate to do – I had to hold back information from a staff member. From Eli, my editor. The newspaper is about to get into a bruising battle with the gas companies and I need to shield the staff as much as I can."

Cass walked over and sat down on the couch, putting Noah down next to a small pile of toys.

This is a mistake, she thought. *Oh well.*

"Would it help to talk about it?" she asked.

Jack exhaled and stared at Cass for a moment, marveling at how much she resembled his late wife Devon and yet was such a different woman.

"It would," he said. "It really would."

Chapter 9

The opponents of the propane and natural gas salt cavern storage project at the north end of Rockwell Valley Lake had been outnumbered, outspent and disorganized until 79-year-old Alice McCallis had joined the fight to try to stop Grand Energy Services from moving ahead.

The opponents were still outnumbered and underfinanced. But McCallis's years as a chemistry and biology teacher and as partner to her late husband, Rockwell Valley accountant Bertram McCallis, helped bring order to the chaos of people who were dead set against GES doing anything with the old salt mines – except maybe mining salt.

Maybe.

Bertram and Alice had spent years sailing their home-built wooden Snipe boat named *John Muir* on the lake. And every spring and fall Alice would take her chemistry and biology classes to the shores of the lake on field trips to test the water and check out the wildlife.

She was credited in the late 1980s with discovering

that the then-operating salt mines were dumping chemicals and salt extraction residue into the lake, killing fish in the process and raising the salinity level of the lake to alarming levels.

Her findings gave government officials enough ammunition that they ordered the company to make expensive changes to the way it operated the salt mines – changes the company eventually decided were too costly.

The 100 or so laid-off salt mine employees still had Alice McCallis on the top of their shit list, even many years afterwards.

Rockwell Valley Police Chief Bobo Caprino's father had been one of those laid-off workers. But Caprino had a grudging respect for McCallis's spunky attitude and keen mind.

That respect was why Caprino defied Rockwell Valley's mayor by refusing to bring McCallis in for questioning about the flares placed under the railroad trestle over the Rockwell Valley State Park gorge.

Instead, he waited nearly two weeks after the incident before he drove out to her house, despite repeated phone calls from the mayor.

Now sitting in her living room, he marveled at numerous photos of McCallis with famous people. Over her piano was a photo of McCallis with former U.S. President Jimmy Carter at some Habitat for Humanity fundraiser.

"Alice, I guess you know why I'm here," Bobo said. "It's about that package of dynamite we found under the state park trestle. The mayor seems to think you had something to do with it."

Alice McCallis stared straight into the police chief's eyes

with a look that Bobo knew had scared the hell out of many generations of high school students. It wasn't just a look, really. It was a penetrating gaze that made Bobo feel like she could laser a hole in his head.

"I mean, I'm just asking some questions, Alice. That's my job," Bobo said, shifting uneasily.

Alice dialed back the intensity of her facial expression and smiled.

"You know, how is it that I never had you in any of my classes?" she asked. "You were certainly on the college track, weren't you?"

McCallis hadn't flinched when he used the word *dynamite*.

But then she doesn't seem to flinch at anything, Bobo thought.

"Well, what you probably don't know – because it hasn't been reported in the media – is the word 'Wolverines' was written on the outside of the dynamite. And that's why the mayor is on the warpath. I am, too. Tag Garber died checking it out. This isn't a prank."

Alice leaned in again, her jaw set slightly.

"Bobo. Hmm... Let's make it 'Chief,'" Alice said. "I have applauded the Wolverines publicly on occasion for some of the things they have done to stop hydrofracking. But I have never endorsed or condoned violence. You of *all* people should know that. And I know Tag Garber's family. They are all good people. So if you want to accuse me of something I think you should get to it. I have a rally to plan to stop that gas storage abomination at the end of the lake.

"By the way," she said, "everyone in town knows that it was just some road flares under the bridge, not dynamite."

Ulysses Returns

Bobo stood up to leave and held his hands up in a motion of surrender.

"Alice, you got me. But the gas companies are still all sore over that Wolverine bunch's antics and vandalism. In Colorado the state police declared them a terrorist organization. I don't need to tell you how determined the gas companies are to stop them."

Alice slipped her arm through Bobo's as they walked towards the door, a gesture not so much of friendship but as one between combatants with mutual respect.

"Chief, we all want to keep this area safe," Alice said.

Bobo slipped his hat on his head as he said goodbye, noticing a photo on the wall in the hallway of Alice McCallis with her arm linked through the arm of a man about Bobo's age. They both had their fists raised in a solidarity salute, huge grins on their faces and a big crowd in the background.

Bobo was backing his police cruiser out of McCallis's driveway when he realized the man in the photo with Alice was Jack Stafford, the publisher of the *Horseheads Clarion*.

Chapter 10

Luther Burnside had dreaded the return of Jack Stafford to the *Horseheads Clarion* from the moment he first heard about it.

He had watched Stafford harass the former CEO, Grayson Oliver Delacroix, and GES with a sharply honed column week after week before Burnside took over.

Now sitting in his corporate office with Rod Mayenlyn, his vice president for public information, Burnside was waiting for some bright ideas of how to get rid of that dread

– and Stafford.

Burnside had initially hoped that the salt cavern propane and gas storage project at the north end of Rockwell Valley Lake would already be functioning – or close to it – before Stafford returned. The handful of activists in Rockwell Valley who Grand Energy Services couldn't shut up had few outlets for their hollering beyond some barely viewed websites and amateurish newsletters.

Most local and regional media were paying little attention to the sign-waving antics of the anti-storage group. The hellacious winter storms that were pummeling the Northeast had people more worried about how to keep warm than where the gas was stored.

And the media weren't paying much attention to GES's plans for a second new pipeline either – a project to carry gas from the planned Rockwell Valley storage all the way to Chesapeake Bay in Maryland, where it could be shipped to sell on the lucrative international market.

Burnside knew that some media types were sniffing around as farmers complained about threats that their land might be taken via eminent domain proceedings. But money could probably keep the farmers quiet.

"So any new bright ideas today, Rod?" Burnside asked.

Burnside had counted on Mayenlyn to come up with some strategies for neutralizing Stafford. Mayenlyn had conjured up a few simple scenarios, including extending an olive branch to Stafford by inviting him to the GES headquarters in Flathead for a talk.

But Stafford's aggressive first column made that unlikely.

"Clear and present danger my ass," Burnside said. "The arrogance of this bozo. We need to slap this guy back hard,

Rod. Hard. And by the way, I want you to find out how in the hell he got ahold of that consultant's report. We paid a lot of money to keep that under wraps. Maybe a phone call to the judge is in order. Maybe Stafford broke some law. Maybe it's possession of stolen property."

Mayenlyn shifted in his chair, wondering himself how Stafford seemed to know so much about what was in the consultant's report about the dangers posed by the salt cavern storage. Because Stafford's newspaper was in New York, and Rockwell Valley was in Pennsylvania, the law was more complicated, he was sure.

Mayenlyn also knew that Burnside was considering going after Stafford on a personal level. But Mayenlyn had dealt with Stafford for several years before Stafford left on his leave of absence while Mayenlyn was editing and publishing an industry-funded website called Energy First America, one of a string of gas industry funded newsletters that were designed to discredit gas industry critics and activists.

Stafford had used his weekly newspaper column to body-slam Mayenlyn and GES repeatedly despite Mayenlyn's best efforts to neutralize the bad press.

And to launch a personal attack against a man who had just lost his wife to a tragic accident?

It would be a disaster, Mayenlyn thought.

"I think our best shot at the moment is to try to divert him," Mayenlyn said. "Or maybe paint his concerns as overblown. I wonder if there is any chance we can get the geologists who wrote that report to recant parts of it. Soften it. It's worked before."

Burnside stood up and waved his hands in frustration.

"Divert? Reminds me a parent trying to keep a child from

throwing a tantrum. Divert them with candy or cartoons. All right, all right, all right," Burnside said impatiently. "But get me some ideas about that diversion quick. We have a corporate board of directors meeting in two weeks and they will not be pleased if the storage project gets reamed again in print."

Mayenlyn stood up and grabbed from the chair next to him the file folder he had brought in as an insurance policy in case Burnside demanded to go after Stafford personally.

In it was an illegally obtained photocopy of admittance papers from a private psychiatric clinic on Vashon Island, near Seattle, where Jack Stafford had spent a week before returning to Horseheads.

The form didn't say admittance for what.

But Mayenlyn knew that for GES purposes, that really didn't matter.

Chapter 11

Oscar Wilson traced his finger over the 2-inch scar above his eyebrow.

It was nearly a year old, but it was still red and angry looking.

Touching it made Oscar's blood pressure rise slightly, too, remembering the brawl at his normally placid Lakeside Winery on the east side of Seneca Lake.

A half-dozen Grand Energy Systems workers, still filthy from working on building some sludge ponds and installing propane storage tanks, swaggered in and started harassing a handful of women who had arrived earlier in a limousine as part of a bachelorette party.

Before Oscar could get out from behind the wine tasting

bar, his 24-year-old niece Lindy was already within a few feet of one of the GES workers, backing him down.

At nearly 6 feet tall, Lindy towered over the man. And from the back Oscar could see that Lindy's broad, athletic shoulders looked up to the task of bowling the much smaller man over if he had the poor judgment to argue.

Unfortunately for him, the GES worker had slurped just enough beer in the truck on the way to the winery that he poked his finger in the middle of Lindy's chest, a poke that resulted in her grabbing his wrist and dropping him to the winery floor in a textbook martial arts takedown.

The rest of what happened remained a little blurry, even a year later.

The other five men backed up as he approached, just like opposing football team players had 40 years before when Oscar was the lead blocker for his best friend in high school, Jack Stafford.

At 6 feet, 4 inches tall and weighing 275 pounds, Oscar even intimidated some of the Samoan players on opposing teams, immigrants to the U.S. who discovered their size made them ideal for American football.

Jack always said it was like following an express freight train down the field, with potential tacklers scattering like rag dolls as Oscar slammed past them. It resulted in a lot of touchdowns for Jack and Oscar's alma mater, Northside High School of Horseheads.

But in the winery brawl, the man Lindy had taken down leaped up off the floor and onto Oscar's back, getting a chokehold around Oscar's fleshy neck.

Oscar grabbed the arm around his neck and swung the GES worker around in a circle several times, unfortunately clipping several wine bottles and expensive glasses on the tasting bar, sending most crashing to the floor.

When Oscar saw that two of the broken wine bottles were his famous and very expensive Riesling called Oscar's Boot, he reached behind and swung his attacker over his shoulder and slammed him to the floor.

One of the other men rushed Oscar with a broken wine bottle, getting in a single slash before Lindy walloped his skull from behind with the Louisville Slugger baseball bat Oscar kept handy behind the bar.

The other four GES workers ran out the door and were later arrested for assault, as were the two injured men paramedics had to carry out on stretchers.

As Oscar traced the scar again, he remembered that Jack Stafford still hadn't returned his phone calls or emails since returning home to Horseheads. Oscar had been the best man at Jack's wedding to Devon. Until the Tonga accident, they had been in touch fairly regularly via email.

Oscar decided that it might be best to simply show up in Horseheads at the *Clarion* office – or Jack's house.

He knew that Devon's sister Cassandra was staying there, helping out with Noah and – he hoped – helping Jack deal with losing Devon.

Jack had come back to his New York roots after a long journalism career in California. At that time he was grieving for his wife Amy, who had died suddenly of colon cancer.

Devon had brought him out of that depression. And when they married and then left with baby Noah for Jack to write a book in Tonga, Oscar thought he had never seen Jack so happy. To lose someone you loved a second time. It was just unthinkable.

Oscar touched the scar again and looked away from the mirror. He saw his niece Lindy staring at him.

"Oscar. Not to ruin your day," Lindy said. "But one of the servers is having trouble with two loud guys at the tasting bar. They're pretty drunk and making rude comments. I think both of them were in that bunch that gave you that scar."

Oscar saw that Lindy had the winery's Louisville Slugger dangling from her fingers.

"Time for a little batting practice?" she said with a grin.

Chapter 12

```
From the Horseheads Clarion

Column One
Horseheads Clarion
```

Wolverines and a deadly prank

```
By Jack Stafford

    If  the  name  "Wolverines"
doesn`t   ring   any   bells,
that`s   because   it`s   been
three   years   since   this
shadowy       environmentalist
group  -  rabidly  opposed  to
hydrofracking for natural gas
- was  busy  across  the nation
```

making mischief, using a variety of dirty tricks to slow down natural gas companies from expanding their drilling – and concomitant pollution.

Some of those dirty tricks were at the level of teenage pranks: Air let of gas company vehicle tires, broken windows at offices, super glue in door locks, even some low-level computer hacking.

Over time the group escalated to destroying expensive equipment and ramped up its *pranks* to dangerous levels, including lighting off spectacular explosions at gas drilling sites.

For the record, none of these pranks resulted in injury to people, just destruction of gas company property.

Police tried unsuccessfully to link the Wolverines to the death of the late Grayson Oliver Delacroix III, the former CEO of Grand Energy Services. He was killed in a spectacular natural gas explosion at his Flathead, Missouri mansion several years ago.

About the same time as Delacroix`s death, the Wolverines disappeared. In the few instances where the name popped up in association with some incident, it eventually proved to be copycats or perhaps a Wolverine-wannabe.

All that is prelude to the fact that the group – or at least the *name* of the group – has resurfaced in Rockwell Valley.

And this time, one person is dead.

As reported earlier this year in this newspaper, Tyrone Arthur Garber of the Central Pennsylvania Railroad fell to his death – or police say might have been *pushed* – from the high railroad trestle that spans Rockwell Valley State Park. He had been checking out a suspicious package on the beams under the tracks. His body was found smashed on rocks below.

The package retrieved by Rockwell Valley Police turned out to be road flares dressed up to look like dynamite.

The word *Wolverines* was written on the outside.

The Rockwell Valley Police are keeping the details of their investigation quite hush-hush, which is understandable.

Less understandable are the grandstanding remarks by Rockwell Valley`s Mayor Will Pennisen. Pennisen is shouting to anyone who will listen that the fake dynamite package represents the opening salvo in some planned eco-terrorist assault against Grand Energy Services` proposed propane and natural gas storage project in the unused salt caverns adjacent to Rockwell Valley Lake.

You might remember Mayor Pennisen also works for GES as project manager.

It`s impossible to say whether the Wolverines have suddenly reactivated. Certainly giving people a fright with some fake dynamite fits with their profile from years past.

But it is also curious that just as public opposition to this risky project starts ramping up, the Wolverines allegedly reappear. It provides a timely diversion to shift the public`s attention away from the manifold safety issues posed by storing the gas below ground in uninspected - and possibly porous - caverns.

Not to mention the safety

of the railroad trestle, which would carry tankers loaded with liquid propane gas.

It also seems like amazing timing as GES steamrolls this controversial project through without sufficient public input or public viewing of studies that show how dangerous this project will be.

Some people are calling for a *more-thorough* assessment, called an *environmental audit,* to be performed by federal officials or a private consulting firm.

In all this, I don`t mean to diminish the death of Mr. Garber.

But his job was, after all, to ensure safety. That`s why he was on that trestle on a snowy January day in the first place.

In his memory, citizens need to keep focused on the bigger picture of defining safety for the people of Rockwell Valley and the surrounding area.

Storing propane and natural gas under pressure in salt caverns most likely should *not* be part of that definition.

Jack Stafford is the

publisher of the Horseheads Clarion *and publishes* Column One *every Friday. He can be reached at* JJStafford@HorseheadsClarion.com.

Chapter 13

Jack sat in his office and watched Eli's fingers flying across the keyboard like a concert pianist as he sat at his desk in the newsroom. Based on his keystrokes Jack could usually tell the difference between Eli writing a story or doing online research.

Eli had developed the *Horseheads Clarion*'s website into a model one national magazine called "a blend of journalistic excellence and electronic art."

Today Jack guessed that Eli was writing a story about Alice McCallis's group pushing for an environmental audit of the entire salt cavern storage project proposed for the north end of Rockwell Valley Lake.

The audit – as proposed by her and the No On Gas organization – would look at the safety of the caverns, the truck and rail transportation issues, the effects on the community from possible air and groundwater pollution and also how the project might adversely affect tourism.

Eli had also told Jack that NOG was worried about the project polluting Rockwell Valley Lake itself. The water in the lake was several hundred feet deep in some spots and very cold. The word *pristine* was often used by people describing it.

"Jack, were you here when Alice McCallis got the state

to shut down the salt mines?" Eli asked.

Jack knew Eli was asking more to make conversation than to seek information. Eli had already amassed a huge pile of clippings on his desk from the newspaper's old-style paper library.

In fact, Jack had just left Horseheads for a newspaper job in California when McCallis started her crusade, though he later read with some satisfaction about how McCallis had taken on the salt mines and won the battle.

"Eli, when you get a minute, come on in, okay?" Jack said. "I want to talk about these Canadian doctors who won't treat people poisoned by tar sands."

Eli waved his agreement with one hand while he kept typing with the other, intent on the story in front of him.

How does he do that? Jack thought. *I can touch-type 90 words per minute, but I certainly can't do it one-handed.*

Before Jack left for Tonga, he had written several columns about the Pennsylvania gag law that made it illegal for doctors to divulge – even to their patients – the names and possible negative health effects of toxic chemicals they might have been exposed to around hydrofracking sites.

Jack's columns had led to a huge national blowup when GES revealed that it was using a genetically modified organism in an attempt to detoxify the fracking chemicals put in the hydofracking chemical cocktail used during drilling. The GMO had started destroying concrete. And in some cases it mimicked a flesh-eating bacteria when it landed on live tissue, prompting GES to go back to its old – and toxic – formulas.

But an email from a Canadian journalist about doctors in Alberta had Jack wondering about medical treatment.

> Unofficially, our doctors are refusing to treat anyone who comes in saying they are sick because of any kind of exposure to anything relating to the tar sands. By the way, my newspaper requires me to call them 'oil` sands. Just thought you might be on the lookout for something similar in the U.S. where your medical care is mostly private and subject to even more pressure.

Jack had just reread the email and was searching for a story in an Alberta, Canada newspaper when Eli came in and plunked down in the chair in front of Jack's desk, a short stack of file folders in his lap.

"The audit story is ready to go," Eli said. "I wrote it myself mostly because I have Jill and Stan and the other two out doing non-gas stories for Tuesday. It keeps me from getting rusty, anyway."

Jack doubted that Eli would ever get rusty at writing, photography or his real specialty of Internet and database researching. The four full-time reporters on the staff loved him and respected his abilities.

Jack wondered if maybe *he* was just a little envious of that.

"So is there any feedback from GES about the environmental audit?" Jack asked. "Someone is going to have to pay for it, and we can bet the town council of Rockwell Valley isn't going to."

Eli flipped open the top folder and read from the story he had just written and then printed out a hard copy. Despite being totally wired into his computers and various electronic devices, Eli made paper copies of nearly everything.

"GES says it doesn't need an environmental audit at all. Big surprise, right?" Eli said. "But Alice McCallis says NOG will consider a lawsuit to force them to do the study."

Jack could tell Eli had more to say but was hesitating. Their last in-the-office conversation about the geologist report on the salt cavern project hadn't ended satisfactorily for either of them.

"Go ahead, Eli. What is it? You look kind of distressed. Spit it out. We can work it out, if it's about that report."

Eli blew some air out and then grinned.

"Not distressed. No, no. And forget that report. I'm crazy happy, I think. Shania told me this morning she's pregnant. I'm going to be a dad!"

Chapter 14

The news about Eli and Shania expecting a baby almost broke the spell that kept Jack in a bleak personal landscape limited to work at the newspaper and a just-beneath-the-surface mourning for his dead wife.

That afternoon when he came home, he scooped up Noah in his arms, hugging him, then threw an arm around Cass, kissing her on the cheek.

"Are you okay?" Cass asked, pushing Jack away.

Then suspiciously, she asked if he had been drinking.

"No, no. Jesus, Cass, not a drop. And yes I am okay," Jack said. "Really okay. Eli told me he and Shania are going to have a baby. Noah, my little man. You will have a cousin, sort of."

He spun a startled Noah around a few times before putting him down, feeling a touch of hope – of fun and anticipation – that he couldn't remember feeling since before Devon had died.

Jack stopped when he saw that Cass was looking out the front window, her arms crossed tightly, just like Jack's mother had 40 years before when he was teenager and she was about to give him a lecture.

He felt his balloon of ebullience collapsing.

"Your friend Oscar called the house today," she said. "He's worried about you and wonders why you haven't called him."

She paused, then turned slightly to look at him.

"And are you sure you haven't been drinking?"

Noah stood halfway between Jack and Cass, looking first at his father, then his aunt who looked so much like his mother. Although he couldn't hear what was being said – nor would have understood it – the vibrations in the air were enough that he started to cry, tiny tears at first that overflowed down his cheeks.

It was one of those moments that get frozen in time in people's memories.

Jack stared at Cass for a moment, then turned, walking into his home office, where he closed the door without looking back.

Noah walked to the door and stood silently looking at it, then back at Cass.

She closed her eyes and wished that this was a stage play in which she was an actress who had just blown her lines.

Or maybe I'm turning into Liz Taylor playing Who's Afraid of Virginia Woolf, she thought.

God.

Chapter 15

Jack showed up the next morning at the newspaper with a huge bag of pastries from Millie's Diner and called a meeting of the news staff.

After brooding in his home office for a half-hour the night before with the door firmly shut – and angry at Cass for spoiling his mood – he went out to apologize, nearly tripping over Noah, who was still standing outside his office door looking puzzled.

Cass was still in place in front of the living room window, too, her eyes looking red.

An hour later the three of them were hurling popcorn at each other while they watched a cartoon video after Cass apologized for sounding like a shrew and Jack apologized for not recognizing her concern was for his well-being.

All Noah knew for *sure* was that smiles were good. And being allowed to throw food at adults? *That* was a lot of fun.

"Do we have an agenda for this meeting, boss?" Eli asked, sticking his head into Jack's office. "Other than eating all these low-calorie foods you brought in."

Jack held up the cream-filled maple bar he was eating,

remembering darkly for a fraction of a second that Devon used to try to keep him from eating the 500-plus calorie sugar bombs he loved.

"We do, in fact. I have a short list of stuff I think we should pursue, but I am leaving the details of how to chase it all to you. By the way, I got this health food across the street. I'm sorry I haven't been very social since I got back. But I must say, Shania looks great. And it's so great she's the manager of Millie's Diner. That's fabulous."

Across the room in the glass-walled conference room, Jack could see that Eli had already assembled the staff – and the platter of food – for the staff meeting.

Two of the people, Jill Nored and Stan Belisak, had been working at the *Horseheads Clarion* before Jack left to write his book. They'd been fresh out of college then, but now, with nearly three more years of reporting, both had developed keen research and writing skills.

The other two staff members, Rue Malish and Keith Everlight, hadn't talked with Jack yet except for an initial handshake. Both had been stealing glances at him for the last couple of weeks, in awe of Jack's reputation as a fighter for good causes and his just-published book.

They had worked for newspapers in Ohio and Michigan, respectively, before Eli hired them. Rue's background in environmental sciences was helping the *Clarion* turn up all kinds of stories. Keith had covered courts and legal issues for a Michigan daily newspaper and was keenly interested in the way gas companies were trampling on individuals' rights in their quest to drill for more gas.

It was a story he had written about the Hutchinson, Kansas, natural gas disaster – and what part salt-cavern storage played there – that prompted Eli to recruit Keith to the staff.

When Eli had hired Rue he thought she might be from his native India. It turned out she was born there but left as an infant. The very slight but pleasing British accent that Eli noticed came from two years spent in Kenya in the Peace Corps, where she worked with British engineers on water and agricultural projects in the villages.

She usually joked that she was glad she had not joined AmeriCorps and been posted to Alabama.

Keith almost didn't get hired because of a swagger that bordered on arrogance, even in his initial interview with Eli. And while he seemed quite athletic and fit, due to the fact that he was barely 5 feet 6 inches in the big-heeled cowboy boots he always wore, Shania thought he might have a little inferiority thing going on, too.

When Jack walked into the room, they all stood up, surprising him.

"Well, I must say I appreciate the gesture, people. But honestly, even though I'm the publisher, when you stand up like that it mostly makes me feel like an old crock," Jack said with a laugh.

"Hell, I *am* an old crock. Sit."

The introductions, story ideas and bad jokes flew around the conference room for nearly an hour, an hour in which Jack could relax and feel all was right with the world. For that hour he forgot all about Devon, Noah's not speaking – even how to approach Cass about asking her to stay on to help with Noah.

The focus of that hour was on keeping the *Horseheads Clarion* pushing against the continued multiple threats posed by hydrofracking for natural gas and how to best use the talented staff that sat in the room.

The list was impressive: a proposed gas pipeline through Rockwell Valley to the salt cavern storage, the salt cavern storage itself, railroad safety, air pollution monitoring and an increase in minor earthquakes believed tied to nearby hydrofracking.

When Jack's cell phone rang and he saw it was Oscar Wilson calling, he excused himself and thanked everyone as he left the room.

"And as a favor, either eat all those damn pastries or get them out of the building somehow, okay?" Jack said as walked out to take the call.

Oscar – as Jack had expected – gave Jack a friendly ribbing for not getting in touch since getting back, then invited him and Cass and Noah to come up to the winery over the weekend.

But Jack's mood darkened when Oscar also told him that he had heard that a second batch of road flares – disguised as dynamite – had been found in a culvert under the gate leading into the Grand Energy Services site at the north end of Rockwell Valley Lake, where the company wanted to store natural gas and propane in salt caverns.

"With the word *Wolverines* on the outside?" Jack asked.

Oscar grunted yes.

"But it's worse," Oscar said. "The guy who told me – he knows people at GES – said the flares had a note attached. It said the next batch would be real dynamite if GES keeps building."

Chapter 16

If Luther Burnside was concerned about the threats against GES and its Rockwell Valley proposed salt cavern storage of propane and natural gas, it certainly didn't show, Rod Mayenlyn thought.

Burnside was dressed this morning in an even *more* expensive silk suit than the last time Mayenlyn had seen him. And Mayenlyn would have sworn that Burnside was starting to deliberately dress so he looked like a Mafia Don – complete with a new haircut that made him look even *more* like his nickname of Luca Brasi, the character from the book *The Godfather*.

A meeting of all the senior vice presidents and their support staff was scheduled for later that morning to go over production reports from hydrofracked wells, the progress on getting permits for liquid natural gas ports on the east and west coasts and a threat assessment provided by GES in-house security services.

The threat assessment was almost a footnote at the end of the longish list that Mayenlyn knew would keep him scrambling on the public relations end for the rest of the week.

"I know we have good folks in our security area. But how should I be spinning these fake dynamite packages? I mean, the last one is some kind of warning," Mayenlyn said. "I would have preferred for these Wolverines to stay dead."

Burnside looked out the window at the parking lot, where many of the executives who would take part in the meeting were just scrambling in from their cars.

He drummed his fingers on the desk, tipped his head and pursed his lips slightly.

Oh Christ! Mayenlyn thought. *I just watched that same gesture in the new Mafia movie about Las Vegas. This is just too much.*

Burnside swung around and smiled at Mayenlyn, shuffling the papers on his desk until he came to a one-page report on the flares-disguised-as-dynamite in Rockwell Valley.

"Rod, I don't know how much you know about explosives," Burnside said. "But frankly, terrorists who really want to blow shit up would use something else. Plastic explosives. Maybe a pipe bomb. Maybe a truck full of fertilizer, like that nut job in Oklahoma City. These are amateurs."

He looked back out the window and drummed his fingers for another moment.

This is maddening, Mayenlyn thought. *Maddening.*

"But I want you to use these two incidents to generate sympathy. And set the stage for the need for more security at all our gas wells."

Mayenlyn was waiting for Burnside to ask him about Jack Stafford again – if he was making any headway in finding a way to neutralize him.

The *Horseheads Clarion* had announced on its front page that it was about to start publishing a series of articles – written by some quasi-attorney reporter named Keith Everlight – about GES efforts to silence critics of hydrofracking.

"Maybe you should take a look into all of the staff of that newspaper and not just Stafford," Burnside said. "I know that editor – what his name, Guppy or something – is some kind of immigrant. It might work to our advantage to tag him as un-American or something. You're good at that."

Mayenlyn felt his face flush. He *was* good at twisting facts and used the supposedly independent website Energy First America to harass critics and discredit a lot of very on-target news reports. The other spin-off websites he controlled were getting plenty of attention on social media, too.

But Mayenlyn was wary of tangling too directly with Jack Stafford and the *Horseheads Clarion*. The newspaper had crusaded quite successfully against Burnside's predecessor and always seemed to be one step ahead of GES.

Stafford had caught GES using hydrofracking wells as dumping grounds for a variety of toxic chemicals unrelated to fracking. Had the late Grayson Oliver Delacroix not been blown into pieces by a natural gas explosion at his house, he would likely have had to eventually face a federal investigation into the scheme.

"Gupta. Eli Gupta. He was born in India but came to the U.S. as a toddler. His journalism credentials are pretty strong. He ran the whole paper while Stafford was off writing that book," Mayenlyn said. "He's some kind of computer genius, too. I don't know about going after him."

Burnside looked out the window again and started drumming his fingers, this time harder.

"Sounds like you admire the little shit. All right. But let's get a story up on Energy First and maybe a couple of the others about how GES won't kowtow to terrorists and plans on ramping up security in Rockwell Valley. Maybe throw in we are considering hiring local people. That might shut up a few more people there."

Mayenlyn nodded his agreement and stood to head down the hall to the conference room where the vice presidents and staff were starting to assemble.

Among his file folders was one labeled "Stafford," which now contained a detailed – and entirely illegal – narrative written by a staff nurse about Jack Stafford's stay at the private psychiatric clinic on Vashon Island.

It had cost Mayenlyn $10,000 to get it. And while Mayenlyn knew it was exactly the kind of dirt that Burnside was looking for, he was holding it back.

Christ, am I growing a conscience? Mayenlyn wondered.

He shook off the thought and headed down the hall.

Chapter 17

```
From the Horseheads Clarion

Column One
Horseheads Clarion
```

Free speech and natural gas

```
By Jack Stafford

   It`s become almost a
cliché for newspapers like the
Horseheads Clarion to have to
remind public officials - and
even readers - how important
the American right to free
speech is.
   So often such reminders come
```

off too preachy, too seemingly self-serving, because the same amendment to the U.S. Constitution that gives *you* the right to say what`s on *your* mind protects the press, too.

But when those rights are threatened, we have a duty to shout it as loudly as we can.

Hello, Mr. Luther Burnside at Grand Energy Services in Flathead, Missouri! Can you hear me now?

In the wake of two incidents in which road flares, disguised to look like sticks of dynamite, mysteriously appeared in Rockwell Valley, GES has somehow convinced a friendly judge to sign an order imposing a quarter-mile *no-protest* buffer from any GES hydrofracking well site, GES business office and even the yet-to-be approved and extremely controversial GES salt cavern storage project at the north end of Rockwell Valley Lake.

There is some question as to whether the judge`s order might even extend to a parked GES truck.

Really.

Verbal protests, waving a sign, or even holding a silent

vigil could result in arrest, the order says.

This would prove extremely awkward if the *Horseheads Clarion* were located in Pennsylvania, not New York.

Our office is across the street from the immensely popular Millie's Diner that is frequented often by GES line workers seeking its hearty food.

That such a draconian order was approved is appalling. It shows the immense power — and even abuse of power — that the company is willing to employ in its quest to drain Pennsylvania's resource of natural gas, leaving the environmental carnage with which we are becoming all too familiar.

For the record, the second *flares-as-dynamite* package was left more than a quarter mile from the proposed salt cavern storage facility, pretty compelling evidence that this latest maneuver by GES has nothing to do with security and everything to do with silencing critics.

Much of that silencing has already been accomplished

with the non-disclosure forms landowners are required to sign when they lease their acreage for hydrofracking. All GES workers are required to sign similar forms. And it`s well-documented how medical personnel are effectively muzzled by a Pennsylvania state law that prohibits doctors from talking about specific fracking-related causes of illness.

They can`t even talk specifically about what`s in fracking fluid with the *patients* they treat for fracking-related problems.

This latest GES ploy is simply tying up some free-speech loose ends. It`s surprising, given the company`s track record, that it hasn`t found such a gas-friendly judge before.

It probably also won`t come as much of a surprise that a series of articles that started last week in the *Clarion* looking into a variety of gas-industry legal issues has already drawn several nastygrams from GES representatives, threatening legal action against the newspaper, staff reporter Keith Everlight and myself.

If it sounds like those

of us at the *Clarion* are not particularly worried by this legal bluster, it's true.

The most recent missive from GES said it would take action against Walter Nagle, too.

If the members of the legal research team working for GES are so out of the loop they don't realize that Walter Nagle - the legendary publisher of the *Clarion* for decades - died four years ago, we probably have little to fear from their legal briefs.

Jack Stafford is the publisher of the Horseheads Clarion *and publishes Column One every Friday. He can be reached at JJStafford@HorseheadsClarion.com.*

Chapter 18

When Keith Everlight was in college, his boxing coach said he had the fastest hands he had ever seen in welterweight, particularly with such power in both of his fists.

Keith left his amateur boxing record of 35 wins and one loss off his résumé when he went job hunting after his first out-of-college newspaper reporting stint.

It hadn't taken long for people in that community

to figure out that he had made the state amateur boxing finals out west only to lose a split decision against a heavy-punching super-middleweight who had starved himself down to the welter division so he could get a shot at an Olympic berth.

Even in that loss, Keith had broken the bigger man's nose – a feat he also accomplished in more than half of his victories.

The last Keith had heard, his super-middleweight-turned-welterweight opponent had ballooned to more than 200 pounds and was working at a Wal-Mart in Bend, Oregon, stocking shelves on the weekends.

It was years of sizing opponents up in the ring, boxers almost always at least a few inches taller than he was, that kept Keith from worrying too much about the two GES workers who had driven their truck up at high speed and slammed on their brakes, nearly colliding with the front of his parked car across the road.

Two hours earlier Keith and Eli had been working on a local angle to tie in with an international story about a natural gas pipeline in Manitoba, Canada that had exploded, bursting into flames and cutting off gas supplies to potentially thousands of people.

It immediately brought to mind the proposal by GES to build a pipeline across miles of rolling hills with dairy farms to bring in fracked natural gas for storage in the salt caverns at the north end of Rockwell Valley Lake.

But Eli wanted a photo of what construction was already underway, even before the permit had been issued for the pipeline that was opposed by many Rockwell Valley residents.

Shortly after Eli took over as editor, he issued every news staff member an expensive point-and-shoot digital camera as standard equipment.

Keith looked across the field at the GES fracking site 10 miles west of Rockwell Valley, where there were several large stacks of pipes that looked like they might become part of the proposed pipeline.

"Hey, Rumpelstiltskin, no pictures," the driver of the GES truck said as he slammed the door to the truck. "This area is restricted by the judge. You're going to have to give up the film."

Keith clicked off a few more frames, then turned the camera towards the two men and pushed the setting to sports mode. When he pushed the shutter button, the small camera rapped off probably 25 photos in a few seconds, sounding like a mini machine gun.

"Hey. I mean it. I want that film, *smartass*," the driver said, still standing by the rear fender of his truck, the hood of which was barely a foot from Keith's car.

The Rumpelstiltskin reference surprised Keith a little, particularly because the man's accent was definitely tinged with a hillbilly twang, Tennessee or maybe Kentucky.

But he knew he wasn't dealing with anyone very sophisticated or he wouldn't be using the word *film*.

Outside of a handful of photo hobbyists, film had disappeared a long time ago. And no media Keith knew used anything but high-definition digital images.

"Hey, *Shorty*. I'm talking to you. You deaf, too?"

Shorty. That's more like it, Keith thought. *His mother probably read him Rumpelstiltskin at bedtime when he was done with his day of torturing small animals.*

Keith turned quickly and walked a diagonal path back towards the driver's side of his car, holding up his press card and I.D. lanyard for the two men to see, waving it over his head without making eye contact.

That these goons were bullies was a given. And by not looking directly at them, he thought they were likely to think he was afraid. And that might slow them down just enough for him to leave.

His theory evaporated when the other GES worker moved quickly on the other side of the road to stand behind Keith's car, blocking his exit.

Keith still opened the driver's door and got in quickly, putting his reporter's notebook on the dashboard, next to a coffee mug-sized figurine of a dog with huge bulbous eyes covering a wide panorama. It looked like one of those bobble-head dog figurines some people put in the back windows of their cars, just a little bigger and definitely uglier.

It also contained a high-definition, wide-angle video camera.

Then the tall driver rapped on his window, hard.

"I'm losing my patience. I don't care who you are. I want that fucking camera now."

Keith rolled down the window a few inches and peered up at the man.

"Look, this camera doesn't have film. But here, I'll take this little card out. See? It's got the pictures on it," Keith said. "It's yours. I don't want any trouble."

He cursed under his breath when the GES worker yanked the car door open and pulled him out by his arm. He took the camera from Keith's hands and looked at it curiously before setting it down on the hood.

"A few minutes ago, maybe I would have done that. But now, little man, I am taking your camera and giving it to my boss. You can't take pictures of our equipment. And if your ass isn't gone in like 10 seconds, you are going to get hurt."

Keith held up his hands in protest.

"I was just here doing my job. On a public road. My boss wanted some photos of where your pipeline is going. That's all."

The GES worker snatched the camera off the hood and walked away, pausing just long enough to turn around and give Keith the finger.

The other GES worker stepped from behind Keith's car to let him back up, laughing.

"Bring your big brother with you next time, Pee Wee," he said.

Definitely Kentucky, Keith thought. *Definitely.*

Keith pulled away, fighting the urge to offer his own single-digit salute out the window but happy he hadn't lost his temper. He had plenty of time to cool down on the drive back to Horseheads.

And he had a great story to write. With video.

Chapter 19

Rod Mayenlyn was rereading the draft of what he thought might be one of the best press releases and website posts for Energy First America he had ever put together.

After Jack Stafford's column basically poked his boss Luther Burnside right in the eye, Stafford became fair game.

And to think I felt a little sorry for the guy, Mayenlyn thought. *Well, we are going to dance.*

Mayenlyn's press release focused on Stafford's claim

that GES was somehow anti-U.S. Constitution. But as a counterpunch, Mayenlyn's press release and website story said that the real enemies were these shadowy Wolverine terrorists. The *Horseheads Clarion* – by not aggressively reporting on them – was encouraging attacks on GES.

"All GES wants to do is keep America on the track towards energy independence," his press release said. "Newspapers like the *Horseheads Clarion* seem to think it's all right to be forced to buy foreign oil or run short on natural gas and propane for heating during cold winter days. At GES, we don't."

Mayenlyn hoped that other media – generally somewhat envious of the *Horseheads Clarion*'s reporting – might turn on the newspaper, taking the heat off GES and the court order that was proving to be more provocative than effective.

Since the quarter-mile buffer zone was reported in the news media, protesters started to flood in from out of the area to support the local activists, creating a huge headache for local police and the GES security forces.

Only a handful of arrests had happened. But some of the people involved were high-profile environmentalists from New York who suddenly began targeting the proposed gas storage facility on Rockwell Valley Lake.

If this hit piece didn't rock Stafford back on his heels, Mayenlyn knew a friendly news producer at a television station in Buffalo who would probably be willing to run with the information about Stafford's stay in the psychiatric hospital on Vashon Island.

The guy loved to quote anonymous sources, Mayenlyn knew. And on more than one occasion, the producer simply made up the sources when he couldn't get anyone to go on the record with the information he wanted to show.

Mayenlyn looked over the material one last time, his finger hovering over the send button which would upload the press release to the EFA website and simultaneously send the link out to every media outlet in the state of Pennsylvania and many in New York's Southern Tier.

He pushed the button and yelled "*BOOM!*" – a habit he had picked up from watching a TV comedian who would punctuate the punch lines of his raunchy jokes.

Mayenlyn was still congratulating himself when his desk telephone rang. It was Luther Burnside's executive secretary, Ida Merganser. She said Mr. Burnside wanted to talk with Mr. Mayenlyn right away and to call him on his private line at his home.

"Any chance you can tell me what he wants, Ida?" Mayenlyn said.

"Not a chance," she said. "Not a *chance*."

Chapter 20

The video from Keith Everlight's dashboard doggy cam had captured some riveting video and good-quality sound of his encounter with the two GES workers.

And since posting it – along with a story and photos about the proposed GES natural gas pipeline – the *Horseheads Clarion* link was being picked up by media all over the Northeast.

Eli couldn't take his eyes off the website tracker that kept a count of how many hits the newspaper's site was getting.

Some media outlets were running stories contrasting

Keith's story about being forced to surrender his camera or get mugged against the EFA's version claiming how pure and noble GES was.

"It's not playing very well for GES," Jack said. "But then, how could it?"

Jack had called the staff together for another combination staff/strategy meeting, sessions he was finding were lifting his spirits, making him feel more and more like he was back in the fight against hydrofracking.

His sister-in-law Cass had noticed that when he left for the office each morning, he had a spring in his step that had been missing since she, Jack and Noah had returned from Tonga.

She knew it made it just that much harder to broach the conversation about how long she would stay on playing nanny and good auntie to Noah. She was falling more and more in love with the child, who still only communicated with her through touching and looks. Noah and Cass had developed their own aunt-nephew sign language.

At the staff meeting, Jack noticed that both of his female reporters were giving Keith reverential looks in the wake of his clever dealings.

The dashboard cam had been a going-away gift from an attorney friend in Michigan who said his had come in quite handy for recording conversations with clients – and occasionally journalists – in his car.

"The only problem is it doesn't have a remote activation switch," Keith said. "I bet Eli can help me with that. And I almost had those guys with the SD card trick, too."

Jack was confused when he saw Eli grin and bow his head as if to take applause.

"GES will buy us a new camera," Jack said. "They have

already apologized and agreed to it. But what about the SD card?"

Rue reached into her bag and handed Eli the company camera she had been issued the day she arrived. Eli snapped it open and popped out two SD cards onto the conference room table.

"I didn't buy these so gas company goons could be fooled. I got them so everyone would have a backup to use if a card failed," Eli said. "But I used that trick in Rockwell Valley when the judge made me sit in a cell at the police station back before you got back, Jack. That's how we had pictures of those GES guys arrested for assault. I handed over the SD card to the judge in court before he made me sit for two hours in a police station holding cell.

"Keith did the same thing. He palmed the one with the still images."

Jack shook his head.

"You know, Walter used to say that age and treachery will always overcome youth and skill. He was full of those kinds of bromides. But I have to say, between the dashboard camera and the double slots for SD cards, you guys are pretty clever. I am so proud of all of you guys. 'Guys' covers the ladies, too."

Jack could see that the staff around the table – Eli, Keith, Rue, Jill and Stan – all looked slightly uncomfortable at the praise.

"No, I mean it," Jack said. "You don't get a lot of compliments from outside the building. So bask in this today. Now let me throw out another of Walter's favorites, 'Great work. Now what have you got for me *today*?'"

Everyone laughed, if a little nervously.

"Well, for Tuesday's front page we have follow-ups planned on the Wolverine dynamite scares, the natural gas pipeline explosion in Canada and that Garber guy who took the header off the railroad trestle," Eli said.

"The police have ruled out foul play. They said Garber most likely just got dizzy and fell. It was snowing that day and it was icy. Plus he had some psychiatric condition that made him afraid of heights, his wife told the cops. He had no business up that high, she said. But no one at the railroad knew about it."

Jack leaned back in his chair and smiled, giving Eli the thumbs up to those and a short list of other stories and photos, including Keith's ongoing series on legal issues.

He stayed behind for a minute as the staff filed out, heading back to their computers and desk.

Eli's psychiatric remark stuck in Jack's head.

I wonder if anyone around here wonders about me, he thought.

Chapter 21

Placating politicians was just part of the job of police chief. Bobo Caprino had that pounded into him from practically his first day on the job as he worked his way through the ranks of the Rockwell Valley Police Department.

But this new Rockwell Valley Mayor was testing even Bobo's legendary patience with continuing demands to use the police department like a private army to go after people who opposed Grand Energy Services's proposed pipeline and salt cavern gas storage project.

Mayor Will Pennisen had called a few minutes ago

to make sure Bobo was in his office so that he could likely come in with yet *another* ginned-up idea to go after the remaining hardcore anti-GES people left in the community.

Between non-disclosure agreements, legal threats, and some extra-legal intimidation that made Bobo uncomfortable, it was amazing there was anybody left to say anything bad about GES or its projects.

A vivid mental image of Pennisen dressed up in Nazi gear smashing windows during the infamous *Kristallnacht* flashed through Bobo's mind until he shook it away.

"Did you really tell Pennisen I was in the office and had no appointments?" Bobo yelled out his office door to the female police dispatcher he really wanted to fire but couldn't.

That's the trouble with having your wife work for you, he thought. *When she becomes your ex-wife, you're stuck.*

As was her custom when pressured by Bobo for anything, the former Mrs. Alicia Caprino leaned back in her chair and flipped him the bird.

"I'll take that as a yes. Thanks ever *soooo* much, *Loretta*."

Another bird flashed from Alicia. Bobo had started calling her Loretta shortly after their divorce the year before, just to irritate. Alicia's mother's name was Loretta and well-known as the biggest bitch in six counties. Maybe in all of Pennsylvania.

The nice thing for Bobo was Alicia would never try to bring charges against her ex-husband/boss for any kind of harassment, because it was equally well-known that Alicia definitely was her mother's daughter when it came to attitude.

Bobo was surprised when he checked his email, hoping

for some emergency – *any* emergency – that would let him escape from Pennisen's visit, only to find a lengthy email from Pennisen sent minutes before, saying meeting in person was unnecessary.

Bobo read it twice, then pushed the print button so he would have a hard copy of the email to put in the locked file cabinet by his desk.

It always amazed Bobo what shit people would say in an email that they would never say in writing. *Except it is in writing anyway*, he thought.

Mayor Will Pennisen's email said he had heard that the group headed up by Alice McCallis was planning on a demonstration the following week at the gates of the proposed salt cavern gas storage at the end of Rockwell Valley Lake. It was a direct challenge to the judge's ruling for a quarter-mile, no-protest zone around all GES facilities.

It wasn't news to Bobo. He had already heard about it from one of McCallis's former high school teacher colleagues whose husband was a GES employee.

But Pennisen wasn't just being a good citizen alerting the police. He pointed out that GES had been quite generous with its donations and equipment. He half-asked, half-demanded that when the Rockwell Valley Police went to deal with whatever the protesters had planned, he wanted them to be in full riot gear in case an "incident" occurred.

Bobo skimmed the rest of the email, full of enough erroneous details about the local protest group to frighten even a right-wing paranoid into overreaction.

But then he reread the line that said Pennisen wanted

every officer who responded to be sure to have the pepper spray GES had donated to the police arsenal – and be ready to use it.

What is this dickhead thinking? Bobo wondered.

After rereading Pennisen's entire email one more time, Bobo sent him a carefully worded response that made Bobo sound like both a good police chief and employee of the town council, responsive to the town's mayor. But it also urged caution.

He printed out a copy of his email, along with a printed copy of a story he had included for Pennisen to read about a pepper spray incident at the University of California, Davis, from several years earlier.

Campus police intentionally pepper sprayed 21 students who were sitting on the ground peacefully protesting, posing no threat. The incident had forced several police retirements, a firing or two and cost the university $630,000 in direct settlement monies to the 21 students who were involved.

Ironically, the cop who was mainly responsible for the incident ended up winning a workmen's compensation claim of nearly $40,000 for the emotional stress he faced after the incident.

"Loretta," Bobo shouted… "Wait, wait! I'm sorry. I meant to say *Alicia*. By any chance can you lay your hands on a copy of our department liability insurance policy?"

He saw her chair lean back. But instead of a bird, he got a thumbs-up.

Progress, Bobo thought. *Progress*.

Chapter 22

When Jack came home from work and spotted two wine glasses sitting on the dining room table with dinner place settings for the three of them, it was a clue something big was up.

For the past few weeks Cass had been ferrying Noah to medical appointments with a variety of doctors to see if they could figure out why he wouldn't speak.

Jack and Cass knew that his hearing was a problem and that symptomatically he acted nearly deaf. But the doctors couldn't find *any* physical cause or physical damage that explained the hearing loss from the trauma of nearly drowning.

In the kitchen, Cass was busy at the stove, Noah right by her legs where he seemed to spend most of his time unless Jack was home. When Noah spotted Jack he hesitated for a second, then walked out and threw his little arms around Jack's legs.

"Whatever you're cooking in there smells delicious," Jack said. "Can I help do anything? I need to do something beside tap on a keyboard."

Cass came out of the kitchen, drying her hands on a small towel, her face a marvel of non-expression.

No hint there, Jack thought.

Like his late wife Devon, she was tall and pretty in a very natural way without any help from makeup or fancy hairstyles.

Tonight Cass had on light makeup, had taken her hair out of the ponytail in which it almost always was contained and was wearing a longish dark dress Jack remembered faintly seeing once before.

Maybe on the plane ride from Tonga, he thought.

Several nights before, she and Jack had talked briefly about a theater group in Rockwell Valley that was looking for a professional director to take over the reins. Cass was certainly qualified, and the discussion that night was all about Noah and what to do with him if she applied. Jack pushed her to think about it, though she seemed more irritated with his encouragement than pleased.

Jack had learned as a young reporter to look for status details that would give away what was going on. It was a lot like being a detective.

But then he realized that because his sister-in-law was a professional actress, director and playwright, he would simply have to watch the show. No reason to try to guess.

Part of that show included Cass giving him a peck on the cheek – the first kiss coming from her direction he could remember. It reminded him of the friendly busses his French *amis* handed out when he been in France years before.

The kiss turned out to be just a warm-up to the main act, which took place at the dinner table when Cass poured both of them a liberal glass of one of Oscar Wilson's wines from his Lakeside Winery as they sat across from each other, Noah at the end in a booster chair.

"You wonder about the wine, I know. And I can see those little journalist wheels spinning like hamsters in cages," Cass said, a hint of smile around the corners of her mouth that Jack was not sure she meant him to see.

"I chatted today with your doctor from the clinic on

Vashon. Actually, I talked with a couple of the staff there. I gave them a synopsis of life here, how you've been, how well you've adapted to being in charge of a newspaper again. And the consensus was you're a lucky man in a lot of ways."

She raised her glass in a toast.

"To one lucky guy and his lucky son," she said.

Jack raised his glass, clicked it lightly, then offered a second toast.

"To you Cass, for holding all this together and for bailing me out from Tonga. And, well, everything else. Right, little guy?"

Cass simply smiled and took a sip of her wine. Then she gave Noah a tiny portion of a vegetarian lasagna, took a little for herself and passed the spoon to Jack.

He wondered if this stage play would have much dialogue.

"In a nutshell, the doctors all agree you are not an alcoholic – but they pretty well knew *that* when you checked out of the clinic and told me so," Devon said. "What they were concerned about is that alcohol might be a trigger for depression – they called it *melancholia*. That's what they called the demon that sent you out swimming in the channel that night."

Jack stirred his food on the plate, avoiding eye contact, so that Cass wouldn't see that he was tearing up.

He didn't need to bother.

"It's okay to cry, Jack. I'm sure Devon told you that maybe 1,000 times. I know she did because she told me. Sisters don't keep secrets very well."

In the course of the next hour, Jack learned that in addition to keeping alcohol out of their house, Cass had enlisted the aid of other people who were around Jack, just to keep an eye on him.

The list was pretty long: Oscar, Oscar's niece Lindy, Eli, Eli's wife Shania and a handful of other community people who were only aware of the drowning tragedy in Tonga that had taken his wife Devon's life but not how Jack had fallen apart.

"Did I get a good report card?" Jack asked, mildly irritated but also flattered that so many people were acting as guardian angels.

"You did. And that's why I wanted to talk tonight about what the next act is in this play," Cass said.

Jack laughed hard enough that tears ran down his cheek a second time. Even Noah, who couldn't hear the words – and would not have understood even if he could – started to giggle.

"What's so funny?" Cass asked.

Jack took a sip of wine, then held it up for another toast.

"All the world's a stage," Jack said. "Are we writing this next act together, I hope?"

Cass lifted her glass and clicked with Jack's, this time her face serious.

"That's what I want to talk about. I want to go home, Jack."

Jack and Cass both looked at Noah at the end of the table, still giggling and now pushing his lasagna around with his spoon.

When he looked up and read the faces of the adults, he started to cry.

Ulysses Returns

Chapter 23

From the *Horseheads Clarion*

Column One
Horseheads Clarion

Politics, pepper spray and clumsy police work

By Jack Stafford

Today`s Column One is early this week. Normally, Friday would be the day for the *Horseheads Clarion* to run this column.

But Saturday`s events at the gates of the proposed Grand Energy Services salt cavern propane and natural gas storage demanded a more timely comment.

The comment?

What in the *name of God* were the Rockwell Valley Police thinking when they used pepper spray on a crowd of mostly senior citizens - and two teenagers - protesting peacefully Saturday?

The protest event was announced a week in advance. Organizer Alice McCallis said she fully expected the protesters to be stopped from approaching well outside the legally questionable quarter-mile "no-protest zone" ordered by a Pennsylvania judge a few weeks ago.

The protest was designed specifically to set up a legal challenge to that law.

Now the courts will also have to consider the separate issue of police brutality and excessive force.

Saturday morning the 21 protesters parked their cars at the top of hill on the road that skirts the north end of Rockwell Valley Lake. They walked down the muddy access road in a heavy rainstorm, past several GES-placed No Trespassing signs on their way to the locked gates.

They were not challenged at *any* point by any GES workers or security people.

When they arrived at the locked gates, they set up a few poster-board signs and waited for area media that had been alerted the night before. Unfortunately the announcement to the press about the protest gave the time for starting a half-hour later than when the protesters *actually* arrived at the gates.

That very human error meant that no media *directly* witnessed what happened.

When television crews arrived from Binghamton and several other Southern Tier cities 15 minutes after the protesters had walked down the same road, they found the access road from the highway blocked. A half-dozen armed, burly GES security people said the media representatives couldn`t pass, noting the quarter-mile exclusion zone dictated by judicial fiat.

A handful of print reporters - including Keith Everlight and Rue Malish from the *Horseheads Clarion* - were also bottled up at the top of the hill.

Keith Everlight`s complete story about what he saw and heard is at the top of this page. But let me borrow a couple of paragraphs.

"Barely five minutes after the press was denied access, four police cars from the Rockwell Valley Police Department - and a black van - arrived with lights and siren on as if there

was a bank robbery in progress.

"When the police got out of their units and a few more officers from the van, they were wearing SWAT-type uniforms and helmets with visors that hid the faces of the individuals.

"One television reporter who had started filming was told she was in the no-protest restricted zone and was threatened with arrest.

"Her camera was seized but later returned, minus its videotape."

The accounts of the protesters differ slightly, but the reports from Rockwell Valley Hospital are consistent: Most of the people – who said they were sitting peacefully on the ground, singing songs written by the late Pete Seeger – were sprayed with a pepper-spray type substance. A Rockwell Valley doctor said one of the teenagers was temporarily blinded but expected to fully recover her sight.

The protesters uniformly agree that they were told by an officer with a bullhorn that they were under arrest for trespassing and violating the

Ulysses Returns

judge`s order about the quarter-mile no-protest buffer.

They also agree that before anyone could even *get* to their feet, one unidentified officer stepped forward and started pepper spraying Alice McCallis in the face.

A moment later, other officers opened fire with their canisters.

This newspaper has – on many occasions – decried the attempts by GES and other gas companies to silence its critics. But it appears the protesters were *deliberately* drawn into a trap to make some kind of brutal point about who holds the power.

Brutal barely describes it.

The protesters` goal was to call attention to a law designed to stifle free speech and get a test case before the courts.

They got their wish.

Jack Stafford is the publisher of the Horseheads Clarion *and publishes Column One every Friday. He can be reached at JJStafford@HorseheadsClarion.com.*

Chapter 24

It was a week of confessions and revelations for Eli Gupta, Rod Mayenlyn and Bobo Caprino.

On Monday Jack confessed to Eli that in fact he *did* have the geologist's report called *A Clear and Present Danger,* about the proposed gas project.

"I'm sorry that I let you think I didn't," Jack said. "I was trying to protect the newspaper – and *you* specifically – because I received it in an email from a source with the consulting firm. I won't say it was stolen. Not *exactly*. But if the consulting firm had claimed that it was, well, I didn't want you dragged into it."

On Wednesday Grand Energy Services CEO Luther Burnside confessed to Rod Mayenlyn that it was a new GES operative named Calvin Boviné – pronounced in French fashion as *Bo-vin-ay* – who had placed the road flare/phony dynamite packages on the railroad trestle and near the proposed salt cavern storage that were blamed on the Wolverines.

"Calvin is keeping a very low profile, as is his nature," Burnside said. "In fact, you won't find him in company records except listed in one spot as a special consultant. But I have some ideas on using him for a few more projects. Maybe even dealing with that asshole publisher in New York.

"By the way, don't ever call him Bovine. Like a cow? He'll rip your head off."

Mayenlyn was speechless, quickly reassessing Burnside's wanna-be Mafia-capacity for intrigue and ruthlessness.

"Okay, the dynamite thing was good, got us *lots* of

sympathy," Mayenlyn said. "But why are you telling me *now*?"

Burnside drummed his fingers on the desk before answering.

"Because, Rod, like they say in the CIA, I want you to 'run' Calvin for me. I don't want to deal with him directly anymore. You'll find he's quite a handful but very, very clever. And I have a project for you to give to him."

Then on Friday Rockwell Valley Police Lieutenant Del Dewitt confessed to Police Chief Bobo Caprino that on last week's raid against the salt cavern protesters, he had allowed Rockwell Valley Mayor Will Pennisen to take part in the police action, donning a police department SWAT team uniform, helmet and face visor.

"Chief, honest to God, *honest to God* had I known that little creep was going to lose it and open up on the protesters with a pepper canister, I would have stopped him. I would not have let him go," Dewitt said. "I should *not* have let him go along. *Period.* I know it. I know it. It was a huge mistake. *Huge.*"

Bobo put his head in his hands for a moment, then looked to make sure his office door was tightly closed so his ex-wife police dispatcher couldn't hear anything. Taking Dewitt's badge and gun – which he was sorely tempted to do – would only make a very public stink about something that maybe, just *maybe*, he could keep contained while he figured out what to do.

"And let me guess. Pennisen said that he was thinking of firing *me* and that he thought you were the best one to step in and take over the department," Bobo said. "But he wanted you do to him a favor first. Right?"

Dewitt's ever-present coffee mug was shaking slightly.

"Yeah. Something like that. Except that he said you were toast no matter what because you are soft on these anti-gas people."

Bobo picked up the phone and left a voicemail message at the mayor's office that he needed to talk with Pennisen right way.

He looked past Dewitt at his wall calendar and wondered if he *could* last 20 more months as police chief to collect his full retirement. Then he suddenly realized Dewitt hadn't said why he had waited until nearly a week later to tell him about the mayor's police play-acting.

"I get *why* you did it Del, really," Bobo said. "Though from my standpoint, you are living proof that some people can be educated way beyond their intelligence. But what took you so long to come in here and tell me?"

Dewitt put his coffee mug on the edge of Bobo's desk, then put his hands together so they *almost* looked like he was about to pray.

"Because I just figured out that Pennisen still has one of our service weapons. One of the new Smith & Wesson .40 caliber units we got from that latest federal batch of surplus stuff. We're one short in the gun locker.

"And he had one on him Saturday."

Pipeline to Perdition

Chapter 1

The staff meetings following the pepper spray incident at the proposed natural gas and propane salt cavern storage site were labeled "Fracking School" by Jack after he reviewed the stories that had been published for a full year prior to his returning to the *Horseheads Clarion*.

"You guys all have tremendous knowledge about how hydrofracking works, how the hydrofracking cocktails pollute and all about the other problems, too," Jack told the news staff in a special Saturday morning meeting.

"The problem is you have started to assume that our readers are keeping all this knowledge rolling around in their heads. You can't. Every story has to have enough in it that people who don't know much can get up to speed. Like the Wolverines and all the havoc they caused. People need perspective."

When Jack first announced they would be holding the two-hour sessions on Saturdays for several weeks – sufficient time to ensure that each of them could explain complicated fracking science in understandable terms – Keith Everlight complained privately to Jack.

"I don't think my stories are too complicated or leave out details," he told Jack, in Jack's office. Keith had his arms crossed tightly as he spoke, his jaw set tight. "People *get* my stories."

When Keith spoke, Jack remembered a conversation he had had with Eli about Keith's tendency take his self-confidence to the extreme.

"Your work is very good, Keith. Very good," Jack said. Then he pushed a copy of the *Horseheads Clarion* across the desk.

"But look at the sentence I circled from last Tuesday's edition."

```
McCallis said the toxic
chemicals from hydrofracking
have poisoned at least a dozen
private home water wells in
the northeastern portion of
the county, where GES just
hydrofracked four new wells.
```

Keith barely scanned at the sentence, then handed the newspaper back to Jack.

"It's perfect. There's nothing wrong with it at all. And Eli edited the whole story anyway," Keith said.

Jack felt his face darken.

Keith's response had two fatal flaws, Jack thought. First, he should have asked what *Jack* thought was wrong. Second, he should *never* have pushed it off on the editor who read it and approved it for publication.

"Aside from the fact that it's your responsibility to ensure your stories are accurate and complete, could you tell me what the toxic chemicals used in hydrofracking are? And where the names are in your story? They sure as *hell* aren't where they belong – right there with your reference to them. Maybe you can show me where they are."

Keith's face reddened and instead of being humbled, he told Jack that there had been so much press about the toxic chemicals in hydrofracking, the specifics were just common knowledge and didn't need to be listed anymore.

That's when Jack blew up.

"*You* are experienced enough to know that's not true. If you do think it's true, we have a serious problem. I want complete stories in this newspaper. If you have a story that says it's hot outside, I want the story to say *how* hot – in Fahrenheit. If the Rockwell Valley town council meeting runs long, I want to read how long, in hours and minutes. And I sure as hell want to know specifics in every damned hydrofracking story. We are publishing stories and photos and videos about an environmental war that the public is losing. *Losing*, Mr. Everlight. I can't have soldiers who don't know how to fight."

The following Saturday at the second session, Jack noted that Keith took careful notes on their discussions about the famous Halliburton Loophole signed into law in 2005 by then U.S. President George Bush giving natural gas companies exemptions to federal clean air and water laws.

And when the staff, Eli and Jack went over several stories from recent weeks that had lacked detail, Keith was quick to offer suggestions on what details needed to be added – and how.

"I am very happy with how much ground we covered in this session," Jack said. "Eli and I are planning next week's focus on some history. One piece will be about how several years ago the gas companies got caught adding all kinds of unnecessary toxic chemicals to the hydrofracking cocktail. It was part of their business plan, getting into the toxic waste disposal business."

Keith raised his hand.

"I remember that whole thing and how the *Clarion* broke the story," Keith said.

"But how do we know that they aren't still doing it?"

Eli and Jack *both* smiled.

"Exactly," Jack said. "That's exactly the kind of questions we need to ask. Actually, Keith, the questions you and Rue, Jill and Stan need to ask. We need to thread those kinds of questions – and information – into stories, into the interviews with gas company people. We need to keep people wondering and asking, too."

When they adjourned the meeting about 11 a.m., Jack offered to take the crew across the street to Millie's Diner to buy them all an early lunch. The staff groaned because they had demolished a huge platter of donuts and pastries that Eli had brought into the newspaper office when they first started.

But they all took Jack up on the offer.

No self-respecting journalist *ever* turns down a free meal.

Chapter 2

After the first few Saturday "Fracking School" sessions, the *Horseheads Clarion* staff went into a frenzy of chasing hydrofracking stories, writing follow-up stories on attempts by Grand Energy Services to stifle gas industry critics and taking a closer look at the details of the proposed pipeline for natural gas to and from the proposed salt cavern gas storage.

Media outlets, first from the Northeast, then the rest of the nation, started asking to reprint stories on their websites or print them in their publications, happy that the *Clarion* was returning to its aggressive stance in its reporting.

GES was keeping its pipeline project very low profile, instead pumping its energy into public relations to promote what a boon the salt cavern storage of propane and natural gas would be.

Without overtly promising it, every GES press release, speech, or public reference to the salt caverns gave the clear impression that natural gas and propane prices would dip for area residents.

"And that is total bullshit," Eli told Jack, sitting at Millie's Diner across the street.

Jack had given up coffee years before and was pleased that Eli's wife Shania – who had taken over as manager of the place while he was in the South Pacific – served his tea in the same New York State Publishers' Association mug that the late publisher Walter Nagle had used for many years.

Getting out of the office mid-morning was a ritual Jack and Walter had established along with Jack's late wife Devon. The corner table where Jack and Eli sat had been the scene of many informal news meetings and planning sessions.

It had even been dubbed "The Horseheads Press Club" by Shania.

This morning Jack and Eli were outlining how to go after the proposed pipeline project to show its impacts without creating too dry a story, peppered with too many details about how many miles it was and how many cubic feet of gas it would hold.

"I know I am demanding those kind of details in stories," Jack said. "And you're doing a good job of keeping these reporters filling in the blanks. But we need a human side to the pipeline, besides explaining why GES wants it so much."

All four reporters had been busy searching public records and within a week were convinced that the Grand Energy Services natural gas and propane storage project was *the* critical component in the GES strategy to ship Pennsylvania gas overseas.

But to get it overseas, it had to get to a proposed LNG port on Chesapeake Bay – or one of the other ports on the drawing boards.

"GES quietly bought up rights to run a spur off their existing pipeline system to the salt caverns," Eli said. "But from the west they have to convince a string of dairy farmers to let them run the line through."

Jack sipped his tea and waited for Eli.

"The thing is, these farmers haven't been keen on hydrofracking at all. Very few gas leases out there. In fact, I talked with a lawyer for one of them who said they organized to fight any attempts at forced pooling."

Jack looked at Eli like he didn't know what it was.

"Yeah, right Jack, like you don't know what forced pooling is," Eli said. "*Please* ... I read your column about it from about four years ago in our files. I'll make sure we explain it in the story."

Jack grinned and waved to Shania for a second cup of tea.

"So we are back to the human side of this pipeline to tell the story. What's your idea, Eli?"

Eli had brought in a file folder with paper clippings from the *Horseheads Clarion* put together by a high school student as a project on hydrofracking. The top clipping was from a year-old business story about a Rockwell Valley dairy farmer who had installed solar panels on the roof of his barn and his house and was now adding a massive solar array on a south-facing slope.

The photo with the story showed a tall man maybe, in his late 30s or early 40s, with a straw hat jauntily perched on his head.

He was standing in front of the under-construction solar array and looked like a proud parent with a child at a kindergarten recital.

"He is our human side, Jack. Lasse Espinola. His dad was Portuguese, his mother Norwegian. Dad's dead, but Lasse, his wife Audrey and his mother still run the 150-acre farm, right square where GES wants to run its pipeline.

"I called him and talked for an hour yesterday. He went to college in California, one of the state polytechnic schools, and studied ag science and – get this – political science."

Jack's tea arrived and Shania squeezed his shoulder before she left.

Another one of my watchers keeping an eye on me, he thought.

"So what's the plan, Eli?"

"We do a series of articles, using Lasse as the human face. And I have an idea for a title: 'Right in the Way.'"

Jack looked out the window at the two Grand Energy Services trucks that had just pulled up with six tough-looking gas field workers piling out.

"A farmer into solar power who's willing to fight to stop a natural gas pipeline. Genius, Eli. Genius."

The GES workers walked up to the diner lunch counter where two of the six stools were already occupied by two well-dressed women who Jack knew worked at a nearby insurance company office. When the women saw the GES workers looming over them, they smiled and hastily picked up their plates and moved to a small corner table.

The GES workers plunked on to the bar stools without even a grunt of thanks.

"I have another story idea to add to your list, Eli," Jack said. "You'll need to call Oscar up at Lakeside Winery about that fight last year. Oscar has been after me to visit him to see the scar he got. I think we need a follow-up story on GES community relations."

Chapter 3

The wiring harness and system controller for the new solar array were on the ground, not just cut away, but sliced into a hundred small pieces, making any repair impossible.

Dairy farmer Lasse Espinola could see that the controller itself, the soul and the epicenter of the array, looked like someone had smashed it with a rock.

This wasn't the work of teenagers, he thought.

The solar panels themselves didn't appear to have been harmed – at least of the ones he could easily see.

The 60 3'x5' panels were attached to a sturdy rectangular metal frame 8 feet off the ground on one end, 10 feet on the other. The height made it possible to drive a truck underneath – and for the cows to walk under easily. Plus the angle made it easy for the winter's snow to slide off.

Since he had built the array and warm weather arrived, some of the herd started using it for shade and shelter. And he had set up a water trough.

Lasse Espinola loved his cows like pets.

He noticed that the cows were on the other side of the pasture this morning, unusual as it was already heating up. The rain in the last few days had made the area around the solar panels into a combination mud-and-cow manure bog, through which Lasse tiptoed, trying to find the most solid ground to avoid sinking into the muck above his calf-high boots.

By the edge of the water trough, he saw huge footprints – left by someone with feet a *lot* bigger than Lasse's size 12 boots.

There's my vandal, Lasse thought. *Bigfoot.*

He smiled when he saw that whoever had done all the damage to his solar array – covered by his insurance – had managed to step in cow manure in several places. In fact, when the sun dried things out, some of the cow pies would have a perfect boot print to take to the Rockwell Valley Police Department.

Not that they would do much. People knew the police, the town government and even the local judges were controlled by Grand Energy Services, whose interests they served – not the public.

After walking around the array twice to satisfy himself that whoever had cut the wires and smashed the controller had not touched the solar panels themselves, Lasse made two quick phone calls.

The first was to his insurance agent, whose main office was in Horseheads. A friend of Lasse's wife answered and offered to help.

She assured him on the phone that his policy covered the vandalism but that he would need a police report before the agency could move ahead to file the claim.

The second phone call was to Lasse's 75-year-old uncle Einar, who had a dairy farm two miles to the east. The day before a visitor from GES had offered him a one-time bonus of $50,000 if he would sign a lease to allow the proposed GES pipeline to cross his land.

When Einar told him his land wasn't for sale – and would never be for sale – the GES man got angry and called Einar a "stupid Swede" and said he would regret not taking the offer.

Einar politely pointed out that he was from Norway, not Sweden, then told him in Norwegian and English to get off his land.

"I even remembered dat word you taught me. I yelled it at him when he stuck his finger in the air."

Lasse pictured the scene.

"Einar, you called him a *dickhead*?"

"Ya, and he was."

Lasse asked if he could borrow a pair of Einar's dogs for an indeterminate amount of time.

"Someone cut some wires on my solar panels last night. I don't think it was kids," Lasse said.

It turned out that Einar had two young Norwegian Elkhounds he was willing to give to Lasse, not loan.

"They like to chase da cows though, you know," he said. "You'll have to work with them."

Lasse laughed and told his uncle he would be over in the afternoon to pick up the dogs.

"Okay, I wait for you," Einar said. "And maybe that big dickhead, he come to apologize for calling me Swede. He was so big he could barely fit into his little car."

Chapter 4

The newsroom was a blur of activity as the staff put the finishing touches on a story about Alice McCallis hit with the pepper spray at the demonstration at the Grand Energy Services salt caverns at the end of Rockwell Valley Lake, where the company planned on storing natural gas and propane.

The pepper-spray incident was several weeks old – almost history in the journalism world.

But the day before, McCallis had been served with a court order banning her from any verbal, written or electronic contact with any GES workers, staff or representatives. And she was to stay away from all GES properties – by the same quarter-mile buffer margin as gas industry protesters.

If she set foot inside that buffer, she could be declared in violation of the court order, arrested and jailed.

The story Rue Malish was preparing pointed out that McCallis lived within a quarter-mile of a GES corporation yard where trucks and equipment were kept – a fact that seemed to have escaped the judge who issued the order or the GES attorneys who talked him into it.

"What is it about that woman that scares these gas company people so much?" Jack asked Rue.

"Well, she doesn't give up, for one thing. She's relentless," Rue said. "Until they put up that other quarter mile no-protest order, she was in front of some GES place nearly every day, posting protest signs, or sometimes with a clipboard and petition to ask people to help stop the gas storage. She posted a lot of videos online until her video camera was stolen. Lately she's been all over that proposed pipeline. She's been helping organize the dairy farmers who own land in the path of it."

Jack gave Rue a thumbs-up and said he looked forward to reading the story the minute it was filed. Jack was cogitating on *his* column for Friday, trying to decide if he wanted to feature this latest legalistic miscue with Alice McCallis – or write about natural gas pipeline safety.

So far GES had pretty much blown off all requests for information about any safety plans for either the proposed salt cavern storage project or the proposed pipeline.

Much of the pipeline would traverse lush farmland and pass through dense woods, if GES was successful in getting it approved. It would need access roads cut all along the pipeline route for maintenance and in the case of a leak – or worse.

The environmental damage caused by building roads and the disruption to wildlife was going to be massive. But so far Pennsylvania environmental regulators only seemed irritated when Jack, other journalists, or environmentalists asked about plans to mitigate those problems.

When Jack had lived near Davis, California for a short time, he remembered that the city had constructed a tunnel under U.S. Interstate 80 so that endangered toads could pass freely back and forth, as they had done before the highway was built.

Imagine Pennsylvania doing that, he thought. *They wouldn't do that much for people.*

Jack's reverie was interrupted when Eli stuck his head in the door and asked if he had heard about the new environmentalist group's report on how much gas was leaking from natural gas pipelines across the country.

"It just came out, and if you were doing a pipeline column, I thought you might want to include it."

The report detailed some of what Jack already knew – that the natural gas coming from the hydrofracked wells was different (some would say more toxic) than gas from conventional wells.

What he hadn't realized was that the pipeline being proposed by GES to run to and from its salt cavern storage was the same size as – and likely of similar construction to – the one owned by Pacific Gas and Electric in San Bruno, California that blew in 2010, destroying 38 homes.

"Eli, sometimes your timing is impeccable. Can you dig through the photo files for me? I think this week I'll have my column jump to the inside of the newspaper. I want to run a picture with it.

"Alice McCallis's predicament will wait for the next column."

Chapter 5

Jack was wrong about Alice McCallis's predicament waiting a week.

Just as Jack's column about pipeline safety hit the streets that Friday morning, Alice was arrested for violating the stay-away-from-GES court order. She had parked her car across the street from the Rockwell Valley GES office in the center of town on her way to the pharmacy to pick up a prescription.

An overeager GES billing clerk in the office saw her park and called the Rockwell Valley Police. The Rockwell Valley PD dispatched an overeager rookie cop who – instead of simply telling Alice she was in violation of the court order and asking her to move her car – puffed up like a blowfish and took her into custody on the spot.

An hour later, Police Chief Bobo Caprino was busy fielding calls from various media outlets – many from out of state – about the arrest of the 79-year-old activist.

"Bobo, you really need to train these boys better," McCallis said, sitting in a chair in his office. "If I had hired a professional public relations team to help me make a splash, I can't imagine they would have done any better."

When she came in – handcuffed – Bobo swore at the young officer, uncuffed her and hustled her into his office, passing by his ex-wife dispatcher, whose smirk was hard to miss.

And Bobo was almost sure that his ex-wife Alicia had placed a phone call or two to a couple of media outlets (using her cell phone so it would be less obvious) just to make her ex-husband miserable.

It had worked.

After talking with the Associated Press, Bobo pushed open his door and asked Alicia to find Lt. Del Dewitt. "Tell him to get his coffee-cup-swinging ass back into the station to help me," Bobo said. Out of deference to McCallis's position sitting in Bobo's office, Alicia didn't give him her usual one-finger salute; instead she let out a sigh strong enough to blow out a window before leaning into her microphone.

"Unit Two, Dispatch. Unit Two, what's your 10-20?"

The radio silence that followed was typical, as most of the Rockwell Valley Police Department did their police business on cell phones to keep it away from snoops who had police scanners.

So Alicia was surprised when Dewitt came on the air and reported in.

"This is Unit Two. I am at the mayor's office. Returning in 15."

McCallis watched Bobo come back in, slum into this chair and run his hand through his thinning dark hair.

"The mayor can't even bring himself down here to ask you to do his dirty work?" she said. "GES is hiring some lazy people these days."

Bobo looked across his desk, feeling a shred of sympathy for GES wanting to muzzle this retired schoolteacher.

"Just shut up. Please? Just shut up. I don't want to put you in a cell. Even though I know you would probably *love* that, wouldn't you?"

McCallis looked at Bobo and grinned, holding her wrists out as if to get the handcuffs put back on.

"I mean it, Alice McCallis. *SHUT UP.*"

Chapter 6

```
From the Horseheads Clarion

Column One
Horseheads Clarion
```

Safety should be GES primary concern

By Jack Stafford

The twin natural gas-related proposals currently facing Rockwell Valley have huge safety issues associated with them.

First is Grand Energy Services` proposed storage of natural gas and propane in the salt caverns at the north end of the lake.

Second is the Missouri-based company`s proposed pipeline to bring gas from hydrofracked wells in the area (and beyond) to the caverns, and then the continuation of that pipeline to a port on the Chesapeake Bay.

Yes, this Pennsylvania natural gas - produced by hydrofracking - is almost assuredly headed for overseas ports, most of them in Asia, where the liquid natural gas (LNG) sells for four or five times what it does in the United States.

The relative safety of the proposed natural gas and propane storage is shrouded in mystery because GES says it is *not* legally required to tell anyone how it might deal with emergencies.

Those emergencies could include fires, derailments of propane railcars, explosions, toxic chemical spills and a host of other frightening scenarios, all detailed in a report called *A Clear and Present Danger,* which this column has already referenced in past editions.

It`s hard to imagine a scenario that would allow GES to keep its emergency plans (if it has them) secret.

But the startling thing is that GES is *right.* Rockwell Valley authorities and various state agencies apparently have no legal clout to require disclosure of a plan of emergency action.

Amazing.

Of course, they *should* have the legal muscle. The facility is going to impact the community just by operating. And in an emergency?

Perhaps officials are overlooking the obvious.

If GES refuses to show how it will prevent explosions and

chemical spills – and deal with fires or train derailments – the permits necessary for this project should forever be tied up in the bureaucracy.

It`s that simple.

The issuance of permits for construction is discretionary and long-established legally. There is no guarantee that when a project is proposed, it will be approved.

So until an *acceptable* safety plan is devised, the *Clarion* suggests that officials bury the whole idea.

The proposed pipeline project is a different case from a safety standpoint, but it is linked directly.

Salt cavern storage in general has had a spotty safety history across the country. It`s difficult to assess the *specific* chances of serious problems in Rockwell Valley simply because every salt cavern`s geology has unique structural quirks. Please don`t misinterpret that sentence. If this salt cavern storage is approved, Rockwell Valley residents will have to live 24-7 with the potential for catastrophe from that point on.

With gas pipelines, the history of problems cuts across the landscape - like the pipelines - and fairly screams from news reports about exploding pipes, spills and continuous leakage into the air.

A recent report from the same consulting firm that drafted *A Clear and Present Danger* about the proposed salt cavern storage pointed out that even in the best of circumstances, there is usually a leakage rate of 4 percent. Some gas pipelines have been found to leak as much as 23 percent.

And all that leaked natural gas finds its way into the atmosphere, where it just adds to our continuing climate change woes.

Right now the U.S. is already crisscrossed with more than 350,000 miles of major gas pipelines, moving gas from region to region. There's another 2 million miles of smaller pipelines for local distributions.

And at least three or four times a month there is a fire, an explosion, or an incident that involves a substantial loss of property and, in many cases, serious injury to people. More pipelines will most likely mean, well, more incidents.

You don't read about these incidents often because they occur in small communities or out-of-the-way places. But every once in awhile there is a big enough blowup that makes national news like the one in 2010 in San Bruno, California.

That blast killed eight people and destroyed 38 homes.

The pipeline that exploded was the exact *same* size as the pipeline GES proposes to run through farmland and woods, through the outskirts of Rockwell Valley proper and then on to the east to the Chesapeake port.

Does it mean it is prone to problems? Not necessarily. But what an odd coincidence.

GES might be in a rush to build this pipeline – and store natural gas and propane in Rockwell Valley salt caverns.

But Rockwell Valley shouldn't be rushed and should demand everything it needs to ensure safety for its citizens.

> It's the best reason for taking our time.
>
> `Jack Stafford is the publisher of the` Horseheads Clarion `and publishes Column One every Friday. He can be reached at JJStafford@HorseheadsClarion.com.`

Chapter 7

It was the issue of what to do with Devon's dog Belle that brought matters to a head for Jack and Cass.

After the end of the third Saturday morning "Fracking School" with Eli and the reporters, Eli told Jack he was worried that Belle, a Labrador Retriever that Eli and his wife Shania had taken when Jack, Devon and Noah left for Tonga, was left home alone for too many hours every day.

"I tried bringing her into work with me, like you and Devon did, but she wouldn't stay put," Eli said. "If the front door opened, out she went. I would find her at your house sometimes, sitting on the porch."

Jack felt guilty that he hadn't even *seen* the dog since coming back. It reminded him that he *also* hadn't yet made a trip up to see his best friend from high school, Oscar Wilson, and his niece Lindy.

And Oscar had been his best man when he married Devon.

An hour after buying the staff lunch again at Millie's Diner, Jack walked up to the front door of his house with Belle the Labrador at his side.

Belle had recognized Jack the moment he walked up the steps to Eli's house, not far from the newspaper. She was a little slower getting up on her feet, he could see. But her wildly wagging tail and barks were just as he remembered.

He didn't bother hooking her to the leash Eli gave him. Belle stuck to his side, walking more than a mile across town just as closely as she had when he and Devon would walk to and from the *Clarion* office every day or when they took walks in evening.

The look on Noah's face was pure joy when Belle bounded into the living room, nearly knocking him down. Belle wouldn't replace his Tongan dog, Tokanga, but they immediately started to wrestle on the floor, love at first sight.

Cass just crossed her arms and leaned against the wall, an enigmatic smile on her face.

Chapter 8

If there was one thing Jack had learned about Cass in the six months or so since she came to Tonga – and then to the U.S. to help with Noah (and Jack) – she would say what was on her mind in her *own* time.

A few gentle parries to her about Belle drew only a small smile that wasn't really a smile at all, Jack knew. It was the actress mask Cass could put on and take off at will.

So it wasn't until late in the afternoon, when Cass pulled out two wineglasses while Noah dozed off on the floor with his head resting on a sleeping Belle the Labrador, that she started to talk. She plopped down on the couch while Jack took the armchair right next to it that had been his father's favorite.

"I feel like such a bitch sometimes, honestly," Cass said. "When you brought that dog in, all I could think was that I had one more damn thing to take care of. And I'm at my limit."

Jack sipped his wine and listened to her soliloquy for nearly a half-hour, a carefully worded recitation of how she felt about her life as a live-in aunt, nanny, housekeeper and medical detective trying to solve Noah's near deafness and lack of speech. And in all of that, her life as an actress, director and playwright had been put on hold.

Completely.

"That's all a long way of saying I really want to go home to Vashon, but I can't figure out how to do it. I guess I feel trapped. Trapped in a golden cage, right?"

When Cass started to cry at that point, Jack knew he was seeing a vulnerable Cass for the first time. Cass barely even cried at the memorial service for Devon in Tonga.

"Noah is so precious, Jack, so precious. And he has stuck so tight to me that I feel smothered sometimes. I'm *not* his mother. I'm *not* your wife."

Jack let Cass ramble again, just nodding his head, knowing that whatever he said was likely not going to be particularly helpful. She needed to work this out in her head.

If he told her she should pack and get home, she would be offended. If he begged her to stay on, she would feel just that much *more* trapped.

Devon. If Devon were alive, this is the kind of thing Devon was good at working out, Jack thought. He felt a few tears welling up in his eyes, too.

"Look, Devon," Jack said. "Sorry. I mean Cass. *Jesus!* Where did that come from? This just brings back how much I miss your sister. I know you do, too."

Cass dabbed at her eyes with a handkerchief she produced magically from somewhere in her dress.

"I have let myself get totally possessed trying to save the world again. It's been my escape. I know it. You know it. But you have helped me so much by taking such good care of Noah and me. I'd still be drunk on Lata Island if it wasn't for you. We can figure something out."

Cass sat back, her face a mask again, though she had a tiny smile working its way up around the edges of her mouth.

"We're almost into summer – the nicest time of the year around here. And I'm wrestling with two serious threats to Rockwell Valley. We will know in couple of months if the boneheads running the gas company will get their way or not. Maybe then…" Jack voiced trailed off. "Maybe then …"

A puzzled look came over Cass at the point, her face glowing with a tinge of redness.

"Where exactly do *I* fit into that scenario, Jack? You mean I just walk out the door with my suitcase when your political life gets settled? This is *complicated,* Jack. Noah complicates this. You complicate this. I care about you, too."

Jack leaned back in the chair and closed his eyes for a second, then leaned forward, putting his wineglass on the table.

"I know this is a mess," Jack said. "If I hadn't fallen apart when Devon died, maybe it wouldn't be like this.

"But I *did* and it *is*. As my reporters say *way* too much, 'this just sucks.'"

Cass got up from the couch, leaned over and gave the still-sitting Jack a hug. Then she felt the muzzle of Belle touching one of her legs, Noah's arms suddenly wrapped around the other.

"What a lovely mess, Jack," Cass said. "Lovely."

Chapter 9

The skinny 19-year-old rental car agent dressed in his father's sports coat at the rental car agency in Binghamton, New York mispronounced Calvin Boviné's name three times in less than five minutes before Boviné finally put the barely shaving kid across the hood of the car he had rented for a week and threatened to rip out his throat.

"Bo-vin-ay, asshole. *Say it.* Say Bo-vin-ay. *Bo—Vin—Ay!*"

He grabbed the kid's head and banged his face on the hood once for good measure.

Why do people go out of their way to screw with me, he thought? *Why?*

It had been a frustrating week in Pennsylvania for Boviné, who had decided to head back to Flathead, Missouri to meet face-to-face with the Grand Energy Services vice president who had some money – and more projects – for him.

Then this skinny pipsqueak at the rental agency tried to charge him $200 to chemically clean the car, which Boviné had to admit did smell pretty *ripe* from manure.

But $200 for a *cleaning? No fucking way*, Boviné thought.

It was the principle of the thing.

GES had given him a bag full of cash – $350,000 – to help convince dairy farmers to sign over rights to allow for a natural gas pipeline to run through their properties.

Boviné was authorized to give up to $50,000 in cash as a signing bonus, making it clear that the money would *not* show up on any records. There would be a separate signing bonus reported to the IRS and paid by GES company check.

It was a sweet deal, Boviné thought. Sweet. Except none of the dairy farmers would buy it. Not *one*. And Boviné had done his best to let them know that if they turned it down, not only would there *not* be an off-the-books cash payment, it was likely the bonus check would be tiny.

And no matter what, the pipeline was coming through, even if GES had to take the land through eminent domain.

Boviné's tough-guy speech had ended at one dairy farm with the owner leveling a double-barrel shotgun at him, ordering Boviné out of the house and off his property.

Boviné had left. But he made it plain to the farmer that if Boviné wanted, he could take the shotgun and shove it up the farmer's ass.

As Boviné walked across the road from the car rental agency to catch a shuttle to the airport, he decided he might just pay that farmer another visit on his next pass through.

He was pretty sure GES would tell him it was okay to take off the gloves with these yokels.

Boviné lived for that kind of action.

Chapter 10

The conference call with Grand Energy Services CEO Luther Burnside and Rod Mayenlyn at the company's Flathead, Missouri headquarters and Rockwell Valley's Mayor Will Pennisen, sitting in his office in downtown

Rockwell Valley, was going well until the issue of the pepper spraying of the protesters came up.

Up until that point Pennisen had been getting mostly praise for making progress on getting permissions for the natural gas and propane salt cavern storage and convincing the town the proposed natural gas pipelines to and from the storage facility would be a boon to the town's economy.

Then Pennisen let it slip that he had actually taken part in the pepper-spray police raid that had gotten national attention.

"Will, did I hear you say you were *there*? With the police?" Burnside asked, his voice betraying his surprise.

"What do you mean you took part? As the *mayor*? I thought it was a standard police action. What the fuck were you doing there?"

Rod Mayenlyn caught Burnside's eye, making a motion that made it clear Mayenyn thought the mayor was crazy.

It took Pennisen a few minutes to get out exactly what his role had been.

After several stops and starts – and an order from Burnside to "spit it out, *Goddamnit*" – Pennisen admitted he had been wearing a police uniform when the Rockwell Valley Police had arrested the protesters at the proposed gas storage site.

"Are you out of your fucking mind?" Burnside shouted.

Rod Mayenlyn started writing feverishly on his notepad.

"Well," Pennisen said, mumbling.

"Well, *nothing*, you moron. I know you can get away with acting like the King of England down there, but you were impersonating a police officer, for Chrissakes, even if nobody raised a fuss," Burnside said.

"If any news media get ahold of this. God. I'd have to fire you. I might fire you anyway."

Pennisen held his breath for a moment, happy he had left out the little detail that *he* was the one who fired off the first canister of pepper spray at the seated protesters, triggering the chain reaction from the *real* sworn police officers on the scene who nervously let go and doused the group when they saw the pepper spray flying.

"Well, I just didn't want the police to wuss out," Pennisen said. "I want to get rid of the police chief, anyway. He's too soft on these people, Mr. Burnside. Way too soft."

Mayenlyn slipped his notebook onto Luther Burnside's desk, his writing shaky but legible.

> **We need to snap a leash on this guy – *quick*.**

Burnside read the note and leaned into the speakerphone mic.

"Will, listen to me very carefully. I am sending Rod down to help with the public relations aspects of this. But for the moment, do not make any moves on the police chief or anything related to those protesters. Understood?

"And, for God's sakes, don't go parading around in a police uniform again. In fact, I want you to get out of the public eye for right now."

Burnside broke the connection, then looked across the table at Rod Mayenlyn, who was sitting very still. Mayenlyn knew that Burnside had handpicked Pennisen to go in and run the Rockwell Valley operation *precisely* because he was such a company man that he would do anything to get the job done.

But it was clear now that Pennisen might also be a little too eager to please.

"Aren't you meeting with Boviné?" Burnside asked, knowing the answer already. "Maybe he should go and check the lay of the land with Pennisen. Take him with you."

Burnside's secretary buzzed the intercom.

"Mr. Burnside, you have a journalist on the phone named Jack Stafford. From Horseheads, New York? He said he wants to talk with you about some report about gas pipeline safety."

Burnside smiled for the first time since he had started the phone conversation with Pennisen.

"Tell him I'm busy, but that you will give the message to Rod Mayenlyn, who will call him back."

Mayenlyn looked surprised, then nodded his head slowly.

"Oh. And while I talk with that jerk, I should feel him out to see what he knows about our crazy mayor," Mayenlyn said. "Right?"

Burnside smiled affirmatively, then turned to look out the window.

He was drumming his fingers on the desk as Mayenlyn walked out.

Dreaming of being a Mafia don, no doubt, Mayenlyn thought.

Only in his dreams.

Chapter 11

From the *Horseheads Clarion*

Column One
Horseheads Clarion

Who should judge Grand Energy Services?

By Jack Stafford

Grand Energy Services proposed natural gas and propane storage project is creeping closer to reality - creeping in via some legal maneuvering that may be legal, but raises some ethical issues.

As reported in the *Clarion* - and other news media - Judge Owen T. Beigenlaw ruled that Grand Energy Services can continue its under-construction project to build a multi-car railroad siding and propane transfer equipment yard adjacent to the salt caverns at the north end of Rockwell Valley Lake. This is the site where GES is planning on storing millions of gallons of liquid propane and natural gas, even though the entire project itself - and whether the storage will be allowed - is still under state review.

The court - and Judge Beigenlaw - are involved because a local environmental group filed a request for an injunction to stop construction, pending state approval for the entire project.

Getting a judicial nod to move ahead with this piece of the project would be akin to the camel getting its nose under the tent, the environmentalists said in legal briefs filed in support of their motions.

The judge didn't buy the argument, however, though he did comment that he had never seen a camel in Pennsylvania.

No kidding.

The judge said in his ruling, "If Grand Energy Services wants to build this railcar facility and *speculate* that it will be part of their larger project when it is approved, it is their right to do so. It's a railroad siding, not gas storage."

And please note, he did say "when it *is* approved," not "*if* it is approved."

That Judge Beigenlaw ruled in favor of GES is hardly surprising. That he has such supreme confidence this controversial project will be approved is troubling.

In a series of articles four years ago in the *Clarion*, it was pointed out that the judge owned a number of gas drilling leases in the Rockwell Valley area but had refused to recuse himself in various civil cases over water pollution, in which GES was the plaintiff.

He has since sold those gas leases.

But this week`s story about his most recent order points out that he also owns a dairy farm through which GES wants to build its natural gas pipeline.

He hasn`t signed a lease agreement yet to let GES put the pipe across his pastures. But then neither have any of his neighbors. Yet.

If Judge Owen Beigenlaw`s name is familiar, it could be because earlier this year he found *Clarion* Editor Eli Gupta in contempt of court when Mr. Gupta walked into Beigenlaw`s court with a camera in a zipped camera bag.

The Rockwell Valley Police Department bailiff challenged Mr. Gupta and said he would have to leave the courtroom. Mr. Gupta said he would put the camera and bag outside, then return. But at that point, the judge intervened and said the act of bringing the camera in was of *itself* contempt. When Mr. Gupta attempted to walk back out of the court, he was handcuffed by the bailiff and detained.

As the *Clarion* story related, Judge Beigenlaw let Mr. Gupta stew in a jail cell at the Rockwell Valley Police Department for a few hours before lifting his contempt order.

As this GES project moves ahead, smart money would wager that there are going to be more legal challenges to many aspects of the proposal. Likewise, the GES proposed pipeline project will likely land in court, especially if the landowners stand firm and Rockwell Valley invokes the law of eminent domain to take the land for the pipeline over their objections.

Judge Owen T. Beigenlaw should recuse himself from all GES matters before he faces a

> legal challenge *himself* for potential conflict of interest.
> He let the camel`s nose under the tent with his recent ruling. He should get out before the rest of the camel sneaks in.
>
> *Jack Stafford is the publisher of the* Horseheads Clarion *and publishes Column One every Friday. He can be reached at JJStafford@ HorseheadsClarion.com.*

Chapter 12

The conference room at the *Horseheads Clarion* was buzzing Monday morning with conversations over stories about a potential lawsuit against Rockwell Valley Police over the pepper spraying, a planned protest over Judge Owen T. Beigenlaw's ruling, arrests around the country where people were protesting the building of gas and oil pipelines – and the rain that had been coming down in buckets for two days.

The thick gray overcast was so low that morning, it looked like you could reach up and touch the clouds.

"You can see where Beigenlaw's ruling is going on the GES project," reporter Keith Everlight said. "Once they put *enough* infrastructure in place out there, it just will make it that much harder to say no to the entire project. Classic developer bullshit move."

Keith's story focused on a series of similar judicial rulings, in the energy sector as well as in housing and other industrial projects. Companies were successful in getting approval based on money they had already invested. Sometimes it was local governments, and almost always courts sided with the developers.

"I did a story in Michigan where a guy built his shopping mall encroaching on a city street," Keith said. "The city paid nearly $2 million to reroute the street when he threatened to simply shut down the project. The city manager said the property tax the city would make more than made up for it. And the developer got an additional 2,000 square feet of rentable retail space. Sweet deal for the crooked developer."

Jack, Eli and the other three reporters shook their heads in disgust.

"And people complain about corruption in Congress," Jack said.

Eli and reporters Rue, Jill and Stan all laid out the various stories they had ready for the Tuesday paper and others they were planning for Friday.

Rue had been trying to talk with Rockwell Valley Mayor Will Pennisen over the weekend. But the normally garrulous mayor was not returning phone calls or emails.

"I saw him Sunday morning across the street at Millie's Diner," Eli said. "He was having breakfast with two guys in suits that sure looked like they were connected with GES."

Jack had been doodling a page layout and suddenly started paying attention.

"They were here, in Horseheads?" Jack said. "Pretty far to go for breakfast, even as good as Millie's. But maybe they came here so they wouldn't be seen together."

Eli smile had started to grow while Jack was talking.

"OK, Eli … what's the rest?"

Eli popped open his laptop and hit a few keys, bringing up a security camera image of three men exiting Millie's Diner. At Jack's insistence, he sent the image to the big-screen TV on the wall, where the image was crystal clear.

"That's Rod Mayenlyn with Pennisen," Eli said. "The other guy I don't know. He looks like a professional football player."

Jack studied the photo for a minute and asked Eli to print out a copy as well as post the photo on the *Clarion*'s in-house messaging system.

"I'd like to know who that big guy is. Maybe he's the guy who was trying to get those Rockwell Valley dairy farmers to sign agreements to let the pipeline go through."

As the staff meeting broke up, Keith saw that he had a telephone message from Lasse Espinola, thanking him for the story the *Clarion* published about his solar panels and solar project at his Rockwell Valley dairy farm.

Keith called Eli over and asked him how to make a high-resolution print out of the photo Eli had just posted on the *Clarion*'s message board.

"I'm heading down to Rockwell Valley this afternoon after deadline and I think I want to show the photo to Espinola," Keith said. "And maybe Espinola's uncle, too. When I interviewed Espinola he said something about his uncle chasing a GES landsman off his property, but it didn't strike me at the time."

Eli and Keith were fussing with Keith's keyboard when they noticed Jack was standing up, talking on the telephone in his office, gesturing in the air.

Then Rue heard him yell, "Call the police! Call them now, Cass," just before he hung up the phone and barreled out the front door.

"What was that all about?" Eli asked.

It was nearly an hour before they learned that someone had tried to grab Noah from Jack's front yard in broad daylight, perhaps stopped only by a barking Belle the Labrador Retriever.

Chapter 13

When Jack got home a half-dozen neighbors were out on the sidewalk in front of his house talking with Cass, who was holding Noah in her arms.

Belle was barking and running around in the yard, acting like it was a picnic. She *loved* all the people.

The Horseheads Police had come and gone already – deciding that it was a false alarm and that the car most likely was just a tourist lost in the labyrinth of residential streets when it had slowed down and stopped right in front of Jack's house.

But Cass was sure she saw a car with two men talking to Noah that quickly drove off when she stepped out onto the front porch.

It didn't help that none of the neighbors saw anything.

"I don't know cars, Jack. It was a dark car," Cass said. "Looked like an American make. I couldn't even say if it was two or four doors. Wait. Four. I'm pretty sure it was four doors."

Nearly four-year-old Noah was clinging to Cass, picking up on her fright as the three of them walked into the house, thanking the neighbors for their concern.

Noah had gone out front with Belle into the front yard to play, his boundary the low, thick privet hedge that separated the yard from the sidewalk.

A small wire chain gate filled the gap between where Noah liked to stand to watch the street and the bushes. The street barely had any traffic, and what there was came through at a very slow clip, thanks to speed limit signs and vigorous enforcement.

Belle's barking was what had alerted Cass to the car outside.

Cass had been working at the dining room table by the window, where she had a good view of the front yard and Noah, when she heard Belle barking. It was a louder, more aggressive sound than what Cass was used to hearing.

"Belle did not like the men in the car," Cass said. "Definitely. She was barking to protect Noah."

Jack made a cup of tea in the kitchen, while Noah climbed off Cass's lap and Belle laid down on the floor.

He was thinking vaguely about all the work stacking up at the newspaper when Cass got up quickly and locked the deadbolt on the door, startling him back to worrying about what had happened.

"I know you and that 12-year-old Horseheads cop probably think I overreacted, but I know creeps. And those guys were creeps."

Jack sipped his tea and put his hand on Cass's arm.

"I absolutely don't think you overreacted at all. If I had been home and that happened, I don't know. I don't know what I would have done. It's just sinking in what could have happened."

Cass put her hand on top of Jack's.

"Thank you for that. The cop and your neighbors were less supportive."

They sat talking about the car, the two men and the police while drinking their tea for a few minutes. Noah sat playing with some blocks on the floor, Belle right at his feet.

Jack kept looking at the deadbolt on the door.

This really scared her, he thought. *Really scared her. Me, too.*

"I need to call the *Clarion* and let them know I'll be gone for the day," he announced.

Jack went into his home office and closed the door before making three phone calls.

The first call went to Eli Gupta, who was relieved to hear that everything was okay. He told Jack not to worry. The newspaper was humming along just fine. And Eli agreed that the incident didn't need any mention anywhere in the upcoming edition of the *Clarion* or on its website. At least not for the moment.

The second phone call was to a house alarm company about which the *Clarion* had done a flattering story just a month before.

The third was to the Horseheads Police to tell them the detail that Cass had left out because she was so shaken.

The driver of the car and the male passenger who talked to Noah were both wearing wraparound-style dark sunglasses – sunglasses on the day that was so cloudy half the vehicles passing by had their headlights on.

Creeps all right, Jack thought. *Real creeps.*

Chapter 14

The letter from Grand Energy Services seemed positive, Lasse Espinola thought at first as he read it standing by his roadside mailbox.

Printed on the letterhead of CEO and Grand Energy Services President Luther Burnside, it offered $20,000 for access across Lasse's land, with promises that the approximately 100-foot-wide swath would be kept clean and truck traffic "minimal, only to service the pipeline."

The $20,000 was a $10,000 boost from the last time GES had approached Lasse but far less than the $50,000, under-the-table payment that Lasse's uncle Einar had been offered.

The contract also made some promises about annual payments, keyed to how much natural gas was flowing through the pipeline.

Lasse only read the first page of the two-page letter before he skipped to look at the draft of a proposed agreement.

```
Because of potential
problems with eco-terrorists,
GES agrees to provide round-
the-clock security for the
pipeline as it crosses your
land.
```

He read the paragraph again and had visions of armed men zooming up and down in the middle of the night alongside the 40-inch pipeline buried in the access corridor.

Then he went back to finishing reading Burnside's letter and found the threat.

> In our review of security
> issues around Rockwell Valley,
> we are increasingly concerned
> about recent incidents police
> call simple vandalism. We
> think it`s the resurgence of an
> eco-terrorist group called the
> Wolverines who caused millions
> of dollars of damage to GES
> facilities several years ago.
> We believe our pipeline will
> help protect your land.

And if I don't sign, well, I'm on my own, Lasse thought.

Since the wires had been cut on his solar array (and the controller smashed), the dogs Lasse had borrowed from his uncle had been on patrol every night. At first the cows were not keen on having the two dogs around. One dog was chased around by a cow upset by its trying to herd her calf.

But the dogs were now bedded down near the barn at night and except for a few drunk teenagers roaring by, it had been quiet.

Lasse was folding up the letter and proposed agreement when his cell phone rang – the ringtone a short clip of the music from an on-demand television series called *Lilyhammer*.

It was the tone alert for Alice McCallis.

Some of his farmer neighbors thought she was a pain in the ass – which she could be.

But Lasse liked her spunky attitude and organizing skills.

Her latest arrest for violating the court order limiting her movements actually boosted her standing with Lasse's neighbors.

They all hated Judge Owen T. Beigenlaw, who over the years had ruled in favor of GES in every legal action the farmers had taken, most of the lawsuits over suspected water contamination from hydrofracking.

"Alice, good morning. Staying out of jail today, I hope," Lasse said as he answered.

Alice's voice gave a half-laugh, half-cackle.

"Well, aren't you the comedian this morning, Lasse. Everything okay at your place this morning?" Alice asked.

Lasse paused for moment, realizing he hadn't gone to the barn yet or heard either dog bark or any other noises.

"I think so. I haven't done my rounds yet. What is it?"

Alice cackled again, then told Lasse that she was just checking in with all the dairy farmers in the path of the proposed pipeline.

"I think GES is about to make another big push to get signed agreements. I heard yesterday from several people that GES has upped its offer.

"But that's not why I called."

Lasse looked towards the barn and was relieved to see one of his dogs coming out, stretching as if he had been sleeping.

"One of my friends at the courthouse – Lasse, do *not* laugh. I do have *friends*," Alice said. "One of my *friends* said that a GES paralegal, or someone with an expensive suit, was going through titles and deeds yesterday, typing a lot on his laptop. Then he went down to the assessor's office."

Lasse thought about calling a woman he knew at the assessor's office who had helped Lasse with filing a tax protest the year before.

"Alice, they should know all that stuff already. I mean. I got one of the new offer letters for an easement."

Alice sighed.

"Yes, of course. They're not stupid about stuff like this," she said. "Just greedy. But my friend at the courthouse said if they want to start eminent domain proceedings, they need the most up-to-date information possible. If not, it can be challenged that way and tied up for a long time.

"What is it young people say these days? I bet GES is about to 'bust a move,'" Alice said. "They are desperate for that pipeline. Oh, and Lasse. I have a court date with the dishonorable Owen T. Beigenlaw at the end of the week. Can you make it?"

Lasse said he would try and then hung up.

He started walking down towards the barn where the dog he had seen stretching moments before was laying on its side.

Even from 100 yards, Lasse could see the dog's tongue was sticking way out and that his body was shuddering and twitching on the ground.

Lasse started to run to the dog, then turned and ran to get his pickup truck.

Chapter 15

Since his close encounter with the GES employees, Keith Everlight hadn't been back across the Pennsylvania state line to visit Rockwell Valley.

He wasn't afraid – not exactly – but his trick with the video camera had made a huge splash across the Internet and in many newspapers and news websites. It had also made him a pretty big target in GES sights.

A letter to the editor sent to the *Horseheads Clarion* from GES took publisher Jack Stafford and editor Eli Gupta to task for letting a staff member "actively engage in unethical behavior" by taking the secret video.

The GES letter neglected to mention the two GES employees' threats against Keith.

Jack set the letter aside and told Keith he would not be publishing it anytime soon.

"Unless I use it in my column to point out an example of GES hypocrisy," Jack said. "And I already have file folders full of those."

Today's expedition had been at Jack's insistence.

Activist Alice McCallis had a court appearance scheduled at which Judge Owen T. Beigenlaw would consider charges of contempt of court against McCallis's getting too close to a GES facility.

Alice – as was her custom – would be representing herself, Keith knew. And that would provide some interesting interchanges between Alice and the judge.

At the last minute, Eli dispatched reporter Rue Malish to go with Keith.

"You never know with that judge or McCallis what might happen. Plus, Jill and Stan have everything under control here," Eli said.

The trip to Rockwell Valley took a lot longer than normal because Keith had followed Rue's advice and was taking a route along roads bordering the farms where GES wanted to put through the pipeline. It would connect the proposed salt cavern gas storage to the hydrofracked wells to the west and a planned Chesapeake Bay LNG export facility.

Along the route, Rue and Keith saw at least 15 GES trucks, most of them with people and equipment consistent with surveying.

At one spot, Keith was pretty sure he saw the two GES workers with whom he'd had the run-in. If they recognized him or his car, they didn't make any sign.

As a precaution for this trip, Keith had removed his dashboard doggy video camera to make his vehicle a little less noticeable.

When Rue and Keith pulled up in front of the Rockwell Valley Courthouse, it was obvious that press coverage of the hearing was not an original idea.

Three television station trucks were in the parking lot tuning their satellite antennas. On the steps, Keith recognized reporters from a half-dozen newspapers standing with another half-dozen people who also seemed to be reporters. The radio folks were trotting about with their recorders on their shoulders, dangling cables and microphones.

"Um, Keith. You didn't tell me we were going to the circus," Rue said. "This is sure going to be more fun than hanging out in the office listening to Eli talk about some new app we have to get."

On the steps in front of the building Keith thought he recognized Rockwell Valley Mayor Will Pennisen, who had been dodging the *Clarion* staff ever since the pepper-spray incident at the salt caverns.

Pennisen was with a Rockwell Valley police officer who was fending off all media from getting very close to the mayor.

"Rue, notice the lack of protesters? No signs, no nada," Keith said.

"I bet they are keeping quiet because the court is within that no-protest zone."

As they walked up towards the steps, Rue took out her camera and fired off a half-dozen shots, zooming in on Pennisen especially.

Then she remembered Eli's run-in with this judge over his camera in the courtroom. She headed back toward Keith's car, parked next to a television van, where the newscaster was having her hair fixed before she did her first standup.

When Rue realized the car was locked, she swore under her breath and turned to go back to get the keys from Keith, bumping *squarely* into the chest of a burly GES worker.

"This *your* car, honey?" the man asked.

He towered over her, and Rue noticed that he smelled faintly of grease and beer.

Another GES worker lurked a few yards away. He looked disheveled and his hands were black.

"Some little shit with a car just like this took a video of me and my buddy. Got both of us in a lot of trouble.

"A lot."

Chapter 16

The phone call from CEO Luther Burnside to Rod Mayenlyn began very politely, with Burnside's secretary going through her normal, formal announcement that "Mr. Burnside is on the line for you. Please hold."

And so Rod Mayenlyn, driving on the highway outside Rockwell Valley within sight of the salt caverns where GES want to store propane and natural gas for export, wasn't prepared when Burnside started the conversation by asking Mayenlyn if he had lost his mind.

"I send you and Boviné to Rockwell Valley to check on that loony-tune mayor I put in as general manager, and the next thing I get a call that someone tried to kidnap that editor's kid. Up in Horseheads. In goddamn New York. Tell me please your mother drowned all the rest of her children and just missed *you* by accident."

Burnside had spent his first years with GES cultivating people all over New York and Pennsylvania, trying to convince them to sign gas leases so GES could hydrofrack for natural gas.

Among those cultivated were police in various towns, easy marks because they truly wanted to believe that the people who opposed hydrofracking were unpatriotic hippies who needed to be taught a lesson.

A retired Horseheads cop called a buddy at the Rockwell Valley Police Department, who in turn called Burnside's private number to let him know about the incident at Jack Stafford's house.

"The police aren't calling it a kidnapping attempt," Burnside said. "But since the woman who lives with Stafford – his sister or something – saw that both men were wearing dark glasses on a day when they needed headlights to drive, they're suspicious," Burnside said.

"Tell me exactly what happened. Exactly. If you're lucky, you'll still have a job."

Mayenlyn pulled over on the highway, smack in front of the access road down to the salt caverns near the shore of Rockwell Valley Lake.

He tried to explain to Burnside that he and Calvin Boviné had driven up just so Boviné could see the house where Stafford lived.

"We didn't do anything but pull up. Really, boss. *Really*. It was Boviné. He told me to stop, and then the idiot rolled down his window and started talking to some kid in the front yard. We didn't know who it was. We're not stupid, boss," Mayenlyn said.

Burnside let 10 seconds pass before he spoke, weighing Mayenlyn's usefulness to GES and Calvin Boviné's special skill set.

"I will be the judge of how stupid you *are*, Rod," Burnside said. "And this was *stupid, stupid, stupid*! What were you doing in Horseheads, anyway? You were supposed to be in Rockwell Valley."

With a great deal of stops and starts, Mayenlyn spit out that Boviné had an idea about setting up Wolverine pranks – but in New York – and leading the police in the direction of the newspaper.

"We know how much Stafford wrote about the Wolverines and how much he made them out to be heroes. Boviné thought he could do a few things and we could lead the police to Jack Stafford, or maybe that editor of his."

Mayenlyn heard Burnside grunt affirmatively.

"Here's the punchline. When Stafford heads off to the South Pacific, suddenly the Wolverines disappear, too," Mayenlyn said. "A coincidence? Or was he involved? Might not matter, if we play it right."

There was another long delay before Burnside spoke again, this time in slightly softer tones.

Slightly softer.

"You just saved your job, Rod. By a fucking thread. And it's because that idea has some possibilities. Just *possibilities*. You are responsible for Boviné, remember? So he works for you, not the other way around," Burnside said.

Yeah, I might be Boviné*'s boss*, Mayenlyn thought. *But he scares the shit out me, too.*

"So, have you even seen Pennisen yet?" Burnside said. "And where *is* Boviné?"

Mayenlyn looked down the road at the gates to the salt cavern storage facility where several GES employees were obviously goofing off – and smoking cigarettes next to a propane truck in line to pick up a load of propane from one of the above-ground storage tanks the company had already installed.

The 30,000-gallon bullet-shaped tanks were put in without any official Rockwell Valley permits, thanks to Mayor Will Pennisen's intervention with the Rockwell Valley building department and its safety officer.

"We saw him briefly in Horseheads. And we have an appointment with him tonight at city hall. I think he said there will be a special meeting or something. After today's court hearing for that old bag that's been stirring up all the trouble. You know, Alice Callister. No, wait. I mean McCallis. I guess the judge is going to put her in jail," Mayenlyn said.

The jail comment got the first chuckle out of Burnside and the first sign to Mayenlyn that his drive-by at Jack Stafford's house would *not* cost him his job, for the moment. In fact, the prospect of McCallis being pilloried – which could take some attention away from the rapid construction of the railroad siding – almost had Burnside in a good mood.

"All right Rod, all right. Now tell Boviné. No. Don't tell him anything. Just check on the mayor, and for God's sake make sure he doesn't do anything stupid. Give me a call tomorrow morning. Early."

Mayenlyn hung up and pulled back out onto the highway, noting that the GES workers were still just standing around, smoking cigarettes way too close to the propane truck – even if it was empty.

If they were any indication of how tight a ship Mayor Will Pennisen was running as GES general manager, Rockwell Valley's GES division might be in trouble, no matter how good a politician he was.

That idea was still floating in his mind as he pulled out and one of the GES workers flipped him the bird.

Chapter 17

From the *Horseheads Clarion*

Column One
Horseheads Clarion

Why buy access if you can take it?

By Jack Stafford

The permitting process for the proposed 40-inch natural gas pipeline to connect existing Grand Energy Services pipes to the proposed salt-cavern storage at the north end of Rockwell Valley Lake is nearing the end.

Thanks to some friendly federal regulators, its approval is likely, though the opponents of the project – including local retired schoolteacher Alice McCallis – are still hoping it won't be built.

McCallis, by the way, is in court today on charges of contempt because she allegedly violated a court order to stay a quarter-mile from all GES facilities, hardly a small feat in an area in which GES owns nearly one-third of the acreage, including several downtown storefronts.

A report on how she fares will be posted on the *Clarion* website.

The pipeline is critical to GES because it wants to store natural gas in those salt caverns, but only as a way station. The gas is destined to travel via a second proposed pipeline to Chesapeake Bay, where a new liquid natural gas port will send the LNG to overseas markets willing to pay a lot more for the natural gas than are the good people of the Northeast.

But there is a stumbling block, about which this newspaper has written quite a bit: Most of the farmers and landowners in the proposed path of the pipeline are not interested in selling easements.

That's not surprising, given how disruptive the construction process is, how much trouble it would likely be to have maintenance vehicles crossing the land, and then, of course, there is the danger of leaks, explosions and fires.

Explosions and fires? Yes. And as news reports about explosions in Manitoba, Canada, New Mexico, Missouri and other places continue to pile up, people in our area have good reason to be nervous.

Incidentally, that Missouri gas pipeline explosion was only 20 miles from the headquarters of Grand Energy Services in Flathead.

In recent months, GES representatives have offered to pay for easements sometimes using tactics more common to time-share sales than normal utility right-of-way negotiations.

One Rockwell Valley dairy farmer says he was offered a bag of cash recently as a signing bonus – cash that the GES landsman said would not be reported to tax officials. A request for GES to comment on what this dairy farmer said received a curt "no comment" from GES corporate headquarters.

No comment? But not a strong denial?

Wow!

The latest twist in all this is that GES is about to launch an attempt to use eminent domain to take the land that it has been unable to buy. Keith Everlight's excellent series several weeks ago in the *Clarion,* "Right in the Way," detailed out the legal side of eminent domain and how it's handled in Pennsylvania.

It would be a big stretch for this out-of-state corporation to fit all the legal rubrics necessary to take this private land and use it for easements to build a natural gas pipeline that would really only benefit the company.

But stranger things have been happening in our justice system.

Just consider the Alice McCallis case today, or what happened in the Cornhusker State.

There in Nebraska, an energy company held *so* much sway with politicians that it essentially was able to get the power of eminent domain transferred to the company itself so the company could do a land grab to get a pipeline built.

If GES does pursue eminent domain proceedings and is successful, the persons forced to give access would be compensated for their land at something generally referred to as *fair market value*.

And there would be no signing bonuses or bags of unreported cash offered. And no way to say no.

Jack Stafford is the publisher of the Horseheads Clarion *and publishes Column One every Friday. He can be reached at JJStafford@HorseheadsClarion.com.*

Chapter 18

Judge Owen T. Beigenlaw peered out from his small office into the courtroom.

It was about half-filled, though he knew a lot of people were waiting outside on the steps or were still in the security line.

His temporary bailiff – Rockwell Valley Police Lt. Del Dewitt – had just come in through the side door used by police, attorneys and a few other people who didn't have to go through the security scanner.

He was about to go out to the bench when he saw Dewitt push the door open to let Rockwell Valley Mayor Will Pennisen in, along with the assistant district attorney who had drawn the short straw today to represent the people.

The assistant DA's face was flushed and the bags under his eyes probably meant he either had trouble sleeping or was nursing a bell-ringer of a hangover.

Beigenlaw watched as the DA winced when the door slammed behind him.

Hangover, Beigenlaw thought.

He waited for Dewitt to close the courtroom doors, which prompted a few protests from the people waiting in line outside to get through the security check.

Then he saw that Alice McCallis was sitting at the defense table, a yellow notepad in front of her filled with scribbled notes on it. And *no* attorney.

McCallis's court appearances were almost always *sans* representation because, for the most part, it made it easier for her to give speeches disguised as legal arguments.

The one time she had appeared in Beigenlaw's court with a lawyer, she fired him mid-hearing, prompting Beigenlaw to threaten her with contempt of court and jail that day.

She hadn't appear frightened that day. Nor did she today.

When Beigenlaw walked in, he noted that almost everyone rose when they heard Dewitt say "All rise."

Alice McCallis seemed to be struggling to get out of her chair and barely stood – a complete *act,* Beigenlaw knew. She was more fit than most women in their 50s.

The courtroom continued to fill while Beigenlaw shuffled papers on the bench in front of him, finally motioning to Dewitt to tell people to sit down.

"I think we can cut right to the chase on this," Beigenlaw said.

"We have the district attorney here, but I don't think we need to go through all the motions, do we, Ms. McCallis?"

Alice McCallis stood up, put her reading glasses on her nose and looked across at the table where the assistant DA sat with Mayor Will Pennisen alongside.

"Your honorableness, it's Mrs. McCallis, as you know, and I would like the district attorney to read the charges against me. Every line. For the record, you know."

The crowd in the courtroom gave out a loud enough murmur that Beigenlaw slammed his gavel hard and yelled, "Order!"

"I will not tolerate any outbursts in this courtroom. None," Beigenlaw said. "And *Mrs.* McCallis, I will ask you to show proper decorum in this room or you will find yourself in a lot more hot water."

Alice continued to stand, turning slightly so the audience in the courtroom could see her better. She got plenty of smiles and another murmur of appreciation that Beigenlaw decided to ignore.

It took the assistant DA more than 15 minutes to read off the details of the incident in which Alice had been taken into custody for violating the judge's order that she stay away from GES properties.

He had to stop twice to take gulps of water from a plastic water bottle, which thirsty *Clarion* reporter Rue Malish dutifully wrote down in her notebook. Only court officers could bring water into the courtroom.

When the DA finished, Alice stood up immediately, only to be told to sit down by Beigenlaw.

"You *will* get your turn, *Mrs.* McCallis."

After the assistant DA's droning reading of the charges, Beigenlaw launched into his own interpretation of McCallis's actions.

"My order was issued for the good of the community – to protect property and persons. That includes you, Mrs. McCallis. Perhaps protecting you from yourself."

Beigenlaw chuckled at his bad joke. He was pleased that McCallis hadn't popped up out of her chair to object to anything that the assistant DA had read – nor had she scowled or made faces during his soliloquy.

Her scowl was reserved for when she looked over at the mayor sitting by the DA.

When Beigenlaw finally paused, Alice stood up slowly in case the judge was just taking a breath.

But he motioned for her to proceed, doing his own eye roll and shaking his head slightly before she even began.

"Your *honor*," Alice said. "I did get that right, correct? Your honor, I was exactly where the district attorney said I was when I was so unceremoniously arrested. I said that in my statements. I would also like to point out – and I did in the statement that the DA chose not to read – that not only am I prohibited from going into the only decent grocery store in Rockwell Valley, but because the hospital is adjacent to a GES truck parking lot, I can't go in there, either."

Beigenlaw looked slightly bored. McCallis had gone over all this when he first issued the order. That time she had left out the hospital part, though. That was slightly troubling to him, though not enough for him to say anything.

"Mrs. McCallis. We have covered this territory before. I issued you an order to stay away – a good distance away – from GES facilities and I remember asking you if you understood. And you said you did. But maybe you didn't or you wouldn't be here facing this contempt charge."

Beigenlaw raised his gavel and gave it a short tap when the crowd grumbled slightly.

"Well, if I get sick, I'll come to your house, your honor. Unless you have leased your property for the pipeline."

The gavel slammed down hard this time when the crowd actually laughed.

Lt. Del Dewitt moved from his position near the back door and came forward, trying to give stern looks at everyone.

He was just at the front of the courtroom when Alice McCallis gave her final words to the judge that day.

"I want to read back what you said a little while ago."

She peered down at her yellow notepad.

"You said your order 'was issued for the good of the community – to protect property and persons.' Is that right?"

She waited for Beigenlaw to grunt agreement.

"Well, I agree with you about the need to protect the community and its people. I just don't believe that Grand Energy Services is the only part of the community that needs protection," McCallis said.

"And the people include *you*, judge. You."

She paused and looked over at Rockwell Valley Mayor Will Pennisen and the assistant DA, both of whom appeared to be close to nodding off.

"I just wonder if the mayor is protecting *you* today, judge," she said.

Judge Owen T. Beigenlaw leaned forward in his chair, intrigued for the first time all morning.

He motioned for her to continue.

"I wonder," Alice said. "I just wonder, you know, why does the mayor have a gun tucked in the front of his pants like a cheap gangster?"

Chapter 19

Keith Everlight had seen a bailiff pull a gun in a courtroom only once before.

In that case the bailiff got so flustered when a suspect in handcuffs jumped up and rushed at the judge that the bailiff dropped his gun on the floor where it discharged a shot that hit a juror in the shoulder.

The juror later won a $400,000 negligence lawsuit, money he used to buy a now-successful fast-food franchise across the street from the courthouse where he was shot.

Lt. Del Dewitt's weapon came out much more smoothly except that by the time it was on its way out of his holster, Rockwell Valley Mayor Will Pennisen had yanked the Smith & Wesson .40 caliber semiautomatic out of his pants and was looking at it like he was holding a rattlesnake in his hands.

He brought the gun up level, looking around, his eyes glazed.

Keith later wrote in the *Horseheads Clarion* that Pennisen seemed as surprised as everyone in the courtroom that he was packing a gun.

And like so many people taken by surprise, he froze, his gun pointed in the direction of Judge Owen T. Beigenlaw, though Pennisen's head was swiveling from side to side.

Dewitt's order for Pennisen to drop the gun was heard by people in the front few rows of the courtroom. Further back, people had already either ducked down below the seats or were heading for the exit door in the back.

The people stampeding out the back door prevented the two security staff outside from coming into the courtroom.

When the first shot hit Mayor Will Pennisen, Judge Owen T. Beigenlaw had ducked below the bench and Alice McCallis was lying prone on the floor under the table.

The second shot missed Pennisen entirely and grazed the assistant district attorney's ear, the bullet lodging in the wall all the way across the courtroom, shattering some wood trim.

The third bullet went wild, too, though it went over the heads of everyone in the room and hit the ceiling, where it split the plaster sufficiently that it rained down on a half-dozen people.

The main headline on the *Horseheads Clarion* story on the website an hour later – accompanied by photos from inside the courtroom taken by reporter Rue Malish's cell phone – was "Shooting gallery at Rockwell Valley Courtroom."

The secondary headline underneath said "RV Mayor in custody – at RV Hospital."

Chapter 20

Luther Burnside could barely read the *Horseheads Clarion*'s account of what had happened in the Rockwell Valley courtroom.

The mayor – *his* mayor, *his* on-site company manager – was sitting in a hospital under guard after a melee that was grabbing national headlines.

And as if that wasn't bad *enough*, Judge Owen T. Beigenlaw – *his* judge, who GES paid enough to fund a posh summer home on Rockwell Valley Lake – had lifted his restraining order "pending review" of Alice McCallis's case.

Repeated calls to Rod Mayenlyn, who was supposed to be on the ground in Rockwell Valley, were going unanswered. And attempts to get in touch with Calvin Boviné though his unregistered cell phone had failed.

One of the GES staff at the main office in Rockwell Valley had told Burnside's secretary that Pennisen's leg wound had dumped a lot of blood on the courtroom floor because the bullet from the bailiff's gun had nicked an artery.

But Pennisen was supposed to recover.

He'd better, so I can kill him, Burnside thought.

Burnside drummed his fingers on his desk, waiting for Mayenlyn or Boviné to surface. He didn't want to deal directly with any of this. But GES phone lines and email inboxes were stacking up with requests from media for interviews about the incident and Pennisen's future with the company.

Because Mayenlyn was missing in action, Burnside had issued a short statement and refused further comment:

> The incident that happened in the Rockwell Valley courtroom today was unfortunate. At this point there are more questions than answers.
>
> To comment further would be premature.

Total bullshit, Burnside thought. *But the media will use it and with luck will just move on to some movie actor's or rock star's latest stupidity.*

Burnside drummed his fingers again on the desk, rereading the story in the *Clarion* by some young guy named Everlight. His name seemed familiar. Then Burnside remembered that Everlight had worked for a Michigan newspaper, hectoring an energy company there over an oil pipeline spill.

We need some outside help, Burnside thought. *Somebody with some credentials and credibility.*

After another round of desk drumming, he remembered a consultant that GES had used in the past, fired, then rehired for a short contract before he moved back to California.

He had been very useful in the days after a New York City school bus got dosed with hydrofracking fluid, resulting in the death of some elementary school-aged children from chemical poisoning. That incident resulted in a huge payout of cash to the parents of the dead children in wrongful death lawsuits.

Burnside pushed his intercom button to his secretary: "I need Michael Ahlbright's contact information. He worked for us about three years ago. Even better, just get him on the phone for me."

He was feeling just a little better, knowing that Michael Ahlbright might be intrigued enough to come back and help. Then he saw another story pop up on the *Horseheads Clarion* website.

It said the gun that Mayor Will Pennisen had pulled out in court might have been stolen from the Rockwell Valley Police Department.

Burnside pushed the intercom again: "And get Rod Mayenlyn on a plane back here as soon as you can find him. An hour ago would be preferable."

Chapter 21

The *Horseheads Clarion* staff meeting was more subdued than normal the Monday after Rockwell Valley Mayor Will Pennisen was shot in the leg by the court bailiff.

Keith Everlight and Rue Malish were still somewhat stunned by what they had witnessed and that the two stray rounds fired by bailiff Lt. Del Dewitt could have hit one of *them*.

And that was before Eli gave them a brief lecture about how he once had nearly been hit in a hail of ricocheting bullets when police and bank robbers got in a shoot-out in Elmira where he was taking photos for the *Clarion*.

Reporters Jill and Stan groaned when Eli told the story. They heard it every time there was a shooting.

Eli, Jill and Stan had worked into the evening, revamping the website and responding to special queries from other news outlets about the shooting.

Jack was still trying to come to grips with the incident with Noah and the two men who might have been there to kidnap him.

"All in all, last week was about a 12 on the 'HSS,' I would say," Jack said.

Eli and all four reporters gave him a puzzled look.

"Walter? The publisher I worked for? He used to say that all the time.

"'The Holy Shit Scale.'"

The fallout from the shooting and other gas-related stories set the staff up for a busy week trying to follow up on several angles.

• The Rockwell Valley Police Department would only say the gun was believed to be one from their arsenal and possibly had been stolen.

• The mayor was in protective custody at Rockwell Valley Hospital in stable condition. And although he likely had talked with police, the news media couldn't get any official statement as to why Pennisen had the .40 caliber gun tucked in his trousers.

- Lt. Del Dewitt was on administrative leave pending an investigation into the incident. He was also refusing to return phone calls. Rockwell Valley police declined to release his shooting range records. It was confidential police information, Rockwell Valley Police Chief Bobo Caprino said.
- Judge Owen T. Beigenlaw was refusing to comment about anything. The court clerk did say he had cancelled his cases for the week. Rue had confirmed that Beigenlaw was seen drunk at a Rockwell Valley bar a few hours after the shooting incident. A waitress said a police car came and picked him up to give him a ride.

"And that's just the easy stuff, right, Eli?" Jack said. "We have all the normal craziness to cover, and I think we should consider following up on this eminent domain stuff, Keith. I know it won't be as exciting as Friday, but you and Rue might like a little less adrenalin depletion."

Keith laughed and gave Rue a tiny smile and nodded. Both gestures were meant in part to say thanks to Rue for not mentioning the altercation Keith got into Friday as they went to Keith's car to leave the court parking lot.

Two GES workers – the ones he had filmed using his dashboard doggy camera – were waiting nearby as Keith and Rue got to the car.

Sitting in the staff meeting now, Keith had trouble not grinning when he thought about the GES worker who came up to the car before Keith got in, thinking this would be a repeat of the roadside incident in which Keith had kowtowed to the bully.

"You're not getting off so easy this time, short stuff," the GES worker said. "You made me look like an asshole."

But when he reached to grab Keith's shoulder, Keith feinted to his right, then threw what some people like to call a *haymaker* punch to the worker's cheekbone.

Rue later said she heard the sound of a sharp crack.

The other GES worker was standing back about 25 feet away and didn't move when he saw his co-worker laid out flat on the parking lot from a single blow.

Keith shut out the memory when he realized Jack had just said his name in the meeting.

"Rue," Jack said. "Do you want to help Keith on making some calls on that eminent domain stuff? It will be interesting to see how soon the good judge gets back on the bench, too. He's always had a drinking problem."

The meeting broke up and Jack went back into his office, hoping for an email or phone message from the alarm company.

Instead he found an email from Cass, who had taken Noah to another ear, nose and throat specialist at a clinic outside of Syracuse. Her brief email was sent from the specialist's office before she and Noah started the drive back.

```
Jack, the doctor confirms
what the last doctor said.
There is no physical reason why
Noah won`t speak.
     She said it might have been
painful to talk for some time
after he was first pulled out
of the water. She said she
could see some scarring on his
eardrums and in his throat,
too.
```

```
Ditto for his hearing.
He should be able to hear
fine. She said the same thing
about us being patient.
I hate doctors.
See you at home.
L. Cass
```

Jack reread the email twice, looking for any hint of good news – other than the fact that Noah didn't seem to be in any kind of pain. Then he telephoned Shania to see if she and Eli might want to come over for dinner sometime in the next few days.

Cass liked Shania – in fact, Shania was about the only real friend that Cass had made since they came back. She had some casual acquaintances around the village, but never had anyone come to the house.

For an actress, she's almost a recluse, Jack thought. *A beautiful recluse who's devoting her life to my son.*

Shania said she would talk to Eli later when Eli wasn't working.

"He's taught you well, Shania. I hated to be interrupted with that kind of question from Devon," Jack said.

The thought of his late wife darkened his mood for a moment, then he thought about Cass again. After she had talked on the phone for what seemed like an eternity with her sister Anne on Vashon Island, she had agreed to stick around through the Christmas holidays, almost six months away.

Six months can be a long time, Jack thought.

And somehow between now and then, she said she would figure out a way to exit gracefully without hurting Noah. Or Jack.

Or hurt herself, he thought.

Chapter 22

> From the *Horseheads Clarion*
>
> Column One
> *Horseheads Clarion*
>
> ## A tale of water and two dogs
>
> By Jack Stafford
>
> Amid all the tales swirling around hydrofracking, the proposals for pipelines and gas storage and even wild courtroom shootouts involving elected officials, we come back to a key element in all of this.
>
> Perhaps *the* key element: Water.
>
> Whether it`s the purity of the jewel called Rockwell Valley Lake, the continued extraction of fresh, clean water out of the lake for hydrofracking, the disposal of recovered (and toxic) gas well water, or plain old residential wells poisoned

by the industrial processes, water is at center stage.

It's easy to forget as you read about – and we write about – court battles over rights of way or arrests when citizens try to protest against the industrialization of Pennsylvania and New York.

But it's there.

The *Clarion* has published reams about the ongoing water-related nightmare in Dimock, Penn., a symbolic ground zero for the anti-hydrofracking movement.

If you have been in a hermitage for the last years, then you *might* have missed that the water wells in that community – many of them, anyway – became contaminated with a variety of chemicals and natural gas when hydrofracking started.

It turned into a huge dustup that drew the attention of the U.S. Environmental Protection Agency, which first promised to help, then later reversed course (thanks to some heavy-handed politics).

As of this writing, the EPA has declared Dimock water clean and drinkable.

It`s not.

But the residents can tell great stories about EPA officials coming to their homes to give them that news but politely declining to drink the tap water offered to them.

They might be easily influenced by politics, but they`re not stupid enough to drink water laced with toluene.

The connection between hydrofracking and well contamination continues to be denied by natural gas companies - including Grand Energy Services. The mantra is that there have been "no definitive studies" to prove that hydrofracking in any way is the cause of these well poisonings.

Tell that to Lasse Espinola, a Rockwell Valley dairy farmer whose land is in the direct path where GES wants to put its natural gas pipeline from the gas wells to the east to its proposed storage to the west.

A few weeks ago Espinola rushed his two watchdogs to the veterinary clinic in Rockwell Valley when they both were stricken as if they had been poisoned.

Espinola has already been the target of vandalism. First a state-of-the-art solar array was damaged. Then his tractor tires were slashed.

When he discovered his dogs writhing on the ground and unable to walk, he assumed they had been fed rat poison or some other toxic chemical.

But the vet had Espinola take his well water to a lab for testing, and the results indicate the presence of heavy metals, toluene, benzene, and formaldehyde.

When hydrofracking started in Rockwell Valley, Espinola had the water in his well tested to establish a baseline.

It was as clean as the water in Rockwell Valley Lake, he says

But that well water is now why his dogs are sick. And unfortunately, now so is his dairy cattle herd, his mother, his wife, and Espinola himself.

Espinola's home is more than two miles from the closest natural gas well drilled by GES. And according to GES, there is no way that the toxins in the well could be the result of drilling - the same stance as it has taken everywhere that hydrofracking takes place.

That response isn`t very comforting to Lasse Espinola and his family.

This specific case will now be added to the hundreds of other reports across Pennsylvania in which formerly usable water wells suddenly have become toxic sewers.

Lasse Espinola says he might join one of the many lawsuits against GES - and other gas firms - to try to collect damages for the poisoning of his water.

He`s not sure. He`s more worried about his family`s health, his health, the health of his dairy herd and even his two dogs, still at the veterinary hospital.

But of one thing he is certain.

He`s not signing *any* contracts for *any* pipelines to cross his land.

Jack Stafford is the publisher of the Horseheads Clarion *and publishes Column One every Friday. He can be reached at JJStafford@HorseheadsClarion.com.*

CANNIBALS AND CHRISTIANS

Chapter 1

The explosion of a natural gas shale well and deaths of three Grand Energy Services workers in Ohio dampened the mood of Michael Ahlbright's first meeting with CEO Luther Burnside at GES Flathead, Missouri headquarters.

Ahlbright had heard the news on his way into the office, a bittersweet drive for him.

Four years before, Ahlbright had been hired by GES as a consultant to determine why the yields of natural gas were falling dramatically at GES wells all over the country. He quickly figured out that a biological agent GES was using in an attempt to neutralize toxic chemicals in fracking fluid was eating the concrete well casings of gas wells.

For delivering *that* bit of bad news, Ahlbright had been fired by the CEO who preceded Burnside.

"A lot of water under the bridge since we last chatted Michael. A lot," Burnside said. "What do you think of the office? After the board named me CEO, I had the place redone. Delacroix had all that Louisiana artwork. What shit."

Ahlbright had been hired by the late Grayson Oliver Delacroix III and wondered what Delacroix would think about Burnside sitting in this office.

And if he ever heard his artwork called shit, *he would have torn your head off*, Ahlbright thought.

"Did the police ever figure out about that gas leak that killed him?" Ahlbright asked. "I remember a lot of speculation that it was that radical environmental bunch, the Wolverines. But then it kind of disappeared."

Burnside adjusted his tie as he looked past Ahlbright to the full-length mirror which he also used to check his facial expressions.

With Ahlbright he wanted to project *friendly* and *collegial*. He had hired him to help straighten out one mess and launch a new project. And Burnside was in need of a smart ally.

"Well, they never *directly* tied it to the Wolverines," Burnside said. "Though I heard informally that it wasn't an accident. There just wasn't enough of the house left to prove anything. Or much of Delacroix either. But that's all history."

Ahlbright listened politely while Burnside talked for nearly a half-hour about the situation in Rockwell Valley: the need for the pipeline, the salt cavern storage, the problem with the mayor and the continued harassment of GES by the newspaper in Horseheads, New York.

Ahlbright took some notes but didn't hear anything he wasn't already aware of.

"I need a *consigliere*, so to speak, Michael. All of these things are too much for me. Too many details. And while I have Rod Mayenlyn helping and the other vice presidents, I need someone closer I can trust to handle the politics and, well, like I said, the details. And *privately*."

Odd choice of words, Ahlbright thought. *Consigliere?*

Burnside readjusted his tie for the third time, looking past Ahlbright again.

"That's why I brought you in on a consulting contract. A lot of what I need you for can be better accomplished with you working off the books, out of the office. It gives you more freedom."

And you deniability, Ahlbright thought.

"Well, I don't hear anything that is all that complicated," Ahlbright said. "The pipeline and the storage are straightforward. I think the permits are wired for those. The mayor? Well, he's a bigger problem, but let's just get him into a clinic. We might even get some sympathy for him."

Burnside looked at himself in the mirror and adjusted his face into a puzzled look.

"What I mean is, sympathy because he snapped with all the pressure put on him by these nut-job environmentalists. And the gun? He was simply carrying it to protect himself. The Second Amendment defense. But he has to play along," Ahlbright said.

Burnside grew a smile.

"I knew you would be helpful here, Michael. Very helpful. I will talk with Rod about the mayor right away. Rod's in Rockwell Valley already. And he can talk with the district attorney and the judge, too. But what about the newspaper? And that ass of an editor who writes those columns?"

Michael Ahlbright looked down at his notepad for a minute, scribbling a note, then met Burnside's eyes.

"I have some ideas. It really helps that Jack Stafford thinks I'm his friend."

Burnside looked in the mirror again and adjusted his smile.

Chapter 2

Weekly social dinners – most often on Sunday evenings – quickly became a part of the landscape for Jack, Cass and Noah, often shared with Eli and Shania as summer progressed. Sometimes the four reporters were invited. And Oscar and his niece Lindy came when their tasting room duties would let them.

Noah in particular liked having Eli and Shania over. The couple would fuss with whatever Noah wanted to play with, no doubt seeing their future when their child was born.

And Belle the Labrador would jump up, bark and frolic when Eli and Shania came to the door, always happy to see them again.

Occasionally she would walk them home and Eli would have to call and let Jack know that Belle seemed to want to stay at their house. It worked well for everyone.

Shania had started watching Noah a few hours most days, getting Noah out of the house. Sometimes she took him to her house, other times just into Millie's Diner, where he would sit at a table and use crayons in a coloring book while Shania worked.

Cass would usually grab the time to work on a new play. But sometimes she drove to Rockwell Valley or Ithaca to meet with people involved in theater groups. When she did, they almost *always* tried to get her to act in a play or agree to be a director for some upcoming production.

Sunday dinners were part social, part child chatter, and part business. Eli and Jack usually retired to Jack's office after dinner to chat about the *Clarion*, news and gossip that might turn into news.

The conversations reminded Jack of when he and Walter Nagle would talk, except now Jack was the publisher and Eli the editor.

The after-dinner chats had leveled the field, with Jack respecting Eli's talents even *more* than he had when he and Devon and Noah had left for Tonga.

"So this Michael Ahlbright is kind of all over the place. But he's not a GES employee," Eli said. "The company PR office said he was hired to help 'facilitate several matters,' whatever that means."

Jack got up and closed the door to his office, drawing a brief look from Cass that was undecipherable.

He reached to pour himself a second glass of wine, then stopped, pouring only some wine into Eli's glass before he sat down.

"Ahlbright was key to us finding out about the bacteria eating the concrete in GES wells," Jack said. "I'm sure you remember him from all that. Then after GES got into hot water over the fracking water spill that killed those children, he went back to work for them as a PR spokesman for a short time. People like him, but Devon never trusted him completely. I didn't either."

Jack wanted to pick Eli's brain about a new book he was reading about the Fukushima nuclear reactor meltdowns when he heard a tiny knock at the door.

Jack was certain it was Noah, who never liked it when Jack closed the door. Noah still wasn't speaking, but in the last two weeks had started responding – by turning his head – to loud noises.

The doorknob turned and Cass stuck her head in the door, Noah standing beside her.

"If you gentlemen are done smoking cigars – or whatever – we have some dessert that Shania brought over that she is ready to dish up," she said. "We'll put the dessert on the table in a just a minute."

Noah looked up at Cass as she finished her sentence and smiled broadly.

Then he bolted, running over to the dining room table where he climbed up into his chair to wait for dessert.

Jack and Cass looked at Eli, then all three looked out into the dining room where Noah had picked up a fork and was waving it in the air like a music conductor while he turned to watch the kitchen.

Before they all dove into a delicious apple cobbler, Jack offered an elaborate toast with dessert wine in honor of Cass and Noah. Each time he said Noah's name, Noah would look at him and smile.

"There are days and there are days. This is a big day in this house for us. Cheers, everyone. Cheers!"

Noah wolfed down a slice of the cobbler while Cass tried unsuccessfully to hold back her tears of relief.

Chapter 3

It had taken some serious political arm-twisting and an unknown amount of Grand Energy Services cash – at least unknown to Rockwell Valley Police Chief Bobo Caprino – to keep Rockwell Valley Mayor Will Pennisen from being charged by the district attorney for carrying a weapon into the courtroom of Judge Owen T. Beigenlaw.

That it went down that way only made Bobo that much *more* convinced of how much influence Grand Energy Services had in his small town.

After a public relations blitz and a press conference *mea culpa* by Pennisen, it appeared that not only would he *not* be charged, he would even keep his elected position and his job as manager of GES in Rockwell Valley.

Amazing, Bobo thought. *Just amazing.*

Bobo's part in the drama was keeping quiet about the gun that Pennisen had pulled out in court.

Bobo sent Lt. Del Dewitt to the press conference to explain the whole thing as delicately – and obtusely – as possible.

Bobo didn't like giving Pennisen a pass on something that would have landed most anyone else in a jail cell, but he swallowed it like he felt he had to swallow so many things.

"There was a mix-up in the records at the police department," Dewitt said to a dozen microphones and a small knot of print reporters. "The gun that the mayor accidentally pulled out in court was an official police weapon. But it was on loan to him for protection because of threats he had received. I was not aware of that loan or I would have understood why the mayor had a gun that day."

The media lapped it up, never asking *who did* authorize the loan of the gun. *The Clarion* did ask but was told the name of the person was confidential. The reporters mostly bought the explanation that Pennisen's in-court crackup was because of pressure over the pipeline and storage projects.

Dewitt's vague references to threats made against the mayor by anti-pipeline and anti-gas storage protesters were featured prominently in most articles and broadcasts.

The press conference resulted in mostly favorable stories and commentaries painting Pennisen as a victim. And his departure to a rehabilitation clinic two days later was portrayed as if he was taking one for the team.

At the microphone that day, the mayor even said, "I shall return," though most of the media were too young – or unread – to get the historical reference to General Douglas MacArthur.

Across the desk from Bobo, Lt. Del Dewitt was holding copies of the *Horseheads Clarion* and several regional newspapers.

"It's pretty goddamn unbelievable that he could screw up that bad and not get tagged for it," Bobo said. "You too, of course. Right, lieutenant?"

Dewitt shifted uneasily in his chair. Since he had winged the mayor in the courthouse shooting, he had been suspended until the day before when a shooting review team from the state attorney general's office cleared him of any wrongdoing.

"You got it chief. And thanks for keeping my shooting range stuff private, too. But, um, not all the press is giving Pennisen – or us – a pass on this," Dewitt said.

Bobo motioned for Dewitt to hand over four newspapers that Bobo then fanned out on his desk.

Three of the four had short accounts about how long Rockwell Valley Mayor Will Pennisen would be gone and that Vice Mayor Pilar Johansen would take over his duties. One published a fawning sidebar story about a mayor in a small town in Kentucky who had gone off the rails shooting up a topless bar. But the story said after he spent a month at a rehab clinic – the same one Rockwell Valley's mayor would go to – he eventually became arguably the best mayor the town had ever had.

Then there was the *Clarion*.

In a column by Jack Stafford titled "No Fracking Way," the publisher of the newspaper ripped into Rockwell Valley's town council for not demanding the mayor resign. It also raised questions – again – about Pennisen's conflict of interest by being both mayor of the town and general manager of the local Grand Energy Services office and construction project.

```
    As controversial as the
pipeline project and the
proposed salt cavern propane
and gas storage are, there is
simply no good reason for Mayor
Will Pennisen to remain in
office.
    Surely there are other
candidates not carrying
Pennisen`s latest bit of
baggage who can step in and
offer the people of Rockwell
Valley some real leadership,
not just corporate obedience.
    Surely the potential
elected official pool is not so
shallow that someone mentally
unbalanced enough to carry a
```

> loaded gun into a courtroom
> should remain in the office of
> Rockwell Valley mayor.
> Surely.

Bobo skimmed parts of the column again, this time running his hand through his hair.

"Well, at least he seems to have bought the part about how Pennisen got the gun," Bobo said. "Right?"

Dewitt nodded.

"Yeah. I think so, but with this Stafford guy, you never know."

Bobo reread Stafford's column, searching for any hints that the Rockwell Valley Police Department might end up in the crosshairs of the *Horseheads Clarion*.

Not finding anything, he chased Dewitt out of the office, checked his email and swore loudly enough that his ex-wife dispatcher leaned back in her chair to peer into the office to see what was going on.

The email on his screen was from a *Clarion* reporter named Keith Everlight who wanted to know if the pistol that Pennisen had carried into court was one of the guns gotten the year before as part of a federal grant – or if it had been purchased with money in another well-publicized donation from Grand Energy Services.

> I`m sure you know, Chief
> Caprino, if it was one of the
> guns from the federal grant, the
> feds might have some questions.

Yes, you little bastard, you're right, Bobo thought. *And if I tell you it was GES funded, I'm screwed, too.*

Bobo got up and walked out to squad room where he knew Dewitt was likely standing, brewing yet *another* pot of coffee.

He was going to pass this little dynamite football off to Dewitt to figure out – or have it blow up in *his* face.

Chapter 4

The idea that he was jealous or envious never crossed Rod Mayenlyn's mind – not consciously anyway.

But Luther Burnside's hiring of Michael Ahlbright to handle some of the more delicate Grand Energy Services matters bothered him.

A lot.

Mayenlyn was especially burned because when the former GES chief executive officer was fired, Mayenlyn used every corporate political dirty trick he could think of to ensure that Burnside took over as acting CEO. Then when the job became officially open – after former CEO Grayson Oliver Delacroix III was blown up in a gas leak at his house – Mayenlyn continued his campaign to keep Burnside in office.

And now here was Burnside, acting like a Mafia don and bringing in Ahlbright.

Calling him his consigliere, *for Chrissakes*, Mayenlyn thought.

But he swallowed any outward signs of that jealousy or envy as he sat in the office of Luther Burnside, with Michael Ahlbright sitting in the chair next to him while Burnside shuffled some papers on his desk.

"Rod, I want you to tell Michael what you told me yesterday. About Stafford," Burnside said. "Michael, you are going to *love* this."

Mayenlyn leaned back in his chair. The day before he had immediately regretted telling Burnside about Stafford's stay in the psychiatric facility on Vashon Island near Seattle. He had thrown it out as a simple chit to try to boost his credibility with Burnside after listening to Burnside wax poetic about how Michael Ahlbright was going to help.

"And that memo? The one with the details about Stafford's case. Let's have a look at it," Burnside said.

The memo wasn't really a memo at all but a narrative written by a staff nurse about Stafford's case.

"I didn't bring the original," Mayenlyn said. "But I have my notes. The original is in my safe."

Burnside's face started to get red until Michael Ahlbright spoke.

"That's smart, Rod. Medical records are volatile. People get quite torqued about their release. And I don't mean just the patients. I mean everybody. No one wants their medical records loose out there."

After Burnside waved his hand at Mayenlyn to continue, Mayenlyn went over the key points in what the nurse had written.

- *Stafford was considered a suicide risk when he arrived*
- *Stafford suffered from clinical depression*
- *Stafford is a high-functioning alcoholic*
- *Stafford took an anti-depressant during his stay*

"She also talked about him having to be restrained in one of those straightjacket things a lot of the time he was in the hospital," Mayenlyn said. "It's a pretty damning report."

The three men silently mulled over what Mayenlyn had said for a moment.

"The question is, what can we do with this?" Burnside said. "I would like to shut that damn newspaper up once and for all. But I don't want any backlash or sympathy for that asshole. Amazing that he can do what he does with that kind of baggage."

Michael Ahlbright asked Mayenlyn to repeat several of the key points.

"I'd like to take a look at the whole written report first," Ahlbright said. "But I think maybe I should pay Stafford a visit. Back when Delacroix was CEO, I helped the *Clarion* with a couple of stories. I *might* be able to talk with Stafford. At least I can take his temperature and see how much of this is real and what we can use."

Burnside started drumming his fingers on his desk in the rhythm that set Mayenlyn's teeth on edge.

"Fine. Rod, give Michael that file. Right now I need to talk with Michael alone for a few minutes."

Mayenlyn stood and walked out, straining to hear what Burnside was saying.

He wasn't sure, but it sounded like Burnside was saying the new pipeline wasn't going to be used solely to transport natural gas from the hydrofracked wells.

Instead it was possible the new proposed eastbound pipeline would move the toxic recovered water to the Atlantic Coast for disposal deep in the ocean, rather than pay to truck it to Ohio to dump into mile-deep injection wells.

Mayenlyn headed down the hallway to the operations office where the schematics for the new pipelines were being kept. The secretary there owed him a favor.

Chapter 5

When the engine of a Grand Energy Services pickup truck parked at a drill site south of Rockwell Valley wouldn't even turn over, a GES mechanic called to fix the truck popped the hood and found that someone had cut several wires.

Damn kids, he thought. *Why not just let the air out of the tires or break a window? Then I wouldn't be dealing with this crap.*

Then he glanced up at the underside of the hood, where someone had painted the word *Wolverines* in big letters.

The mechanic had been with GES for nearly 10 years and remembered seeing *that* spray-painted name plenty four or five years before, when he had fixed trucks and other vehicles that had been vandalized.

At one point, he remembered, the group was blamed for blowing up some GES facilities.

He looked around nervously, but the only other people were four uniformed roughnecks working on equipment around the site.

He relaxed.

Fifteen minutes and a half a roll of electrical tape later, the mechanic was pleased that when he turned the key, the truck roared to life.

Satisfied that the truck was running well enough to take to the main GES shop, he put the truck in reverse, *immediately* hearing a series of sharp popping sounds as he felt the truck shudder.

He jumped out to see that three of the four tires on the truck were flat – the victims of neatly placed 4-inch spikes. The fourth spike had fallen over and didn't enter the tire.

The mechanic had just pulled out his cell phone to call the main office to report what had happened when he looked on the ground under the truck.

On the gravel someone had spray painted the word *Wolverines*.

In smaller letters underneath were the words *We're Back*.

Chapter 6

```
From the Horseheads Clarion

Column One
Horseheads Clarion
```

When a 'win-win' is really one-sided

```
By Jack Stafford

    When    landsmen    started
traveling  the   country   roads
of  Pennsylvania  and  New  York,
trying to get property owners to
sign  contracts  giving  natural
gas   companies   the   right  to
```

drill on their lands, it seemed like *such* a gift.

The hubbub was all because the now familiar technology known as hydrofracking made it possible for the companies to get at the natural gas locked deep in the Marcellus Shale, thousands of feet down.

It seemed like another gold rush, except this time the gold was natural gas.

Because the landsmen were good salesmen – and the property owners for the most part distrusted attorneys – many owners signed gas leases, unaware just how much more the contracts benefitted the gas companies than the property owner.

All that is history, a sad history with which people who signed *those* contracts have to live.

Today most gas company landsmen complain bitterly about the cottage industry that has grown up around gas leases designed to protect property owners: attorney specialists, consultants, contract experts and legal advocates.

Being a landsman isn`t as easy as it used to be when they

just had to show up in a fancy pickup truck and wave around a sheet of paper with a lot of numbers on it.

But today's tale is of a Rockwell Valley rancher who thought he had covered himself quite well three years ago but now can't get a bank loan to buy some much needed equipment.

His gas lease - which applies to just a tiny portion of his 500-acre spread - gave the company the right to use his property as collateral for loans. His entire piece of property is encumbered, not just the corner 10 acres he agreed to let Grand Energy Services use to drill for gas.

The company is using his land - and perhaps the land of other Rockwell Valley property owners - to raise capital to build the proposed pipeline from the gas wells to the proposed salt cavern storage at the north end of Rockwell Valley Lake.

The rancher's name isn't printed here because he is understandably embarrassed.

He didn't read the fine print that gave GES this power, which he *now* understands was a huge mistake on his part.

The issue isn't the lack of due diligence on the part of one of our neighbors. It's that GES didn't alert him to this clause that unbelievably encumbered his property for nearly $1 million without telling him.

But there is a second, seedier twist to this tale.

When the rancher first found out about his property being used as collateral, he contacted GES to complain. After being passed around from GES office to GES office, he talked with the individual in charge of getting easement rights for the proposed natural gas pipeline from GES wells to the proposed salt cavern storage.

He told the rancher that GES *might* be able to purchase his needed farm equipment for the rancher, in exchange for his signature on an easement agreement for the pipeline.

Yes, you guessed it: An easement agreement that would be *very* favorable to GES.

"The asshole had the balls to say it would be a 'win-win,'" the rancher told the *Clarion*.

A win for GES perhaps. But the rancher would still have his property encumbered. And it raises a variety of legal issues, including the rancher's ability to sell off any portion of his acreage - something he has been planning to do for several years.

In coming weeks, the *Clarion* will publish a series of articles about eminent domain and these kinds of contorted legal agreements that many Rockwell Valley and New York property owners have signed.

The articles have been researched and written by reporters Keith Everlight and Rue Malish.

The title of the series came easy after reviewing this rancher's plight and that of others: *Fracking Justice*.

Jack Stafford is the publisher of the Horseheads Clarion *and publishes Column One every Friday. He can be reached at JJStafford@ HorseheadsClarion.com.*

FRACKING JUSTICE

Chapter 7

The staff meeting at the *Horseheads Clarion* had erupted into a babbling debate that mixed history with current events with newsroom philosophy.

Eli Gupta finally pulled rank and said that the newspaper needed to take a closer look at the latest incidents involved the Wolverines.

"I hate to throw my managing editor card down here, but we *have* to look at this. There's something going on," Eli said.

The four reporters groaned, looking at each other to see which of them might be willing to devote any of their already overcommitted time to pulling together a story about the Wolverines.

Eli looked nervously at Jack, who hadn't said a word.

"Okay, let me wade in for a minute on this," Jack said. "Eli and I were front and center earlier when these Wolverines were waging a low-key guerrilla war against GES and other gas companies. It certainly bears a look. But I have a question, Eli. You live on your computer and I haven't heard you mention the Wolverines. Has there been any chatter, any instances anyplace else recently? Like Colorado? They were really active there."

Keith Everlight's face lit up with the smug look that Jack and Eli hated. But it answered the question for Jack before Eli had a chance to answer.

"Actually, no," Eli said. "All the websites I check for this kind of stuff haven't had anything. No national reports from any news media. All we have is the local incidents, like that GES truck."

Jack leaned forward and tossed his yellow notepad on the table.

"You might remember I wrote a column months ago – not long after that road-flares-disguised-as-dynamite stunt – that was skeptical that this was really the Wolverines we wrote about. I am still skeptical. Which is why we need to look at what's going on.

"We still have a story, folks, no matter what. Maybe we need to talk with Alice McCallis."

Jack waved his hand at Eli, giving him back the floor. And for a moment Eli waited silently for one of the four staff writers to volunteer.

Finally Stan and Jill – who had been on staff as brand-new reporters back when the Wolverines were active – raised their hands.

"If we can work on this together, I think we can do it justice," Jill said. "It's going to take talking with the GES people. So I think that leaves Keith out."

Keith blushed. From the look on Jill's face, it seemed likely Rue had mentioned his altercation after the Rockwell Valley courthouse shooting.

Jack's cell phone beeped, the third text he had received during the half-hour meeting. The first two had been newsy updates from Cass, who was busy lining up yet another round of doctors and medical specialists to look at Noah. The third was from Lasse Espinola, saying his two dogs – poisoned by drinking contaminated well water – were recovering slowly, but he wanted to talk to him about Jack's last column.

As the staff filed out, Eli stayed to debrief with Jack while Jack called Lasse.

"This will be quick, Eli. If not, I'll call him later," Jack said.

The phone call with Lasse Espinola wasn't quick, but was interesting enough that half-way through Jack put his phone on speaker so Eli could hear too.

"Lasse, say that again so my managing editor can hear."

"Well, my uncle Einar read your column and then looked at the contract GES wants him to sign. You know, the contract to allow the pipeline to cross his land? It says just like your column did. GES could borrow against his farm if he signed it. And it wouldn't need his permission."

After Lasse hung up, Eli looked up at the ceiling and then back at Jack.

"Okay, we'll put the Wolverines on hold for a little bit," Eli said. "I think we have 30 or 40 people in the path of that pipeline we need to contact to see what their contracts might say."

Chapter 8

The news that the salt cavern propane and natural gas storage had received *all* the necessary state and federal approvals to start construction had Grand Energy Services CEO Luther Burnside in a particularly ebullient mood.

In fact, he was close to giddy with delight, thinking about not only the triumph but the big cash and stock bonus that would be his.

Although he had known from the start – thanks to *generous* amounts of cash, campaign donations and plain old arm twisting and political leverage by GES that both propane and natural gas storage would *eventually* be approved, it was just one more persuasive argument in favor of starting the construction of the natural gas pipelines to and from the facility.

The approvals ramped up the pressure to get the pipelines operational right away.

Burnside had called Rod Mayenlyn at home early that morning, directing him to get a press conference together for later that day at GES headquarters.

Burnside wanted to get this bit of good news out to investors right away. Plus, he knew that the people who owned property along the pipeline route would now want more money, not knowing that GES was ready – if it needed to – to file a legal brief asking for a sweeping judicial order for eminent domain to cover all the land.

That order would only be needed if Michael Ahlbright's alternative plan didn't work.

A somewhat groggy Mayenlyn convinced his boss that the place to hold the triumphant press conference was actually *at* the salt cavern storage site in Rockwell Valley, not GES headquarters.

"It will be like a ribbon-cutting sort of thing," Mayenlyn had said. "You know, lots of media, balloons." The image made his head hurt even more than the whole bottle of excellent Riesling he had imbibed the evening before.

"We can set it up for two or three days from now. Friday would be best. You can fly in and it will give me time to get all the media coverage going. This could get national attention because of the pipeline connection. Congratulations, chief."

Burnside balked at first. He wanted to grab a little glory immediately. Then he thought about the new $6,000 Italian suit delivered to his Flathead home the day before.

Perfect for television, he thought, looking at himself in the mirror across his office, adjusting his smile to show his teeth. *Perfect.*

"Okay, Rod, but one more detail. I know we usually try to exclude Jack Stafford from all our events. But this time I want you to invite him personally. I want to see the look on that asshole's face when I talk about the project."

Chapter 9

They were about 15 minutes into their conversation at Millie's Diner before Jack thought it was odd that Michael Ahlbright had chosen Jack's home turf to drop such a huge bomb.

When he had called the day before, Jack thought Ahlbright wanted to talk about the approval of the salt cavern gas storage, knowing that the *Clarion* would be supportive of activists' rumblings about filing a lawsuit to stop it. Ahlbright had, at times, been helpful to the *Clarion*, even when working for GES.

But after the first few minutes of normal meet-and-greet chit-chat, it was obvious that Ahlbright wanted to convince Jack that he was there to try to protect Jack from getting hurt by the revelations Grand Energy Services was considering making public about his hospital stay on Vashon Island.

Ahlbright said GES wanted to spin a case that he wasn't fit to be editor of the newspaper and certainly not fit to be throwing stones at anyone.

"Michael, I appreciate this heads-up. I know you work directly for the new CEO. I guess he's not that new. But if I hear you right, your boss and GES are just *considering* going public with information about me. Considering."

Ahlbright held up his coffee mug and waved to Shania.

"Yes. I told Burnside that GES shouldn't get into the mudslinging business, but he's a pretty volatile guy, Jack. He acts like he's the Godfather from that movie sometimes."

Jack made his own motion towards Shania, holding up his teacup while he thought carefully about what Ahlbright was implying.

"I know that your new boss's nickname is Luca Brasi. But the last CEO – Delacroix – was a pretty big asshole, too. And he was damn smart about politics. He wouldn't have sent someone to *threaten* me, Michael. I'm surprised you would do it."

Jack stared straight at Ahlbright, who looked down to his coffee mug to avert Jack's gaze.

"*He* didn't send me to do anything Jack. I'm here on my own. In fact, Burnside thinks I'm up here to check on the gas storage facility. This is just between us. Really. We are definitely on opposite sides of the gas issue, but I have always admired your willingness to stick your neck out."

Jack and Ahlbright suspended their conversation while Shania poured the coffee and more hot water for tea in Jack's mug.

"Okay," Jack said. "Maybe I'm a little oversensitive these days. But last month I thought someone was trying to kidnap my son. Then today you tell me that GES has somehow gotten my medical records. I'm beginning to think I'm not paranoid at all."

Paranoid? Ahlbright thought. *Nope, that wasn't in the nurse's narrative. But 'close to a psychotic break' was.*

"I *hate* this kind of stuff Jack. I thought GES was playing things straight or I never would have taken this contract. But if you do back off some on the hyperbole – particularly naming *Burnside* so much it would help. Burnside has a huge ego. He gets wounded way too easily. If you could dial it back – just when you use his name – I'll do my best to convince him to bury whatever document he claims he has."

"Shred would be nicer. But thank you, Michael. That's a nice offer."

The two men chatted for another 15 minutes or so, laughing occasionally. And to anyone watching, it was just a couple of old friends reliving some shared history.

But while Michael Ahlbright was busy spinning in his mind about what he would tell Luther Burnside about Jack, Jack Stafford was busy spinning an idea about the GES threat of a personal smear campaign.

Michael Ahlbright and Jack Stafford shook hands as they parted outside Millie's Diner, each man lost in his own thoughts.

Chapter 10

Jill Nored had run across the book at the public library, her favorite place to go on lunch hour or when she simply needed some time to think outside of the *Horseheads Clarion*.

Most of the staff usually rolled across the street to Millie's Diner for lunch. But Jill preferred the library's silence – and the serendipity of finding some book she might never run across searching online.

Plus, she was trying to drop 10 pounds.

But now she was anxiously waiting for Jack to get back from his lunch from across the street at Millie's with his son Noah and sister-in-law Cass. Jill had met Cass only a few times, but whenever she thought about her, the word "elegant" came into her mind.

Jill was a full head shorter than Cass, so it might have been Cass's height that influenced her. It might also have been Cass's slim athletic build.

And she always has such great-looking hair, too, Jill thought.

Jill was startled when her mental vision of Cass morphed into the *real* Cass, standing right in front of her desk, with Noah at her hip. Noah was peering at Jill with big blue eyes.

"You reading Norman Mailer?" Cass asked. "He's not someone I would have thought you would spend much time with. Any time, really."

Jill shook her head, partly to say no and partly to shake off the surprise of Cass being in the office. Jill looked past Cass and saw Jack wandering around in his office, looking for something.

"No, this isn't the book by Norman Mailer. Jut a similar title. But the subtitle gives away what the book is really about. It's by a Pennsylvania professor, Charles Avery Sawmill. He studies energy and environment stuff."

Cass picked up the book, looked at the cover and then flipped it over to read the book description on the back.

```
Cannibals and Christians: The
Extractors vs. The Sustainers
```

> compares the myriad differences between the people involved in extraction industries and people who believe in sustainable technologies and lifestyles. The book is the result of 10 years of research conducted across the globe and looks at the influences of culture, technology, history, wealth and politics. Cannibals and Christians: The Extractors vs. The Sustainers offers insight into the reasons behind the clashes we see worldwide over natural resource use and suggests solutions for the reconciliation of these two very disparate philosophies.

"Wow, this sounds like the kind of book Jack reads all the time. I can barely get him to watch a movie at night," Cass said. "He's so immersed."

Cass looked at Jill who was blushing.

"Oh … You got this for *Jack*. Hey, no need to blush. I'm Jack's sister-in-law, not his wife. I don't get jealous."

Jill blushed even deeper and excused herself to go to the ladies room just as Jack came out of his office.

"What's up with Jill?" Jack asked. "Is she sick?"

Cass handed Jack the copy of *Cannibals and Christians: The Extractors vs. The Sustainers* that Jill had picked up at the library.

"I believe Jill got this for you and wants to talk about it," Cass said. "And no, it's not the Norman Mailer collection of essays. This one looks interesting."

Jack looked at the book and could tell from Cass's expression that there was something else going on but knew better than to bother to ask.

It *did* look like an interesting book and might even make the basis for a column.

But that would be in the future.

"It looks interesting, Cass, but can you come into my office before you go back home? I have something I want to show you."

Now it was her turn to be curious.

Chapter 11

The virtually untraceable GES cell phone that Calvin Boviné used to keep in touch with Rod Mayenlyn had gotten wet the night he had crawled through a puddle to get underneath a truck at a GES gas well site.

The puddle was a lot deeper than it seemed in the dark and Boviné's trousers got thoroughly soaked in the mud and water around the truck.

Days later – when Boviné called and left a message for Mayenlyn about the big press conference at the Rockwell Valley salt cavern storage site – his message came through garbled.

And when Mayenlyn attempted to call Boviné back a few hours later to ask him what he wanted, he got a message that the phone was out of service.

Damn cell phones. Always out of range, Mayenlyn thought.

Mayenlyn tried a few more times – even Thursday, the day before the press conference – but gave up because he had too many details to deal with to pull off the conference. Plus, he had to double check arrangements for the limo scheduled to pick up CEO Luther Burnside at the airport at 9 a.m.

Mayenlyn also had to make sure that Burnside's penthouse suite at the newly remodeled 250-room Rockwell Valley Lakeside Hotel was ready with the flowers and champagne he had requested.

Burnside's wife – a reclusive woman only a few of the GES top brass had ever met – was not coming with him.

But Mayenlyn noted that his female executive secretary and assistant – Ida Merganser – was on the list for a suite adjacent to Burnside's.

The mid-day Friday press conference – including a celebratory reception at the hotel for local dignitaries that evening – was proving to be a bonanza for the hotel. In addition to all the out-of-town media who were booking rooms, a number of state officials were coming in.

And the town government had commissioned a local sign company to make a 20' wide by 40' tall vertical banner to drape down across the front of the hotel that said "Congratulations to Grand Energy Services and CEO Luther Burnside."

Mayenlyn had agreed to have the town council stand on the hotel balcony to cut a ribbon to unfurl the banner in a brief ceremony just at the start of the reception.

Some of the press events and speeches were planned for the GES salt cavern site. But this kind of showy stuff would make for great television, Mayenlyn knew. And because it was happening late on Friday, it was likely the banner unfolding would run several times on Saturday television broadcasts when there is so little news, most small market news directors were desperate to fill air time.

Time to breathe, Mayenlyn thought late Thursday night in his hotel room in Rockwell Valley. *Just one press conference tomorrow followed by one big party.*

He fell asleep wondering if he had forgotten something.

Chapter 12

Rockwell Valley Police Chief Bobo Caprino had just finished dinner and his third beer. He was also getting ready to settle in with a rerun of *Law and Order* when his phone rang and Lt. Del Dewitt's I.D. popped up.

Bobo frowned at the phone. He had strict orders with the night dispatcher and everyone on the force never to call him after hours unless it was a major problem. He fussed like it was an imposition, but in truth, his night vision had gotten so bad he hated to drive after dark and would have to ask a unit to pick him up.

Dewitt was back working a day shift. But for the past week he was at the department office most evenings, too. The squad room chatter was he was having trouble with his wife. But Bobo didn't ask and didn't really want to know.

Bobo let the phone ring right up until the last ring, then slid the bar to answer it. Whatever Dewitt wanted was probably important. And after the debacle with letting the mayor go on the protest arrest – and the whole business with the gun – Bobo told Dewitt to keep him in the loop.

"Hello, hello," Bobo said. But he had missed the call. "Damn it."

Bobo went back to the start of *Law and Order* when the phone made an odd beeping sound, a sound that had Bobo confused until he realized that it was Dewitt again. This time he was trying to Skype.

Bobo searched the face of the phone, finally finding the button to answer the Skype call. And suddenly there was Dewitt's image in front of him, still in uniform.

"Hey Chief, I am sorry to bother you at home. I tried to call," Dewitt said.

Bobo grunted, wondering if his side of the camera was working. He had on just his undershirt and boxers – his relax-at-home clothes.

"I missed the call, sorry. But what's with the Skype? Just trying to be fancy with the tech, Del?"

Dewitt disappeared from the screen for a moment and Bobo watched as the image suddenly starting swinging around, then bouncing, then suddenly steady again. Finally Dewitt's face appeared, the tables of the department's tiny crime lab in the background.

"Sorry, chief. But I found something today I thought was kind of, well, weird. You get time to look at this stuff when you can't go out on patrol."

As if you ever *go out on patrol anymore,* Bobo thought.

"I was looking at the photos we took at the GES well site. The one where the engine was sabotaged and the tires got flattened? Anyway, one of the guys took pictures of the footprints in the mud around where the truck was parked. It would have been nice to actually have a cast to compare though," Dewitt said.

Bobo looked at the screen while Dewitt held up several photos of the footprints.

After the third photo, Bobo asked Dewitt what his point was.

"Sorry, chief, look at these first," Dewitt said.

And for another minute or two, another set of photos flashed in front of the screen until Bobo cried uncle.

"Del, fascinating. Great. I get look to look at footprints in the mud while I'm trying to drink a beer. The short version, please."

"Sorry again, chief, it's late and I didn't have enough coffee today. The first pictures were from the GES well site, the second set from Lasse Espinola's farm. I've adjusted the photos on the computer to double check, but I'm sure now."

Bobo stared at his nearly empty beer bottle, then asked Del to spell it out – again.

"Well, without actual physical casts to compare, I couldn't take this into court. But I'd say the footprints are the same. I think whoever hit the GES drill site also ripped up Espinola's solar stuff," Dewitt said. "The tread looks like an exact match chief. Exact."

Bobo pondered that for minute.

"Del. That's just goddamned fascinating. But the GES vandalism was supposed to be linked to those environmental whackos who put the fake dynamite under the railroad trestle and in the culvert out by the salt caverns. It doesn't make sense that they would destroy solar power equipment," Bobo said. "And how many people wear a boot with that tread? Really, Del. Been shopping for boots lately?"

This time it was Dewitt's turn to let some time pass before speaking.

"That's why I called, chief. I told you it was *weird*." Dewitt's face disappeared and was replaced by two photos of boot prints. He held them up for a full 30 seconds, long enough that Bobo found himself peering, closely comparing the two photos.

"Look at these pictures side by side. Same tread, like I said. Exact. But they are the exact same size, too. That's why I think it might be the same guy. Lots of people wear that kind of waffle tread boot. Sure.

"But not very many have feet this big," Dewitt said.

"I would bet the guy who vandalized the truck and Espinola's ranch wears a size 23 boot – maybe bigger. He must shop for shoes the same place circus clowns go."

Chapter 13

```
From the Horseheads Clarion

Column One
Horseheads Clarion
```

A sort-of private word with Clarion readers

```
By Jack Stafford
```

```
   Journalists often have a
hard time telling their own
stories. It`s an occupational
byproduct of listening so much
to - and reporting on - what
other people have to say and
do.
```

But today I want to share with you some details of a tragedy I experienced just before returning to the *Clarion* earlier this year.

I will explain later *why* I am sharing these details today.

Regular readers know that I left the *Clarion* several years ago on a leave of absence, traveling to a small island in the South Pacific nation of Tonga where I wrote a book titled *An Endless Quest for Hope and Solutions.* I lived on the island with my wife, Devon, who had been a reporter at this newspaper, and our infant son, Noah, who is now almost four years old.

A week before we were scheduled to return to the United States, my wife, my son Noah and a Tongan friend (a very experienced boater and island guide) were aboard a sailboat crossing the channel from our home to the main island in the group to run some errands. It was also so that Devon and Noah could say goodbye to some friends. A powerful, unseasonable rain-and-wind squall came up so suddenly the boat capsized. And in moments, my wife Devon - a very strong swimmer - disappeared beneath the waves.

Only through Herculean effort was my son Noah saved by our Tongan friend.

Those are the facts of what happened that day.

But I want to share what happened in the days and weeks after.

Simply put, I fell apart.

My wife Devon and I were as close as any two people can be. And our son was a miracle we celebrated daily. My emotional reaction to her being so suddenly snatched away defies any description.

Even now, many months later, it`s hard to describe how hard a blow her sudden death was to me.

Our many Tongan friends tried to help. My sister-in-law flew in immediately to help.

After a few weeks, my sister-in-law convinced me that leaving Tonga would be best for Noah and me. Simply mourning wasn`t healthy. I needed to get back to work, back here to Horseheads. Back home.

When we returned from Tonga, we went to the Seattle area

(where my late wife Devon had lived). I checked myself into a hospital - yes, a *psychiatric* hospital - for treatment of depression.

I can't say enough good things about the professional attitudes - and kindness - of all the doctors, nurses and counselors who in the space of weeks brought me out of the darkness that had enveloped me. And here in Horseheads, the warm welcome my son and I received upon returning earlier this year - and continue to get daily - remind me how good it is to be alive, even as much as my son and I miss my late wife.

All that is prelude to why suddenly *today* this sad episode is prominently featured among the rest of the *Clarion*'s news.

I was approached recently by an individual claiming to be in possession of medical records from my hospital stay. And the individual said the group he represents would make a very ugly public splash about the fact that I had been treated for depression unless I was willing to alter this newspaper's news coverage.

```
    The precise legal term
for this is the threat of
blackmail, of course. Though
threat of extortion fits, too,
as he sought favorable news
stories and editorials.
    There's nothing ugly about
being treated for depression -
or seeking such treatments.
    Nothing.
    But threats of blackmail
and extortion?
    Ugly, very, very ugly.
    And for the record, this
columnist - this newspaper
- does not respond well to
threats of any kind.
    Ever.

    Jack Stafford is the
publisher of the Horseheads
Clarion and publishes Column
One every Friday. He can
be reached at JJStafford@
HorseheadsClarion.com.
```

Chapter 14

A crowd of maybe 500 people milled around in the parking lot outside the Rockwell Valley Lakeside Hotel late Friday afternoon as a half-dozen Rockwell Valley officials crowded out onto a high hotel balcony where a banner was furled.

Most of the people in the parking lot had missed the noon press conference at the Grand Energy Services salt cavern propane storage site where CEO Luther Burnside had given a *much* shorter-than-expected speech about the many benefits the salt cavern storage would bring to Rockwell Valley and the area.

Rod Mayenlyn had written Burnside's nearly 50-minute talk with the emphasis on construction jobs generated, permanent jobs for people to work at the site, the money that would pour into the community for building materials and strong hints that by storing millions gallons of propane and natural gas in the caverns, local heating costs would be lower in the winter.

But Burnside had a problem delivering the speech.

He was too furious with the column he read by Jack Stafford that completely sabotaged his plans to use Stafford's stay at a psychiatric hospital as leverage.

That son of a bitch did everything but say it was us, Burnside thought. *And, of course, where in the hell is Michael Ahlbright?*

Things started to go sideways for Burnside when in his pique about Stafford, he *departed* from reading the prepared text of his speech handed out to the print reporters and the television and radio media at the site. They looked confused when he said the project would hire 150 people during the construction phase when the prepared speech said 50. And the number of permanent, on-site jobs was listed as 10 on the prepared text in the reporters' hands. Burnside said GES would hire "40 or 50 people.

"And that's just the start, my friends. Just a start," Burnside said.

What was supposed to be a carefully managed press event devolved quickly into a shouted question-and-answer session into which Mayenlyn eventually had to step and extract Burnside by telling the reporters any discrepancies between the prepared remarks and Burnside's speech would be explained in detail in a press release later that day.

"CEO Burnside was given some more up-to-date figures earlier today. But I promise the exact numbers by the reception," Mayenlen said.

But Mayenlen's explanation didn't make the news — only video of a very flustered Burnside appeared on a half-dozen newscasts later that afternoon, looking like he didn't understand his own company project.

And to add insult, as he made his way to the limousine to take him to Rockwell Valley Lakeside Hotel, a huge raven expertly dropped a neat plop of bird crap onto the shoulder of Burnside's suit.

None of the video cameras caught it, however.

Tales about the speech debacle trickled over into the parking lot of the hotel, where Alice McCallis and a small knot of anti-gas-storage protesters were holding court with the reporters, giving their version of what was really going on with the project.

McCallis and the protesters stood outside the GES salt cavern project gates on the highway, waving signs during the press conference. But they weren't allowed into the project area where Burnside melted down in front of the cameras.

"I think you got to see how fast and loose these gas people play with the facts," McCallis said. "But besides that, those much touted construction jobs? The ones the CEO seems to know so little about? Those will all go to out-of-state people, not Rockwell Valley or even New York workers. The same for the fulltime jobs."

On the edge of the protesters several Rockwell Valley police officers lurked but kept their distance.

CEO Burnside was standing mid-parking lot, surrounded by GES vice presidents and a handful of recently hired private security staff.

McCallis was just explaining to the reporters how unlikely it was that propane prices would go down as result of the storage when a loudspeaker barked.

Rockwell Valley's Vice Mayor Pilar Johansen – standing in for Mayor Will Pennisen – shouted to the crowd that it was time to unveil a small thank-you to Grand Energy Services for its perseverance in pushing the salt cavern propane storage project through.

The vice mayor had brought along the town's five-foot-long ceremonial scissors, better suited for cutting ribbons than lines holding banners. But after a few tries she managed to cut one side, then the other, unfurling the 20-foot-wide by 40-foot tall vertical banner, which rolled out as neatly as the sign company had promised.

What the company had *not* promised – or known – was that the word *Wolverine* was now scrawled in blood-red letters, with a giant W at the top, the rest of the letters running down the entire length of the banner, obscuring much of the message that said "Congratulations to Grand Energy Services and CEO Luther Burnside."

The gasp that initially came out of the crowd was quickly replaced by laughter, followed by more than a dozen wolf whistles, catcalls and few shouts of *Wolverine*s!

The people of Rockwell Valley knew a good joke when they saw one.

Chapter 15

The banner with the red spray-painted name Wolverine was still hanging off the balcony when Jack and Cass arrived.

The town council members had set it up to drop and hang from the balcony but didn't make arrangements for how to retrieve it.

Keith Everlight saw Jack and came over, the grin on his face as big as if he had pulled off the stunt himself.

"You should have seen the look on Burnside's face. Honestly. I thought he was going to explode," Keith said. "And yes, before you ask, I snapped several photos. But it will be all over the television, too."

Jack was concerned about the sudden appearance of the Wolverine name on the banner – certainly it was in keeping with the kind of tricks the group had done when it first popped up. But before the group disappeared it had moved from pranks to vandalism to blowing things up.

"Let's keep an eye on how the Rockwell Valley Police handle this. Maybe check into that pickup truck vandalism," Jack said. "In the meantime, let's get inside and eat some GES food and drink their wine."

Keith, Jack and Cass started forward just as the perplexed town council finally decided to simply cut the banner down and drop it to the ground.

Unfortunately they neglected to tell the people directly underneath the heavy banner, who suddenly found themselves covered – and in several cases knocked down – when it tumbled from the balcony.

"Is it any wonder this town is in such bad shape?" Jack said.

The GES security men – and the Rockwell Valley Police – were stationed around the doors of the hotel, requiring everyone who entered to provide identification. Jack, Cass and Keith were let in right away, though Jack's press I.D. raised the GES security man's eyebrows.

Alice McCallis's protesters were turned back, first because they carried protest signs, later when GES security said they weren't on the guest list.

Later that night two television stations ran footage of McCallis being forcibly turned back from the door, following by footage from earlier in the day when CEO Luther Burnside announced that the reception at the Rockwell Valley Lakeside Hotel was open to all people of Rockwell Valley.

"It's a truly communitywide celebration," he had said. "Everyone is welcome."

Inside the celebration, Keith took Jack aside and told him he felt uncomfortable – and more than a little hypocritical – munching GES food, drinking imported vodka and French wines while on the prowl for stories.

"Keith, if a little Grey Goose vodka and tonic would sway your ability to write a fair story, I would agree," Jack said. "But it won't. And I hope you mention that they were serving only French wines at this soirée. There's nothing local, either from around here or from our New York Finger Lakes at the bar. Not a single local wine."

Across the room, Luther Burnside studied Jack, even as he chatted with reception attendees. Cass noticed it as she was picking up some shrimp from a buffet table next to a man who introduced himself as a longtime Rockwell Valley resident.

"My given name is Melvin, but my friends all call me Bobo," he said. "Some people might not think that's an improvement, but I hated it when my parents called me Mel. I don't really know why. Lived here all my life."

Cass chatted with Bobo while she watched over his shoulder as Luther Burnside stared at Jack. Cass though Burnside looked like a brute.

And that suit! Cass thought. *Hideous. He looks like he's auditioning for a part in Goodfellas.*

Two other men came up and starting talking with Burnside, one who obviously worked for Burnside, based on his fawning nervous approach. The other looked like he might have once played professional football. He seemed disinterested in the event and looked uncomfortable in the ill-fitting suit he was wearing.

"Um, nice to chat with you, Miss,?" Bobo asked.

"Walsh, Miss Walsh," Cass said. "It's actually Cassandra. I live in Horseheads."

Jack caught Cass's eye and waved for her to come over and meet some of the "No On Gas" protesters who had slipped past the guards and were enjoying the GES-paid-for food and drinks.

She excused herself, and Cass and Jack watched Burnside trying to be affable and upbeat, but after being slapped down twice in one day, the steady redness of his cheeks told the real story.

Cannibals and Christians

"How did you like chatting with the police chief?" Jack asked. "He looked like you had him in your spell."

Cass looked startled.

"Police chief? I thought he was a businessman trying to pick me up," she said.

As they chatted, Keith wandered over and said he had talked with Eli – home with Shania in Horseheads watching Noah and Belle the Labrador. Eli had been watching a 6 p.m. newscast that ran a two-minute segment on the noon press conference and the Wolverine banner.

"Eli said he forwarded you the link from the station's website. Even the anchor looks like she was trying not to laugh."

Cass smiled as she watched Rockwell Valley Police Chief Bobo Caprino suddenly put his plate down on the buffet table while he half-walked, half-trotted towards the men's room at the back of the banquet hall.

That's what he gets for shoveling in so much shrimp with hot sauce in a couple of gulps, she thought.

"What's so funny?" Jack asked.

"A shrimp 911," she said. "I'll tell you later."

Chapter 16

Bobo Caprino's normal diet of beer and takeout food from Rockwell Valley restaurants hadn't prepared his stomach for the three glasses of smooth French champagne and several generous helpings of fresh shrimp he wolfed down at the GES community reception and celebration of approval of the salt cavern gas storage facility.

Towards the tail end of his conversation with a dreamy-looking tall woman who said she was from Horseheads, he felt his bowels give the kind of warning twitch that he was about to be struck with what his father had always called "the galloping trots."

And so while the party outside was raging, he was in a stall in the men's room, his pants around his ankles, listening to a gurgling sound in his lower intestine.

Christ, I'm putting out as much gas as a GES well, he thought.

Bobo normally stayed away from these kind of social gatherings – particularly ones like this that were fraught with politics. But with Mayor Will Pennisen sidelined because of his gun-in-court stunt, Bobo wanted to be sure that the GES big chief saw him. If a new general manager was put in Pennisen's place – and maybe a new mayor, too, if Pennisen resigned – Bobo wanted Luther Burnside to know who he was.

Bobo was just trying to come up with some way to casually approach Burnside to introduce himself when the door to the adjacent stall was pushed open forcefully and then slammed shut and locked. His neighbor dropped his trousers quickly and plunked down on the toilet seat.

Too much shrimp, too, I bet, Bobo thought. *We could have a run on these toilets before the night is over.*

The two men sat in their stalls, both farting enough to keep a party of teenagers in stitches, until the man next to Bobo grabbed several handfuls of toilet paper, cleaned himself off and stood up, pulling up his trousers.

Bobo was still in the throes of getting rid of the last of the gas bombs in his bowels when he glanced at his neighbor's shoes.

Jesus Christ! Bobo thought. *This guy's feet are huge! Shit. What was it Dewitt said? 'Clown shoes'?*

The door to the other stall opened quickly and the man was gone before Bobo could get himself together enough to stand.

Bastard didn't stop to wash his hands either, Bobo thought as he cinched his belt.

A few minutes later, Bobo was out in the ballroom searching for Lt. Del Dewitt, who had been squiring a couple of the Grand Energy Services staff around all day. Since Bobo had made his dash to the toilet, another 100 people or more had come in to the reception, filling the room to its capacity. It was difficult to move at all.

Bobo finally stepped outside to call Dewitt on his cell phone.

"Chief, what is it? I thought you were at the reception."

Bobo peered through the glass, trying to see people's feet.

"Del, listen. I was just in the men's bathroom. I saw a guy with huge feet. Gunboats. He could be our Wolverine vandal."

Dewitt moved behind a room divider so he could hear better.

"What's he look like Chief? I have four men with radios and radios with earpieces. We can position them at the exits."

"Del, I didn't actually see all of him. I was in the crapper and all I saw was his shoes. Never mind that. Just look around for some guy with huge feet. We need to check him out. Quietly."

Ten minutes later, Bobo was squatting on his haunches, scanning the crowd at knee height, drawing stares from anyone who looked in his direction. He was about to drop to his knees when his cell phone beeped with a text message from his lieutenant.

> **Over by the podium. Standing next to me.**

Bobo stood, noting that the woman from Horseheads he had been chatting with was looking at him with a concerned expression on her face. Across the room, he spotted Dewitt, who gave him a friendly wave, like they were at a baseball stadium and Dewitt had saved him a seat.

What the hell, he thought?

He pushed through the crowd as gently as he could. Many people were still eating and drinking.

He had to stop twice, just long enough to exchange pleasantries. He hoped that Dewitt had the good sense to detain Mr. Big Feet until Bobo could get there.

And when he finally popped out the other side at the podium, there was Dewitt with a champagne glass in his hand, held in pretty much the same casual fashion as he clutched his coffee mug all day at the police station.

Next to Dewitt was Grand Energy Services CEO Luther Burnside himself. And beside Burnside was a tall, beefy-looking guy sporting the huge shoes Bobo had seen in the stall next to him in the men's room.

"Here he is now, Mr. Burnside. I'm sure you know my boss, Chief of Police Melvin Caprino. And boss? Let me introduce Mr. Calvin Boviné, a GES associate."

Chapter 17

It wasn't until the Wednesday afternoon staff meeting that Jack, Eli and the four reporters were able to catch their breath.

Jack had been fielding phone calls and emails about his column, many of the inquiries wanting to know if it was Grand Energy Services who had leaned on him.

Keith had put together several stories about how far along GES already was on the salt cavern propane storage project – with work that was done prior to the actual approval.

Jill and Stan were covering how angry activists from all over Pennsylvania and New York were threatening so many legal actions it was like bats flying in a swarm of insects.

But unlike the efficient nocturnal animals, the threats were just that – threats.

"The anti-storage group got caught flat," Jill said. "They had some big fund-raisers set for next month. And an environmental group had said it would kick in money. But now? Now no one is returning phone calls about any possible legal actions. Everybody is just plain old *mad*."

After a few minutes of early meeting kvetching, Eli asked Rue for an update on the eminent domain situation along the pipeline route from the gas wells to the storage site.

Rue had taken over the legwork on that part of the story, going to Rockwell Valley and contacting GES attorneys who were supposed to be working on filing legal documents to grab the land if the landowners continued to balk.

An expected last-minute flurry of offers to purchase the easements had not materialized.

"And I thought the GES people would be all over it. I mean, they must know that with the storage going in for natural gas, it puts pressure on regulators to approve the pipeline. And if it's approved, the courts are going to go along," she said.

Keith gave a short laugh.

"The courts! They'll go along with anything the gas industry wants in the entire state. Rockwell Valley doesn't have a chance," he said.

Jack Stafford was scribbling on his legal pad while the staff bantered, with Eli occasionally bringing the conversation back to specific stories and deadlines.

When there was a lull he finally jumped in, asking Stan to kick in with his assessment.

Stan Belisak was the quietest member of the staff, though his reporting was solid. His new nickname – bestowed by Keith – was Ghost. After Keith's various run-ins with GES workers and staff in Rockwell Valley, Eli had started sending Stan on trips to the town and out to talk with farmers.

When Stan went to town meetings, most of the time no one realized a reporter was even present. At least not until the next issue of the *Horseheads Clarion* came out or something popped up on the website.

"It's too quiet," Stan said, getting a big laugh. "No, not in here. I mean about the pipeline and everything. Now that the storage for natural gas has been approved with the propane, GES should be going nuts to get that pipeline approved. They should have guys out there with bags of money again. We're missing something."

Jack leaned back in his chair and looked around the table. The staff wasn't used to Stan saying a word, which might be why they all looked pensive, as if they were weighing what Stan had said.

"Exactly," Jack said. "Thank you, Stan. I've been thinking the same thing. When they got the approval for the storage, we didn't really see it coming. Not that quickly, anyway. And we didn't understand there was no traction for a court fight. But this is a planning meeting, too. So Eli, what's the plan?"

Before Eli could answer, Jack's cell phone beeped. He glanced at it and saw that it was a text from Lasse Espinola. Jack and Lasse had had a nice phone conversation over the weekend, in which Lasse offered up how sorry he was about Jack's wife Devon passing.

```
Call me when you can.
Uncle Einar can see the
pipeline being built.
```

"Eli," Jack said. "New plan. First, have someone call Lasse Espinola and ask him what his uncle has to say about the pipeline."

Chapter 18

The anger Luther Burnside felt didn't *show* at all.

And so Rod Mayenlyn and Michael Ahlbright were nearly relaxed, thinking that their respective personal storms from the past week had passed.

At least they *were* relaxed until Burnside let loose with a tornado of foul language, a prelude to a scathing double tongue-lashing.

"I wanted to talk with you both together because – God help me – you represent what this company considers to be its brain trust," Burnside said.

"After the last week, I think brain *fart* might be a closer assessment."

For the next 20 minutes, Burnside unloaded, first on Mayenlyn for not controlling Calvin Boviné, then on Ahlbright for miscalculating Jack Stafford's reaction to the threat of his psychiatric records being revealed.

"Do you have any idea what an ass I looked like in front of those Rockwell Valley yokels when that banner came rolling out? And done by my *own* employee? Christ, I would almost rather have it be the *real* goddamned Wolverines."

Burnside had taken Rockwell Valley Police Chief Bobo Caprino aside at the reception after Mayenlyn confessed that it was Boviné who had done the banner. Burnside convinced the chief to let both Wolverine matters simply drop.

He promised heads would roll at GES headquarters and the persons responsible would be fired. Burnside made sure he swore a few times in the conversation so the chief would believe him. And he hinted that he and the chief and GES had a rosy future ahead of them now that gas was flowing and the storage facility was operational.

But Bobo was less amenable to forgetting the vandalism incident at Lasse Espinola's farm that he was sure Boviné was connected to. Burnside said he would deal with it directly, promising that GES would offer restitution if needed.

But what about the fake dynamite? Bobo asked.

Burnside said that *was* the work of the *real* Wolverines. "I might have some overzealous people with poor judgment on my staff, but that threat of explosives was real eco-terrorism," Burnside said. "My people had *nothing* to do with it. You have my word on that.

"Besides, I'm sure you know what *that's* like, chief," Burnside said, looking directly at Lt. Del Dewitt. "Having staff show *poor* judgment."

The chief wasn't entirely mollified, but the champagne encouraged him to bow to the politics of the situation.

At least for the *moment*.

Bobo realized he was feeling a little sick to his stomach. And not just from the food.

Jesus, he thought. *Am I getting an attack of conscience?*

He shook his head and walked back to the bar to grab a glass of club soda.

In Burnside's office, Michael Ahlbright listened to Burnside's tirade against Mayenlyn and braced for his own trip to the woodshed. Ahlbright knew he had miscalculated on two fronts.

First, he should have known – because of prior dealings with Jack Stafford – that Stafford would never back down based on personal pressure. Stafford had a romantic code of honor that would never let him protect himself if it meant others would suffer.

Second, when Ahlbright more carefully studied the documents given to him by Mayenlyn, he realized GES would have put both corporate feet into a giant legal cow pie if it publicized *any* of it. The documents were not official – even though they were on letterhead from the psychiatric hospital. They were way too good to be true, he thought, something that was confirmed when Mayenlyn told him GES paid $10,000 to obtain them.

Worthless, he thought.

Ahlbright listened as Burnside railed at him, saying that GES "had lost its advantage" and "appeared to be a bully" by what Stafford had published in his column.

But as Burnside appeared to running out of air, Ahlbright offered a gentle defense and a strategy.

"I'll take my lumps for not realizing what a Boy Scout Stafford is," Ahlbright said. "Fair enough. But he didn't name us because he couldn't. I made damn sure we could deny everything but the cup of coffee I had with him. No email trail, no phone messages, except to set up a meeting between old friends. He didn't see what we had. Period."

Burnside leaned back in his chair, mollified slightly and worn out from his soliloquy.

"So here's my suggestion," Ahlbright continued. "We're already on track to have the salt cavern storage ready by early December. We won. *We won.* Let's start hammering about how it's supposed to be a real cold winter again – a record-breaker – and GES is doing everything it can to make sure we have extra propane and natural gas ready to help. That's the message. Something like, *Our Gas Will Keep You Warm.*"

Mayenlyn leaned in and agreed.

"I think he's right, chief. We need to go on the PR offensive with our message. But Michael, is it really forecast to another ball-breaker winter?"

Ahlbright laughed.

"Who knows? But nobody will debate *that*. Everyone just wants to know they will be able to keep warm."

Ahlbright and Mayenlyn both noticed that Burnside was looking at himself in the mirror again.

Crisis averted, they both thought.

Chapter 19

```
From the Horseheads Clarion

Column One
Horseheads Clarion


   The hills are alive -
with a new gas pipeline

By Jack Stafford


   It`s been a long time since
this columnist went to one of
those county fairs where a
slick, quick-handed carnival
worker used sleight of hand to
shuffle in a shell game, asking
people to tell under which
shell a pea was located.
   But the people of Rockwell
Valley    were    unwittingly
```

involved in such a game in recent months, played quite cleverly by Grand Energy Services.

While Rockwell Valley residents were protesting the overland route of a proposed natural gas pipeline to run to the just-approved natural gas and propane storage at the north end of Rockwell Valley Lake, GES was quietly buying up easements slightly to the south.

The farmers and landowners along *that* route apparently have few qualms about the 40-inch pipeline, access roads and industrial paraphernalia that will be part and parcel of the project.

But what about the many various state, federal and local approvals that are needed?

The *Clarion* discovered this week that an amended application is on file - one that reroutes the pipeline away from dozens of recalcitrant property owners to land where GES has *already* secured easements. Approval of the amended application will require study, of course. But the smart money says that it will be approved and likely on a fast track.

GES and its natural gas project are popular with the regulators who have to give the pipeline project the green light.

This switch in pipeline routes – detailed out in stories in today's *Clarion* – was first discovered by a dairy farmer who alerted this newspaper that all kinds of pipe and heavy equipment were being delivered just over the hill from his farm. Since receiving that call, our photographers documented the scene with some of the photos you see on the front page. Plenty of other photos of the pipe, earthmoving equipment and a freshly cut road are on our website.

It's doubtful GES would be investing in so much infrastructure and equipment purchase if it wasn't dead-on sure that this new route will be approved.

A GES source – who asked to remain anonymous – said it expects to be sending natural gas through the pipeline before Christmas.

But there is one wrinkle in the new route that has *already* raised the ire of local environmentalists and others who have a fondness for Rockwell Valley Lake.

Because of the change of routing – and geography – GES is requesting permission to place a half-mile-long pipeline along the bottom of the lake north of the Rockwell Valley village shoreline in the relatively shallow water.

That area is shallower because of sediment from Rockwell Valley Creek.

The shallows – actually 40-50 feet deep in some areas – are favorite fishing spots year round, with fisherman anchoring boats all across that patch, pulling in bass, Northern Pike, and a variety of trout. The pipeline will require some kind of exclusion zone – marked with ugly floating warning buoys, no doubt – to keep fisherman away from the pipeline`s route.

The Rockwell Valley Chamber of Commerce – normally a cheerleader for all aspects of natural gas drilling and the gas industry – is appalled at what the chamber calls "visual pollution" by the buoys, especially because of the proximity to the Rockwell Valley Lakeside Hotel.

The need for that underwater pipeline is the one aspect giving hope to local environmentalists. They think it will give them a wedge to file a legal challenge to halt the project. But given the success rate of such challenges in the past, Rockwell Valley residents should prepare for a flurry of construction - and even dredging of the lake right in front of the hotel - in the coming months.

That`s what happens when you don`t keep your eye on which shell has the pea underneath it.

Jack Stafford is the publisher of the Horseheads Clarion *and publishes Column One every Friday. He can be reached at JJStafford@HorseheadsClarion.com.*

Chapter 20

Noah sat in Jack's office Saturday morning at the *Horseheads Clarion*, fiddling on a tablet computer Jack had bought for him the week before.

As Noah's hearing slowly returned, he was showing interest in all kinds of aural stimulus. Much to Jack's chagrin – and Cass's delight – Noah *loved* opera and would swing his hands around in the air as if directing the music whenever Cass put it on at home.

Noah was watching some YouTube videos of people cooking while Jack sat in the newsroom chatting with Eli. Noah had just discovered YouTube and was having a great time navigating through videos.

"As quickly as he's picking up how to use that tablet, I think you better put some software on there to keep him from stumbling onto some porn site," Eli said.

Jack watched Noah's finger sliding around on the screen, the sound of people singing coming from the tablet.

"That's exactly why I brought the tablet in," Jack said. "Plus Cass is down in Rockwell Valley today as a consultant with an anti-fracking theater group. That's why the little guy is with me."

After months of almost solely playing nanny to Noah, Cass had started meeting with a newly organized theatre group of mostly college-aged amateurs from New York and Pennsylvania who were putting together a series of one-act plays about hydrofracking, climate change and other environmental issues.

Their idea was to make the plays amusing enough to reach a broad audience, but also pack an informative, satirical punch.

Cass was writing a lot of the dialog and stage direction, which was making evenings at home fun for Jack as he shared content and context for the activists' hyperbole. Noah would watch Cass and Jack acting out scenes, clapping his hands from time to time.

"So, Shania was telling me about the plays and stuff," Eli said. "I hate to bring this up, but she also said Cass had told her a month ago she was thinking of leaving. Going back to Washington."

Jack looked back into his office to make sure Noah was still busy on his tablet.

"Well, that *was* her plan. But that was before this theater gig started. Now she hasn't said anything and she is all wrapped up with these plays."

Eli turned and tapped a few keys on his computer, biting his lip slightly – a habit his wife Shania kept telling him was a bad thing to pick up. He tapped a few more times and then spun the computer around for Jack to see.

Jack expected to see some special software for Noah's tablet computer.

But what he saw was a video of a male police officer in Texas who was questioning a journalist who had been shooting video and still photos of an oil pipeline fire near Eagle Ford.

The police officer was upbraiding the journalist – a freelancer – for shooting the video, saying she was in violation of some Homeland Security regulations about photographing "critical infrastructure."

The officer seized her camera, not realizing that the woman had a second camera recording the whole episode.

"I wonder if she had a dog-on-the-dashboard like Keith's," Jack said.

Eli started to laugh, then stopped.

"I've started collecting data on these kind of incidents. It's pretty amazing how often this is going on. I'm thinking of having Keith and Rue start asking our local cops about this stuff. But I am almost afraid to have them ask."

Jack nodded agreement.

"Yes, we don't want to give them any ideas. But then with Judge Beigenlaw, I imagine anything goes."

From Jack's office, the sound of a Rocky and Bullwinkle cartoon came wafting out.

"Your son has good taste," Eli said.

Jack's phone beeped with a text message.

"Fan mail from some flounder?" Eli said.

"Oh Eli, you are going to make a great father," Jack said. Then he frowned as he read the text message from Cass.

```
Some of the actors just
got arrested!!!!! We were
practicing a skit on the town
square. The police said we
didn`t have a permit. I`m okay.
But I need to stay here to help.
```

Chapter 21

Rockwell Valley Police Chief Bobo Caprino was at his department desk trying to sort out exactly why his officer decided to stop a bunch of young people from doing some kind of impromptu play in the town square on Saturday.

As best he could ascertain there had been no formal citizen complaint filed. It was in the town square, where, theoretically, free speech was allowed. And at least a dozen people were standing around watching, most of them reportedly enjoying the performance.

Then he remembered the ordinance that Mayor Will Pennisen and his cronies had pushed through last winter, even waiting for the press to leave before taking it up. It required *anyone* wanting to use the square for "political purposes" to have a permit, issued by the mayor's office, of course, rather than the chief of police, who normally handled such things.

It's a bullshit law, Bobo thought. *And now we've stepped in it.*

It wasn't until this morning that the officer's report on the incident made it to his desk, where he read that two young men and one woman were ordered to stop their little play on the bandstand, pending obtaining a permit.

"Subjects were talking about hydrofracking," the report says. "Upon hearing several minutes of their exhibition, it was determined it was political in nature and they were not in compliance with the town ordinance."

A woman – maybe in her late 30s – had argued with the officer that they were just practicing their lines and that it wasn't *really* a public performance, just practice.

But the three actors starting ad-libbing and including the Rockwell Valley police officer as a comic foil in their skit. He lost his temper, and with the help of another officer called to the scene, arrested the three of them for disorderly conduct.

Thank God they didn't grab that woman, too, Bobo thought. *We don't need that kind of trouble.*

Lt. Del Dewitt swung into the chief's office, a file folder in his hand and his ever-present coffee mug in the other.

"It looks like they sat in our holding cell Saturday for just an hour, chief," Dewitt said. "Judge Beigenlaw said he wouldn't advise holding them over the weekend without a hearing. And he wasn't about to hold a hearing. Probably had a date with a martini."

Bobo looked over the file, swearing under his breath.

"Del, I'll delegate it to you to talk to our guys about this. But for Christ's sake, that ordinance says that a first offense is a goddamn *citation*. Worst case, those kids should have gotten a ticket. In fact, *did* they get a ticket?"

Dewitt sat down and stared at the chief.

"You're right, chief. Absolutely. But, well. Our guys *were* kind of provoked by the kids. Real smart-ass college kids. The judge said to just kick them loose with a lecture. Which is what happened. No tickets."

Bobo scanned the document quickly again, his eyes lighting on a list of witnesses who had been present in the town square and saw the three taken into custody. The witnesses all volunteered to give statements. And the report noted that the first name on the list *insisted* on giving a statement and had urged the officers to make the arrests.

The name at top of the list was Will Pennisen, Mayor, Rockwell Valley.

The next name reminded Bobo of his stomachache at the Grand Energy Services party: Cassandra Elena Walsh of Horseheads, New York.

"Alicia!" Bobo shouted out to his ex-wife dispatcher. "Could you call the good mayor and see if he has a free moment to meet this morning?

Alice rolled her chair back to look into the office and gave a non-committal nod.

"Del, put down the coffee and go with me over to his office," Bobo said.

"I might want you to shoot him again."

Chapter 22

Cass was badly shaken by the arrests of the young actors in Rockwell Valley's town square.

Although she had seen plenty of protests – and even participated in some in Seattle – she was stunned by the rough treatment she witnessed.

"These cops were, well, it was like they were on *drugs* or something. They acted so angry. But it wasn't an act. It was real," she told Jack. "They told me to walk away or I would be arrested, too."

For Noah's sake, Cass swallowed any display of her anger and anxiety until Monday morning when, at Jack's request, she came to the *Clarion* staff meeting.

"I think you need to convey to my reporters and staff what happened – what you saw and felt," Jack said. "I'm so sorry."

They walked from their house and dropped Noah off at Millie's Diner with Shania. Noah walked immediately back behind the counter to the high-chair-stool combination Shania had brought in for him weeks before. He sat behind the counter coloring in a notebook atop the back counter, content to watch (and now listen) to the hubbub of the diner. Cass wasn't too happy with the seemingly endless supply of hash brown potatoes, bacon and whole milk that Shania gave Noah. But his almost four-year-old metabolism burned it off fast and she was grateful for the help.

In the *Clarion* office, Eli rounded up the staff and hustled them into the conference room as soon as Jack and Cass walked through the front door. As was Eli's custom, he carried his laptop computer with him, both for note taking and reference.

"Okay," Eli said. "We've got a bunch of stories to talk about, including a new report about the rash of earthquakes in Ohio. But Cass is here today to talk about Saturday's arrests in Rockwell Valley. Welcome, Cass."

Although she had spent countless hours on stage, this particular morning Cass found she couldn't summon the actor's protective mask she relied on. Her words spilled out in a torrent, held back since Saturday night because she didn't want to upset Noah – or Jack – with how frightened she had felt because of the way the police acted.

"It wasn't like they were *physically* intimidating, exactly," Cass said. "In fact, neither of them was much taller than I am. But it was their voices. I swear, they kind of growled when they spoke."

For 15 minutes Cass talked about how the first patrol unit came up with its lights on, letting its siren chirp a full 30 seconds before the officer got out of the car, still leaving the roof lights flashing.

"I don't care if you were just walking your *dog* around that town square, the way the cop arrived – really, it was more like he made an entrance – was intimidating. Everyone in the square area *froze* when the car arrived."

The arrival of the second Rockwell Valley police officer moments later was the same, except that officer pulled his nightstick out as he got out of the car.

"It was like there was a fight in progress and he was ready to wade in. But that's not what scared me," Cass said.

When Cass stepped between the police officers and the actors to try to explain what was going on, she was told by the baton-wielding cop that she was obstructing justice and if she spoke again she would be arrested.

"Actually, he said if I opened my 'big mouth' again, I would be arrested.

"Then I was told to leave. 'Get your goddamn hippie ass out of here' was what he said, actually."

As a few tears had started to well up, Jack offered Cass the handkerchief from his pocket.

"I think they would have arrested me if I hadn't started talking to the Rockwell Valley Mayor," Cass said. "I recognized him from the pictures you've published. I walked over to him and I saw he had his cell phone in his hand. I think he was the one who called the police. He seemed to be enjoying the whole thing. He had kind of an idiot's grin on his face."

Jill had written down most of what Cass had conveyed, not sure how it might work into a story. But it was good local background that tied in with reports of police across the country ramping up actions against peaceful protesters. Some of the video footage of those encounters was breathtaking, most of which was linked on the *Clarion* website.

It was fast becoming a national story that oil and gas companies were having more and more influence with local governments, often hiring off-duty police officers to work as company security.

It seemed to Jill that a lot of these cops were having trouble distinguishing exactly who they were working for – and when.

Eli stood up and thanked Cass for coming in, and she and Jack headed back to Millie's Diner to have breakfast and retrieve Noah. He was scheduled to spend the rest of the day at the *Clarion* in Jack's office. Staff members had decided Noah made a good newspaper mascot.

Jill wondered if anyone else noticed Jack was holding Cass's hand as they walked across the street.

SEDITION

Chapter 1

Eli Gupta had been resentful at first that Jack Stafford had come back. Not that he didn't admire Jack or feel awful about Devon's death.

Eli had run the whole newspaper the entire time Jack was gone, with minimal guidance from Jack and Devon in faraway Tonga.

But now Eli realized Jack's return as publisher and editor allowed Eli to spend time again where he was most comfortable: at his computer keyboard carrying out a half-dozen searches simultaneously and pulling it all together for news stories.

I'm a computer geek and a pretty damn good one, he thought.

Before Jack got back, Eli often felt strangled by the responsibilities of management, compounded by getting married to Shania, who sometimes was unhappy with Eli's long hours at the newspaper.

On this quiet Saturday morning Eli was alone in the office while Shania was across the street, ensuring that

Millie's Diner would run smoothly for the day while Eli chased twin ghosts across the Internet landscape.

The first was about the Ebola virus outbreak in Sierra Leone that had spread to other African nations and totally slipped the grasp of the normally efficient World Health Organization. It was labeled an epidemic. Privately health officials were terrified that the virus might mutate and be transmitted through the air, turning a relatively small outbreak into a worldwide pandemic.

Unlike Ebola outbreaks since the 1970s, this time infected patients were getting into heavily populated areas where a combination of poor medical facilities and lack of understanding about the disease was causing a massive spike in cases.

The thread Eli was chasing had to do with several Ebola patients who had been brought to the United States amid plenty of screams by people concerned about the virus getting loose in the U.S.

Eli had compiled a list of sources – and stories already published – in which medical authorities were dismissive of fears that the virus would get loose in America. Most of them cited data about how contracting Ebola was actually difficult, given that contact with the bodily fluids of infected people was the only way the disease spread.

But Friday afternoon Keith Everlight had gotten a tip from a source at Grand Energy Services that one of their top international division corporate managers in Nigeria might have been exposed to Ebola. And if so, GES might be bringing him to Rockwell Valley Hospital's new isolation unit, built as part of a recent hospital renovation.

At Jack's insistence, Eli was also trying to track down instances in which viruses similar to Ebola had mutated, changing the way they were transmitted among humans.

His search was complicated by the sheer volume of data and medical opinions.

The second ghost Eli was tracing was more political and shadowy.

In fact, most of what he was reading was coming from apocalyptic websites and fringe groups whose paranoia was often staggering. Still, sometimes they were onto something, holding a tiny nugget of the truth.

For months, many of these websites were overflowing with rumors that the federal government, either through Congress, the White House or some powerful agency, was readying a massive assault on civil liberties, all in the name of national security.

The militarization of local police departments, an issue made more relevant by the shooting of a teenager in Ferguson, Missouri added fuel to that fire.

Then Eli nearly spilled his coffee when he checked out one of his usual go-to websites, *Veritas For All*, a collective site run by some anti-government, anti-corporation types from all over the U.S.

VERITAS FOR ALL

The specter of yet another U.S. government intrusion into civil liberties that has been circulating for the last two months has finally been named. A longtime *Veritas* contributor

> has pried it out of a Congressional staff member who apparently *still* has a shred of a civic conscience.
>
> It's called the Industrial Sedition Act.
>
> The few details we know are mostly too sketchy for *Veritas* to report today. But with a name like the Industrial Sedition Act, it's going to be ugly. And it most likely is tied to energy policy and energy transportation, our source says.
>
> Start revving up the search engines for that name or its acronym, ISA.
>
> As always, we will tell you what we know, the second we do.
>
> And we trust you will do the same for us.
>
> *In Veritas*

Eli immediately started searching both the Industrial Sedition Act and ISA, running mostly across references to the federal Sedition Act of 1918. That act was meant to stifle criticism of the government in wartime and was passed in the closing days of World War I, Eli noted. But it was repealed by 1920, though some government types had wanted a peacetime version to silence the more radical newspapers and particularly to shut down a growing foreign language press.

When Eli searched for ISA it brought up references to restaurants, gardening clubs, surfers, sociologists and just about everything else.

Interesting that the Veritas references haven't popped up yet, Eli thought.

He remembered that Shania had said something about grabbing some lunch — at the diner, of course — and then maybe taking a drive up to Seneca Lake.

With the baby due in December, she wouldn't be doing any wine tasting, but she still liked to listen to live music that most wineries featured on Saturday afternoons and evenings.

Eli was just closing up a few applications when he noticed his coffee mug started to shake slightly, then harder, making tiny chocolate-colored waves before slopping slightly over the edge.

He looked out the window to see if another one of the huge GES supertanker trucks hauling fracking wastewater had rumbled through when the ground shook again, this time harder and causing his coffee mug to dance right off the end of the desk.

No way, he thought. *An earthquake? Here?*

Chapter 2

The earthquake wasn't quite a California-style, glass-shattering, sinkholes-in-the-pavement event. But it was enough that it got everyone's attention — particularly people opposed to the natural gas and propane storage at the north end of Rockwell Valley Lake.

It was just that kind of earthquake that could be enough to crack open the walls of a salt cavern to allow a propane or natural gas leak that would likely end in disaster.

The Monday following the 3.0 magnitude temblor, Alice McCallis and two dozen protesters marched through Rockwell Valley's downtown with the goal of walking the 10 miles north along the shore of Rockwell Valley Lake and ending up at the highway gates to the proposed salt cavern natural gas and propane storage, where they planned a loud rally.

McCallis's earlier arrest for violating the court order that said she had to stay a quarter-mile away from all Grand Energy Services facilities was still loose in the legal system with no determination yet in her case.

"Let them arrest me again," she told her fellow marchers, speaking through a bullhorn. "Maybe there will be another earthquake and GES will be swallowed up as retribution."

The march had been hastily called. But because the earthquake had most New York and Pennsylvania media outlets on high alert for stories, Rockwell Valley was playing host to several television stations, some metropolitan newspapers and even a National Public Radio stringer who vacationed annually in a cabin on Rockwell Valley Lake.

The interest in the protest had been piqued by simultaneous protests in Texas and Ohio over earthquakes in the three weeks prior. A Texas quake had flattened the walls of an elementary school classroom, injuring five children and their teacher, who were buried in the rubble and rescued by firefighters.

Texas legislators had already been talking about having to rebuild schools to California standards, with the funds to come from a special severance tax on oil and gas wells.

Gas industry officials, including Grand Energy Services' Luther Burnside scoffed at the idea and bristled at the notion of a special tax.

"There is no shred of proof that our gas wells are in any way connected to that tragic Texas earthquake," he said. "None. This is just a way to squeeze more money from our energy companies."

At the Lakeside Winery on the east side of Seneca Lake, Oscar Wilson had lost several dozen bottles of his best Riesling, creating a glass-and-wine mélange that drew enough fruit flies that the cleanup crew wore masks to keep from ingesting the tiny bugs.

He had been on the phone with Jack Stafford on Saturday when he felt the earth move under his feet.

At the *Horseheads Clarion*, the earthquake had knocked a clock off a wall in Jack's office but only caused minor damage to the plaster walls of the newsroom. It also shook violently enough that Jack's favorite coffee mug went sliding off his desk to the floor where it shattered on impact.

The *Clarion* had published online stories that same day about the entire area, with sidebar articles about a number of industrial gas wells in Pennsylvania that had suffered damage. One of the most alarming was a report about a break in the wall of a fracking wastewater holding pond at a GES natural gas well site.

More than a thousand gallons of wastewater had poured out through the breach, down a hillside and into a small creek that was a feeder for Rockwell Valley Creek – a creek that fed directly into Rockwell Valley Lake.

"GES says it contained the water before it hit the creek," the story said. "But farmers downstream report hundreds of dead fish floating on the surface."

But at the *Clarion* staff meeting, Keith Everlight said he wanted to keep after the seismology people to pinpoint more exactly where the epicenter was, so far only vaguely described as on the Pennsylvania-New York border, near Rockwell Valley.

"A Cornell geologist told me where GES has been drilling, the rock strata is like Swiss cheese," Keith said.

Chapter 3

```
From the Horseheads Clarion

Column One
Horseheads Clarion
```

A new fissure in the earthquake debate

```
By Jack Stafford

    In the wake of last
week`s earthquake, people
in the Central New York
and Pennsylvania areas are
justifiably nervous about the
likelihood of another quake.
    They should be.
```

But here's an interesting twist. For years hydrofracking proponents have claimed that hydrofracking has *nothing* to do with the spike in earthquakes that have dogged the tracks of gas rigs.

A recent report actually supports *part* of that contention.

The report says that the pumping of millions of gallons of water and toxic chemicals into the ground in the hydrofracking process - all aimed at loosening that natural gas - is mostly likely *not* the direct cause of the spike in earthquakes experienced in many of the 34 states where hydrofracking has become prevalent.

Instead, the report puts the blame on the *injection* wells used to dispose of the toxic wastewater that comes back up along with the natural gas. That water - millions of gallons - is forced under high pressure down into these injection disposal wells. And to no one's surprise (except for the companies drilling the wells), the process is causing temblors, some small, some *not so small*.

We were lucky that we had a small one here in New York and Rockwell Valley.

Let's hope it wasn't a harbinger of things to come.

In Oklahoma the U.S. Geological Survey said one area of the state that historically has experienced one to three quakes of a 3.0 magnitude per year jumped to an average of 40 per year since 2009.

Guess when hydrofracking - and the use of deep injection wells to get rid of wastewater - got started?

As this is written, reports are coming in that the entire Sooner State seems to be shaking with a reported 150 small earthquakes this week.

This week. And so far, small quakes. But for how long?

Consider too, hydrofracking drilling continues pell-mell across the state, and so does pumping the wastewater into the nearly 5,000 deep injection wells in use.

With those numbers, earthquake insurance is probably getting *very* expensive for Oklahoma residents.

Many other states — historically relatively immune to earthquakes — are crying uncle, too. Ohio, Kansas, Colorado and Texas (among others) are screaming about the connection between hydrofracking, the injection wells, and the increasingly powerful earthquakes.

It seems like Mother Nature is trying to make a point as these toxins are poured into her rock strata.

All of this comes back to the law of unintended consequences, of course.

The natural gas companies are trying to fill a need — and let`s face it, reap big profits — and didn`t set out to cause earthquakes, whether it`s through the hydrofracking process or these injection wells.

But they did.

And like the ongoing heated dialog about polluted ground water, it would be best for the gas companies — including Grand Energy Services — to stop with the blanket denials and try to fix the problem.

In the meantime, the residents of Rockwell Valley

and along the Southern Tier of New York are cleaning up from the first arguably big quake in many years. Perhaps we have been spared most of this quake activity largely because the wastewater from hydrofracking goes to Ohio for disposal.

That could all change in a heartbeat, however.

If Ohio decides it`s tired of being the Northeast`s hydrofracking wastewater toilet, gas drilling companies in Pennsylvania and New York could find there is need to inject that water closer to home.

And if the report is accurate, earthquakes will most assuredly follow.

Unfortunately, in its *skimpy-to-nonexistent* safety planning for the recently approved natural gas and propane storage in salt caverns adjacent to Rockwell Valley Lake, GES neglected to even *mention* earthquakes and earthquake preparedness.

It might want to rethink that.

A seismologist from Ohio State says with the Ohio quakes growing in strength, one might

> trigger a *massive* temblor that could rock even the fault lines that underlie the salt caverns in Rockwell Valley, Pennsylvania.
>
> It is unlikely, he admits.
>
> But the earthquake Saturday should remind us that quakes don`t respect state borders or other political geography.
>
> *Jack Stafford is the publisher of the* Horseheads Clarion *and publishes Column One every Friday. He can be reached at JJStafford@HorseheadsClarion.com.*

Chapter 4

Jack Stafford and Oscar were supposed to just have lunch the Saturday after the quake. But they ended up at Jack's house instead for a party that started out small but ended up with Jack, Oscar, Oscar's niece Lindy, the four *Clarion* reporters, Eli, Eli's wife Shania and, of course, Cass and Noah.

Belle the Labrador Retriever was in heaven with the hubbub and so many people to throw a tennis ball for her in the front yard. Jack eventually had to tell everyone to give Belle a rest. She was getting too long in the tooth for that much running but would *die* rather than not chase a ball.

Oscar told anyone who would listen about the crashing bottles he watched during the earthquake. But most of the winemaking equipment was undamaged, meaning the fall harvest would be easily handled.

He had brought a case of his famous Oscar's Boot Riesling to Horseheads as a gift for Jack and Cass – and just in case a party got going.

When Oscar arrived Lindy was already playing with Noah while Cass and Shania were throwing together the fixings for a late-afternoon Italian dinner.

For Jack, it reminded him of dinners he and Devon had hosted for Oscar and many of the same people before Jack and Devon and Noah headed to Tonga. When Cass walked through the kitchen door into the dining room wearing an apron that Oscar had given Devon, Jack felt his heart give an arrhythmic flip.

The printing on the apron said, "Life is too short to drink cheap wine."

Eli fiddled with the controls of the new 60-inch flat-screen TV Jack had bought the day before. A big-box store in Elmira was selling off its stock at low prices – with no guarantees – because the televisions had fallen off stock shelves in the quake.

Eli had checked out the set at the store for Jack and declared it undamaged and well worth taking a chance on, given the 50 percent discount.

"Whoa, look at this," Eli said, as the satellite TV connection kicked in and a national news channel's program blasted into the room, silencing all the social chatter.

A news anchor with an eerie resemblance to the famous Walter Cronkite was reporting on a rally in front of the

White House in Washington, D.C. An angry crowd was demonstrating against a proposed oil pipeline and the event had turned into a shoving match between protesters and pro-pipeline demonstrators. Police were wading in, trying to break up fights.

"What's that?" Jack asked Eli. "Is that the D.C. protest? That was supposed to be a peaceful sit-in."

Cass and Shania shuffled plates onto the table and called everyone over.

"Time for food," Cass said. "And you news hounds? Please! Can we turn that off while we eat?

The group gathered around the table, doing the where-should-I-sit dance, the television volume turned very low.

Then the volume suddenly roared again and Jack spun around at the sounds of people screaming.

Noah was standing in front of the TV, the remote control in his hand. He was mesmerized by the live report showing the swirling crowds being pummeled by a water cannon mounted on a truck, operated by police in full riot gear.

Jack ran over and picked up Noah, turning down the volume but unable to look away.

"Jesus!" Jack said. "This looks like a something from the Deep South in the 1960s. Like something that crazy sheriff would do. What was his name? Bull Connor? It's like that."

Shania took the remote control from Jack's hand and clicked off the television.

"I'm sorry, but I think we should just have a nice meal," Shania said. "You can all make the world a better place with some pasta in your stomachs. Besides, look at Noah. That scared him to death."

Jack was pretty sure Noah was not really frightened. But Jack was deeply disturbed by what he had seen. He was baffled why the D.C. police would go to that extreme. The D.C. cops were used to demonstrations. They were often held up as the models of restraint for other big cities. And most U.S. presidents never wanted images like what Jack had just seen linked to their administrations.

Jack felt the hair standing on the back of his neck.

Eli had briefed him about the *Veritas* website claims, which for the moment was way down the *Clarion*'s priority list. On the front burner was confirmation that a GES employee reportedly infected with Ebola would be arriving at Rockwell Valley Hospital – if he survived the long flight on a private jet from Lagos, Nigeria.

But the water cannons slamming protesters against the White House fence fit with some of the radical chatter Eli was talking about from *Veritas For All* and other websites. He began mentally adding up the incidents of anti-citizen, anti-civil liberties events.

He suddenly wasn't hungry.

Chapter 5

The walls of the conference room at Grand Energy Services in Flathead, Missouri were covered with colorful maps and charts – a display of pipelines proposed and those already built across the United States.

GES's wholly owned pipelines were highlighted in red. Pipelines through which GES-generated gas or oil flowed were blue. An elaborate color scheme for other pipelines made the walls seem like they had been decorated by the

Rainbow Coalition – an observation a GES vice president *unfortunately* quipped loud enough that Grand Energy Services CEO Luther Burnside heard it when he walked in to join the meeting in progress.

"Very funny," Burnside said, his face turning red. "Just *fucking* hilarious. I wish your division could be as good at business as you are at being a comedian, Rogers. Maybe you can get a job doing standup comedy somewhere. You might need one."

Rod Mayenlyn and Michael Ahlbright watched Burnside's face, then glanced at each other.

Burnside had been touchy for weeks, even though the work on various GES projects was going well.

"One week and Rogers is gone," Ahlbright whispered to Mayenlyn.

"I give him three days," Mayenlyn whispered back. "And let's make it $100, okay?"

The rivalry between the two men had been fading as they realized it was in their best interests to carefully manage their respective relationships with the mercurial Burnside.

Several high-up staff members had been fired by Burnside in the last month, often over trivial things.

Mayenlyn was pretty sure that Burnside's irritability was because his executive secretary, Ida Merganser, had broken off their long-standing – and *supposedly* secret – affair.

The only reason *she* wasn't fired was because she had stashed plenty of GES confidential documents that predated Burnside taking over as CEO. Plus what she had set aside since Burnside succeeded Grayson Oliver Delacroix III was enough to get Burnside indicted for any number of illegal corporate moves.

The joke about the Rainbow Coalition might have soured Burnside, but the rest of the staff and vice presidents were enthusiastic. The engineers and analysts presented information on how fast the various pipelines were being constructed, and target dates for starting operations and linkups were being moved up, not delayed, as was the usual scenario.

It was up to Ahlbright to deliver the bad news on behalf of the vice president in charge of strategic pipeline planning. He had called in sick that morning, saying he didn't want to infect anyone with a flu bug.

More likely he didn't want to get his ass kicked, Ahlbright thought.

"I'm going to have to be the wet blanket today," Ahlbright said. "I'm standing in for Pipeline Paul today."

Ahlbright noted that everyone *except* Burnside smiled when he used the vice president's in-company nickname.

"As rosy as these guys have painted things, Paul's report is about a couple of specific holdups – big ones – in the Midwest by activists. And in Pennsylvania, there's a threat, too," Ahlbright said. "Basically, the people are using the usual bullshit tactics, like chaining themselves to the pipeline pieces or camping out inside the big pipes so we can't connect them."

Burnside waved his hand at Ahlbright to stop his narrative.

"I know you are a stand-in, but Michael. Why can't police just get rid of these people? They are trespassing."

Ahlbright flipped a few pages in the report, knowing the answer but wanting to quote directly so that Burnside's wrath might be directed at the absent Pipeline Paul.

"Here it is," Ahlbright said.

> Local authorities in Nebraska, Oklahoma and Texas are reluctant to move in without further legal authority or legal mandate. The pipeline sections are on federal land, and while we hold the right-of-way documents, it`s less clear legally about the company ordering action. Requests for federal clarification - and action - are pending.

To everyone's surprise, Burnside smiled, a big grin that even made the vice president who had made the crack about the Rainbow Coalition breathe a little easier.

"Those goddamn feds. Well, legal staff is already working on this. It's not as serious as Paul thinks. Let's move on," Burnside said.

The meeting droned on for another half-hour with arguments over the speed of gas and oil flows, delivery dates and contracts before Burnside waved his hand impatiently.

"I need to leave, so Rod, you chair the balance of this meeting. Give me a report later."

Everyone stood while Burnside got up and walked out the door.

Ahlbright held the door for the CEO as he walked through it. He gave Ahlbright a regal nod as he passed.

Ahlbright held the door open a crack as he watched Burnside walk down the hallway to his office. When

Burnside opened his office door, he could see Calvin Boviné sitting in a chair waiting.

Boviné's eyes locked on Ahlbright's for fraction of a section.

Now what? Ahlbright thought.

Chapter 6

Professor Charles Avery Sawmill was flattered when he got a phone call from Jack Stafford, the publisher of the *Horseheads Clarion* newspaper.

Stafford said he was reading a copy of Sawmill's book *Cannibals and Christians: The Extractors vs. The Sustainers* and wanted to chat with him about it.

Sawmill had considered including a short section on Stafford and the *Clarion* in the book when he talked about the impact of media. But when he was drafting *Cannibals* the media section was getting too long, and Stafford was off in the South Pacific, *very* hard to contact.

"I'm enjoying your book, professor. *Really*. Your approach about the two basic camps is a great way to explain it," Jack said.

Sawmill's book was starting to get some traction – a review in the *New York Times* had been promised and anti-hydrofracking groups were starting to pass it around and talk it up, too.

He was mostly retired from Central Pennsylvania University and had moved into his family cottage on the shore of Rockwell Valley Lake, not far from the house where Alice McCallis lived.

"The one part of the book I wanted to chat about was the piece about Luther Burnside, the CEO of Grand Energy Services," Jack said. "You made a marvelous case that these gas and oil company CEOs are like Roman emperors in their power and the way the use it. Or abuse it, I guess. But I was a little surprised when you said Burnside could be considered a modern *Caligula*. I'm not sure I would have chosen him as Burnside's Roman avatar."

Sawmill laughed, having heard that from other readers. It had taken him hours – and throwing a staged temper tantrum – to get his publisher to include that section in his book *exactly* as written. He told his publisher if that section was edited out, it would void their contract and he would take his book elsewhere.

"Well, the truth is, I think Burnside *is* an egotistical madman, though I don't say that quite *that* directly," Sawmill said. "I just use examples to say that he's erratic and even dangerous. Like Caligula was dangerous. You obviously know your ancient history, Mr. Stafford. Some people thought I should compare him to Nero, because of the old story about letting Rome burn. In this case, he's helping set it on fire."

This time it was Jack's turn to laugh.

"Actually, I knew Caligula was a bad actor," Jack said. "I see that in your author's note that Burnside and GES declined to cooperate with your research.

"Have you heard from GES or Burnside since the book came out last month? I'm pretty sure I am going to write a column bouncing off some of your thoughts. And I would like to include a reaction from him or GES. But to be honest, they really don't talk to my newspaper – or me – if they can avoid it."

Sawmill flipped through the papers on his desk before he answered. He had the envelope he had found in his mailbox. The only writing on the outside of the envelope said *Sawmill*. Inside was a photocopy of a recent San Francisco newspaper article about a long-shuttered – and very controversial – 1970s-era drug rehabilitation program.

The story was about how militantly the rehab program treated its critics. In one case, the story said, a lawyer suing the program found a rattlesnake in his mailbox.

"I haven't heard from GES," Sawmill said. "But do you know anything about a group called Synanon?"

Chapter 7

It was rare for anyone to beat Eli into the *Horseheads Clarion* office any day of the week.

So it was a big surprise when Eli found Keith Everlight already tapping on his keyboard shortly after 7 a.m. with a steaming mug of coffee on his desk.

Eli could tell from the look on his face that he was dying to tell someone – anyone – about something.

"So Keith, what's with the early bird stuff today? It's Wednesday and not even deadline day," Eli said.

Keith leaned back in his chair, waving to Eli to come over to his screen.

"I saw this posting on *Veritas* at 3 a.m. this morning," Keith said. "The damn garbage truck made such a racket outside my window I couldn't get back to sleep. Anyway, read it and then I'll give you the rest of the news."

VERITAS FOR ALL

The same Congressional staffer who spilled the beans about the Industrial Sedition Act told *Veritas* that the details of the proposed law are being drafted completely back-channel in a secret, *off-the-books* Congressional committee called the Committee on Energy Security and Eco-Terrorism.

You won't find that committee listed anywhere in any Congressional directory. Forget a web search, too.

Veritas was able to get hold of one sliver of the proposal thanks to the staffer who is risking a lot leaking this information:

> "Sections 114A-D: It is a federal offense to photograph vital natural resources or energy transmission systems or to republish or reproduce documents describing in detail any such systems."

Always,
In Veritas

Eli read the *Veritas* posting a second time and plopped down in the chair next to Keith.

He knew that when Jack arrived in the office, he would have all four reporters – and Eli – scrambling to dredge up some details about this supposed Industrial Sedition Act. Jack had been pretty skeptical because of *Veritas* being the only media getting any information out.

Reporters Rue and Stan – with some help from Jill – had used all their contacts in New York and Pennsylvania governments to get some hint of information. Calls to the various House of Representatives' offices and even the U.S. Senators' resulted in pleas from the staff that they had no idea what the reporters were talking about.

One chief of staff of a U.S. Senator from Pennsylvania told Jill that the *Horseheads Clarion* should pay more attention to the *real* news: how much hydrofracking was helping the state's economy.

"You said you had some real news," Eli said. "Don't keep me waiting, I've only had one cup of coffee this morning."

Before Keith could answer, Rue, Jill and Stan came through the door at the same time, jamming the doorway like actors in a television comedy sketch.

The three reporters looked as startled at finding Keith and Eli there as Keith and Eli were seeing the three of them coming in nearly an hour before the office opened.

"We all saw the same thing on *Veritas* this morning," Jill said. "At about 3 o'clock. I think the Rockwell Valley garbage truck woke us all up rumbling through. Anyway, when we saw the *Veritas* thing, well, we texted each other and agreed to get in early – before Jack."

Eli laughed.

"Let's get some coffee into us before Jack gets here," Eli said. "But one of you has to write a story about that noisy garbage truck. Apparently it woke up half the town."

Eli and the other three reporters headed to their desks until Eli realized that what with his early morning foggy brain, he had forgotten to have Keith say what else he knew about the Industrial Sedition Act and what *Veritas* had claimed on its website.

"I'd like to wait for the staff meeting now," Keith said, turning on his most smug look – a look that drove Eli crazy.

When Keith realized Eli was about to explode, he held up his hands in mock surrender.

"Okay, okay. ... The short version is that this ISA is designed to basically put all energy facilities – including the companies drilling and exploring and storing product – under federal protection," Keith said.

He paused for dramatic effect until Eli looked like he would explode.

"And my source says the language being tossed around in that secret committee is that it is all 'in the interest of national security.'"

Eli walked over to his desk, where he tapped the mouse to wake up his computer. His screensaver photo of Edward Snowden – the famous leaker of information about NSA spying, popped up.

You warned us, Eli thought looking at Snowden's famous face. *And it's only getting worse.*

Chapter 8

From the *Horseheads Clarion*

Column One
Horseheads Clarion

Laws made in secret don't benefit the people

By Jack Stafford

Newspapers do not like to report on rumors. At least this newspaper doesn't.

To do so gives validity to what frequently turns out to be simply malicious gossip - and frequently wrong to boot.

And that's why until today, the *Horseheads Clarion* has held off on mentioning something called the *Industrial Sedition Act*.

The ISA, as best this newspaper and other news agencies can determine, is a proposal being drafted behind solidly locked doors in Washington, D.C. Its intent - again, as best as can be determined - is to drape all U.S. energy production and distribution of energy in the mantle of "national security."

What that means in practice is shrouded in the same secrecy as almost all details about the ISA.

Almost all details.

This past week, thanks to some excellent investigative reporting by Keith Everlight, we know that the name of the Congressional committee working on this proposal is the 'Committee on Energy Security and Eco-Terrorism.` That name actually popped up first on website called *Veritas For All*, the work of a collection of citizen journalists around the U.S. who share information.

Mr. Everlight was able to confirm the existence of the committee. He was also able to confirm that committee members are taking their cues from the energy industry, shutting out any other influences.

In fact, at least half the committee members are actually *energy company representatives.*

Perhaps not surprising also is that Mr. Everlight was able to confirm that at least one member of the committee is a high-ranking executive with Grand Energy Services.

This newspaper has chronicled the power and influence of the energy lobby and energy companies for years, pointing out how that power and influence got energy companies exemptions from federal clean water and clean air acts. Those exemptions opened the door to hydrofracking for oil and natural gas, arguably the greatest manmade threat to our environment we have ever faced.

And to add insult to that injury, the poisons pumped into the ground (added to the millions of gallons of fresh water used in the hydrofracking process) are legally kept confidential by the energy industry. They claim trade secret status.

Even so, citizens all over the U.S. are battling with energy companies over polluted water, air pollution, unwanted pipelines and a plethora of social, cultural and economic problems associated with the industrialization that has accompanied a gold-rush mentality.

State laws in virtually all cases have favored the energy companies, allowing them nearly free rein to drill next to schoolyards, under people's homes and even in the shadow of hospitals where people made sick by hydrofracking are being treated.

But apparently it is not enough.

This Industrial Sedition Act in all likelihood will prove to be an attempt to silence critics – with threats of being charged with federal crimes related to "national security" – and to shroud energy companies in even more secrecy.

Already the term "eco-terrorist" is being applied by local officials in Rockwell Valley to just about anyone who picks up a protest sign.

We have witnessed the disturbing trend of the militarization of our local police forces in recent years, a development directly fed by the federal government providing sophisticated military hardware while also funding additional purchases to encourage police to believe they are more army than peacekeepers.

> The situation in Ferguson, Missouri last year is a textbook example of that.
>
> So is what happened in Rockwell Valley when the police let fly with pepper spray on peaceful demonstrators.
>
> Should this so-called Industrial Sedition Act crawl out from under the rock where it is being hatched, we hope citizens will add their voices to this newspaper in opposing it.
>
> These energy companies don`t need any more protections. If any protection is needed, it is us from them.
>
> *Jack Stafford is the publisher of the* Horseheads Clarion *and publishes Column One every Friday. He can be reached at JJStafford@HorseheadsClarion.com.*

Chapter 9

The last time Rockwell Valley Judge Owen T. Beigenlaw was in Police Chief Bobo Caprino's office, the judge had been stinking drunk from sipping four Café Royales with his lunch at the Alibi Bar and Grille in downtown Rockwell Valley.

As was his custom, Beigenlaw would slurp a few drinks with lunch, then get a police cruiser to drive him back to the courthouse where most afternoons he was handling traffic cases – including drunken driving.

On the afternoon in question, the officer sent to act as Beigenlaw's taxi had the good sense to bring the judge to the police station to sober up instead of dumping him on the courthouse steps.

Today Beigenlaw had asked for a conference with Caprino, police Lt. Del Dewitt and Rockwell Valley Mayor Will Pennisen about the proposed federal Industrial Sedition Act, as well as what Beigenlaw called some other "delicate legal matters."

Conference, my ass, Bobo thought. *This is a lecture about how we all need to dance when Grand Energy Services calls a tune. And delicate is not in the judge's vocabulary.*

"I think the likelihood of the ISA getting through Congress is very dubious," Beigenlaw said. "But the little that I can glean about it says it could be very useful in keeping things moving more smoothly. So we have to be hopeful."

And who is 'we' exactly? Bobo thought.

If there was any tension among the men because of the incident in the courtroom when Pennisen pulled out the pistol he stole from the police and ended up getting shot by Dewitt, it didn't show.

To Bobo, the four men could have been discussing where they might hold a bocce ball tournament or a friendly poker game – not how to skirt the civil rights of Rockwell Valley citizens.

As Mayor Pennisen twisted his neck left and right, Bobo noticed Pennisen's eyes seemed slightly glazed. Since Pennisen had returned from his legally mandated time in rehab, he had been taking several different mood-controlling medications that seemed to moderate his near-frothing diatribes whenever names like Alice McCallis came up.

"Owen and I were just talking about that woman. That Alice McCallis," Pennisen said. "Owen still has her case under advisement since, um, well. ... But he told me he's ready to drop the hammer on her for protesting again. She's threatening to go out in a rowboat and drop anchor where the pipeline is being built in front of the hotel."

Bobo looked over at Lt. Del Dewitt, hoping Dewitt would somehow figure out a tactful way to suggest that the conversation they were having was way out of line and that they could all – Judge Owen T. Beigenlaw included – end up in front of a grand jury for conspiracy to violate civil rights.

Jesus, Bobo thought. *The judge could get tossed off the bench.*

The thought made Bobo smile, which Pennisen misinterpreted as being supportive.

If Dewitt picked up on any of Bobo's thinking, it didn't prompt him to speak up. Instead, Dewitt stared into his coffee mug for most of the conversation, looking longingly at the door from time to time while he tried to figure out how he could escape long enough to go refill his cup.

"Judge, you know this department will carry out any legal orders," Bobo said. "And we will arrest people for illegal demonstrations, of course. But right now Alice McCallis is not doing anything we can go after her for. And I'm more than a little uncomfortable talking about her like this."

Pennisen's eyes came back into focus as his expression went from blank to a fierce frown, the same frown Bobo remembered Pennisen almost *always* featured prior to his medical stint.

"Uncomfortable. You are *uncomfortable*?" Pennisen said, half shouting.

"Well, *wah-wah-wah*, baby Bobo. *Jesus Christ*! My company has millions riding on that pipeline and getting our salt cavern storage in place before the end of the year. And you're worried that some crone is going to be upset because we won't let her go play *Greenpeace* in the lake in a canoe. I think you need to get your priorities straight, Chief. *Straight*."

Judge Beigenlaw stared at Pennisen for moment, remembering that his own political aspirations were linked to GES and that as long as he treaded carefully, no one was going to challenge his rulings – or his gas-industry-funded move up the judicial ladder.

As it was, most of the people of Rockwell Valley and the surrounding area had become so dependent on GES for their livelihoods, protesters were mostly considered a pain in the ass.

"Chief, the mayor's a little excitable and stressed," Beigenlaw said, shooting Pennisen a look that clearly said *shut up*.

"I just wanted to have this chat because I think you need to understand that with or without the ISA, the popular mood has swung solidly in favor of everything GES is doing here, and we need to support that. Within legal bounds, of course."

Pennisen's eyes glazed again as Beigenlaw reached into his briefcase and pulled out two separate court orders.

He handed copies to Dewitt with the original signed versions to Bobo.

"These are dated tomorrow. The top one says, essentially, if Alice McCallis *farts* anything about GES loud enough for someone to hear it, I want her arrested for contempt of court," Beigenlaw said. "And the second details out that the rest of Rockwell Valley is for all intents and purposes declared a no-protest zone, at least against Grand Energy Services. The second is an *order of protection* for all GES employees in this region – which extends to where they work and where they live."

Bobo studied the documents, then glanced over the shoulders of the three men sitting in front of him.

His police dispatcher/ex-wife Alicia had leaned back in her chair far enough that Bobo could see she was flipping the bird in the direction of his office – aimed *not* at Bobo, this time, but clearly at the mayor and judge.

Atta girl, Alicia, Bobo thought. *Atta girl.*

Chapter 10

The second earthquake in less than a month shook the Rockwell Valley region and up through the Finger Lakes with decidedly more power than its little brother had.

A bank in Rockwell Valley had three large plate glass windows blow out onto the street. Rockwell Valley High

School's gymnasium roof partially collapsed. And a 100-foot smokestack at a salt processing plant near Watkins Glen toppled into Seneca Lake.

Authorities reported about 50 injuries, including three Grand Energy Services workers who were badly hurt when a section of a 40-inch-diameter pipeline rolled off a truck in a field outside Rockwell Valley, pinning the three men beneath it.

It took two hours to free the men, whose legs were crushed by the weight.

In the *Horseheads Clarion* office, the staff was putting things back together from the temblor that had tipped over a bookcase and knocked out the building's electricity for two hours.

"The seismologists are still trying to pinpoint the epicenter," Keith Everlight told Jack in the conference room. "But it started within 75 miles of here."

Jack, Eli and Keith had dispatched the other three reporters to different areas to gather information and get photos. Keith had volunteered to stay behind to rewrite, edit and be the central collector of stories and photos.

Eli was putting together reports from the region for the *Clarion's* website.

"The first quake seemed like it was a fluke. Absolutely," Keith said. "But in less than a month? Another quake? This goes beyond weird."

Eli tapped on his laptop keys, surfing some area websites and blogs, emailing various people for permissions to use the photos of earthquake damage and also telling them the *Clarion* would be posting links to their pages.

Newspapers in Ohio, Oklahoma and Texas were contacting the *Clarion* for permission to reuse many of the photos and were seeking some exclusive shots, too.

Quakes in those states – generally smaller than what walloped Central Pennsylvania and New York – had become so commonplace that an entire cottage industry of people who repaired earthquake damage to houses had sprung up.

The staff was so focused on getting the earthquake stories and photos up and running that Jack nearly missed the email from Prof. Charles Avery Sawmill.

Sawmill always left the subject line of his emails blank – a habit that often sent his emails to spam folders of recipients of his electronic correspondence.

And so it was that Jack didn't read the email for nearly an hour until he, Eli and Keith took a break from the earthquake coverage to head over to Millie's Diner for some food.

```
Mr. Stafford: I just
received a phone call from my
neighbor Alice McCallis. She`s
been arrested. She was very
upset and said something about
'martial law` being declared.
It sounds like a job for a
journalist to check out. Best.
C. Sawmill
```

Chapter 11

Noah did his best to get his father off the couch to play with him. But Jack's headache was pounding.

Sedition

Exactly *what* was going on in Rockwell Valley was murky despite the best efforts of Keith Everlight to find out by telephone. After Keith spent a frustrating hour of playing telephone tag with various Rockwell Valley officials, Jack dispatched him to go to the Pennsylvania town and try to meet with Alice McCallis and Prof. Charles Sawmill.

Keith had been unable to even find out via telephone if McCallis was still sitting in jail or had been bailed out.

Jack turned on his side and watched Noah sitting on the floor nearby playing with a box of wooden blocks – blocks that had been Jack's when he was a child. The box was upended and Noah was stacking the cubes, sometimes pausing to look at the letters or animal images on them.

Cass was sitting in the dining room, tapping on her laptop computer. She had started writing a play about a community in crisis and was very secretive about what she was putting together.

Jack had offered several times to read it. But she said the creative process required that she not show it to anyone until she thought it was ready.

"I doubt you show your first draft of your column to anyone before you polish it," she would say.

On the couch Jack smiled thinking about that, the first genuine smile he had cracked since getting the email from Prof. Sawmill about Alice McCallis.

I only ever write one *draft*, Jack thought. *But then, I'm not writing a play.*

Jack wasn't sure if it was the headache or the glass of wine he had when he came home, but watching Cass typing away, jotting handwritten notes on a notepad, looking up at the ceiling for inspiration all reminded him so much of his late wife Devon.

Devon had sat at that same table, banging on the keys with the same intensity that Cass was now. And because they looked so much alike, Jack wondered what Noah thought.

But when Devon was there, she was writing news stories and crunching numbers, Jack thought.

Cass looked over at Jack with a quizzical look on her face, then smiled, putting her hands together along the side of her head to signal Jack to close his eyes and sleep so he could get rid of his headache.

Noah saw her motion and put his head down on the floor as if to take a nap.

In the last few months Jack and Cass had settled into a careful domestic routine that to strangers looked as if Jack and Cass were husband and wife and Noah their child.

The three-way affection among them was visible to everyone. When they walked around Horseheads – frequently with Belle alongside – they drew smiles and plenty of friendly chatter.

But Jack and Cass struggled with the domestic setup.

One night after drinking a very uncharacteristic second glass of wine, Cass confessed that she had been jealous when Devon married Jack.

"Not that it was *you*, if that makes sense. Just that she was getting married and was so damned happy," Cass had said. "And when you moved to that island in Tonga? I couldn't write a happier ending for any play."

As Jack slept on the couch and Noah dozed on the floor, that conversation replayed in a dream for Jack, except that Cass and Devon were both in the dream. And Noah wasn't a four-year-old but a teenager, a handsome tall teen that looked strikingly like Cass, not Devon.

The dream startled him awake.

Jack looked and saw that Cass was gone from the table, sending an odd twinge of anxiety through him when he couldn't see where she was at the moment.

He tried to shrug the feeling off, but it stayed with him until he heard some banging in the kitchen and Cass singing to herself.

He dozed right back off and didn't wake up until dinner was on the table.

Chapter 12

Keith Everlight thought that *martial law* was an overly dramatic characterization of what was really going on in Rockwell Valley.

After the initial email that sent him catapulting to Rockwell Valley several days in a row, Keith reported that the town was quiet – perhaps eerily so. But commerce and normal day-to-day life continued.

The late October sun was just setting as Keith drove out along the shore of Rockwell Valley Lake for a visit with retired professor Charles Avery Sawmill to talk about a second threatening letter that had appeared in his mailbox.

Keith had just finished a somewhat unsatisfactory interview with Police Chief Melvin "Bobo" Caprino about Judge Owen T. Beigenlaw's judicial order that activists claimed was stifling protests.

The order reminded Keith of regulations college campuses often put into place aimed to limit free speech to certain areas of campus and only allow that with a permit from the police department.

In Beigenlaw's order, all marches and rallies required approval of the chief of police.

Alice McCallis's group, No On Gas, found out-of-town legal counsel to challenge the law, but it was slow going.

Chief Caprino had been quite cagey in his responses to Keith's questions. But he told Keith despite the flap being created by McCallis, no one had actually come in and even *requested* a permit for a rally or march.

"If they don't ask, how can I even consider if it will be safe," the chief said.

Keith's questions about the constitutionality of the judge's order drew blank stares from Caprino and his lieutenant, called in to the conversation.

"We're cops," Lt. Del Dewitt said. "Not constitutional scholars. As long as the judge's order isn't overruled, we have to abide by it. I think you need to talk to the judge."

Keith thought so too, except that the judge refused to grant an interview.

When Keith asked Caprino and Dewitt what they thought about the threatening documents that Prof. Sawmill had received, they gave him more blank stares.

"If Sawmill is getting some kind of threats, he hasn't told anyone in this department about it," Caprino said. "Not a word. He is getting a little old. Maybe a little paranoid, too. Maybe it's a disgruntled former student."

It was dark by the time Keith drove past Sawmill's mailbox, a gaudily decorated Pink Flamingo on the state highway. Sawmill had told Keith it was a gift from a sister in Sheboygan, picked up at a curio shop in Montour Falls, New York.

Keith stopped in the middle of the deserted highway and backed up the 100-plus yards to the entrance to turn in.

The slightly inclined gravel road was like hundreds of others that dotted the lakeshore of Rockwell Valley Lake, all leading down to cottages and a handful of year-round homes like Sawmill's. Sawmill's directions said his house was off a small spur to the north and marked with the pink flamingo sign.

As he approached the house, Keith saw it was dark inside, though he thought he could make out a small car parked next to the house. A handful of solar fixtures on the deck put out a feeble amount of light, but the house looked deserted.

Keith left the car running with his headlights pointed at the deck while he checked his cell phone.

Dammit, he thought. *No service and no Sawmill. I wonder if he is slipping a cog and forgot. I know we had appointment.*

He turned off his car lights and then his engine and rolled down his windows. Keith knew he was right on time. But people who live in rural areas like Rockwell Valley sometimes aren't always as punctual as people in a city might be.

Keith was exhausted after starting out his day at the newspaper office at 6 a.m., helping Eli to lay out pages for Friday's issue. Keith had become the unofficial assistant editor of the paper, fulfilling all of his reporting duties and adding layout and headline writing to his workload.

He dozed off, thinking about a headline he had written that morning.

Keith couldn't tell how long he had been asleep when a crashing sound woke him. He was disoriented and the pitch-black night made it worse. He fumbled for a flashlight in his glove box as he turned on his headlights.

In the doorway leading onto the deck, a man was lying face down on the boards, his legs still inside the house.

He jumped out of the car and was walking quickly towards the man he was sure had to be Professor Charles Avery Sawmill when he felt someone give him a hard shove from behind, knocking him to the ground.

Whoever knocked him down grabbed his head with two hands and slammed it down into the dirt three or four times.

As Keith pushed himself up onto his hands and knees, he heard two sharp reports of shattering glass.

My headlights, Keith thought.

It was pitch black again when Keith felt the first sharp kick to his ribs.

Chapter 13

The two-patient room at Rockwell Valley Hospital had just enough room for Jack and Eli to squeeze in and sit down in the chairs by the beds.

Prof. Charles Avery Sawmill was propped up in the bed by the window, his face puffy and forehead bruised. The nosepiece of his glasses was taped together with some white adhesive tape. He was sound asleep with an IV bag connected to his arm.

The hall nurse said he had been given a sedative and would most likely sleep until morning. But he was stable and the doctors thought he would be fine.

In the bed closer to the door, *Clarion* reporter Keith Everlight was sporting much more serious bruising on his face, a broken nose and – according to the emergency room doctor – possibly a broken rib.

"His right hand is hurt, but it's a sprain, not broken," the doctor told Jack.

Keith checked in and out of consciousness for the first hour after Jack and Eli arrived, a combination of pain medication and adrenaline depletion.

But in bits and pieces he told them about seeing Sawmill on the deck and then being attacked.

"Whoever hit me was big. Really big. As in heavy – big and tall," Keith said. "He started knocking me around pretty good. But I blinded him with my flashlight long enough for me to get in a couple of shots to his temples. I hit him in the ribs a couple of good ones, too. I hurt my hand on his hip."

When the call came in to Jack from the dispatcher at the Rockwell Valley Police Department, she told Jack that the man who had attacked his reporter was apparently wearing a ski mask – something that Professor Sawmill had said, too.

A badly injured Keith had gotten Sawmill into his car and driven out without headlights to the highway.

"A truck driving by saw them driving down the road with Sawmill holding a flashlight out the window," the Rockwell Valley Police dispatcher said. "When he got a good look at them, he called us and an ambulance."

Rockwell Valley Police Lt. Del Dewitt told Jack the Rockwell PD figured it was most likely a burglary gone bad and the assailant was just a thief who had panicked.

"We don't have the resources to station an officer at the hospital," Dewitt told Jack on the telephone. "But I wouldn't worry, whoever did this is long gone, I'd say."

Jack and Eli told the hospital's part-time security officer — a fit 65-year-old Vietnam veteran – they were worried about Keith and Prof. Sawmill.

He promised to keep an eye out.

"Anybody bigger than a Munchkin goes near that room, I'll take care of it," he said. "Plus, we have a new orderly working nights who played college ball. He's from Samoa. No worries."

Chapter 14

```
From the Horseheads Clarion

Column One
Horseheads Clarion
```

Martial law and civil liberty

```
By Jack Stafford

    Several weeks ago, the
Clarion was alerted by a handful
of Rockwell Valley residents
that citizens believed they
were about to be placed under
martial law.
```

Sedition

Martial law, in case that term is foreign, is the imposition of military power, usually over a town or region.

In this case, hysteria overcame reality. There were no plans for soldiers with tanks or guns to march in front of the Rockwell Valley Grocery Mart or the Rockwell Valley Savings and Loan or to defend the Rockwell Valley Courthouse from marauders.

What prompted the overreaction was announcement of a court order issued by Judge Owen T. Beigenlaw that said there could be *no* demonstrations or political gatherings in Rockwell Valley without the written permission of the Rockwell Valley Chief of Police.

Elsewhere in today`s *Clarion* there is a story explaining in detail that Judge Beigenlaw does not have the authority to unilaterally make such laws, even though the Rockwell Valley Police, so far, act as if it is legal.

The larger question to ponder – beyond the judge`s legal ignorance – is, how did we get to this point?

After all, in recent years energy companies have all but written the laws *regulating* themselves. And fawning federal agencies approve proposals for oil and gas pipelines, storage facilities, and ocean ports to export liquid natural gas with the speed of summer lightning.

Sometimes faster, it seems.

They have what they want, but tucked in their amazing arrogance is that they also don`t want anyone to utter a bad word.

Weeks ago hundreds of peaceful protesters at the White House in Washington, D.C., were fired upon with powerful water cannons by riot-gear-clad police, injuring dozens, including children. The protesters` crime? It was having the temerity to oppose a controversial oil pipeline that *non*-oil industry-funded scientists *agree* will be a disaster for the environment.

In Rockwell Valley, the same judge who wants to quash demonstrations slapped a restraining order on activist Alice McCallis so restrictive that she can`t go to Rockwell Valley Hospital without risking arrest. And yes, the judge is aware and has declared his indifference.

Then just last week, a 77-year-old retired Central Pennsylvania college professor was attacked in his home.

How does that fit?

Prof. Charles Avery Sawmill is the author of the new book on U.S. energy policy titled *Cannibals and Christians: The Extractors vs. The Sustainers.* As you might guess, the book is not particularly kind to people who drill for oil and natural gas, but it is more inclined to laud efforts of people to protect the environment and sustainability.

Rockwell Valley Police say that the man who assaulted Sawmill was likely a burglar. But as our story said last week, *Clarion* reporter Keith Everlight managed to scare off the attacker after struggling with him, but not before being badly injured himself.

That doesn`t sound like a thief involved in a snatch-and-grab. It sounds more like it could be a bit of personal payback to Prof. Sawmill for his penning passages like this published in *Cannibals and Christians*:

> The oil and gas barons in the U.S. today act with the same impunity as Roman emperors did 2,000 years ago, fearless of any force, except stockholders intent on quick profits at the expense of the environment and the poor. They cannibalize the earth, destroying irreplaceable natural resources without understanding that one day they – and their regal descendants – will have fouled their water and air, too, making the earth unfit for everyone.
>
> *Jack Stafford is the publisher of the* Horseheads Clarion *and publishes Column One every Friday. He can be reached at JJStafford@HorseheadsClarion.com.*

Chapter 15

Phone calls from Luther Burnside on days that Jack Stafford's column was published were a routine part of Rod Mayenlyn's schedule.

And so it was on Friday that Burnside was frothing into the telephone about Stafford's latest broadside.

"It's bad enough that that odious book by that *academic-know-nothing* is getting some traction," Burnside said. "Now Stafford has to chew on us just as the Rockwell Valley Town Council starts to get cold feet."

The normally tame Rockwell Valley Town Council was suddenly finding its spine – in part a reaction to the court order by Judge Owen T. Beigenlaw limiting any public demonstrations unless approved by the police chief.

It was one thing for Grand Energy Services to throw money and jobs around to keep people quiet. But a few people had started grumbling about "constitutional rights" sufficiently to get people wondering what they had signed up for and what they had given up for the veneer of prosperity.

A local music group's song, "I Owe My Soul to the GES Store," got so popular so quickly that many people around town were humming the tune, a musical takeoff of the 1950s song "Sixteen Tons," performed by the late Tennessee Ernie Ford.

For nearly two years the council had rubberstamped everything Grand Energy Services wanted for both its salt cavern storage of propane and natural gas and permits for the pipeline to bring in natural gas from the west.

But a final permit to deed over a large tract of Rockwell Valley-owned property – critical for the building of a 20-acre brine pond for the propane storage system – had become a debatable issue.

At the council meeting earlier in the week, Mayor Will Pennisen had to pull several *out-of-order* parliamentary moves to stop Alice McCallis and a group of anti-pipeline and gas storage people from making a plea to the council to refuse to approve the brine pond permit.

He got away with it largely because the town council members knew even less about *Robert's Rules of Order* than did Pennisen.

But the best Pennisen could do was delay the matter for one week. If it had gone up for a vote after he rudely shut down Alice McCallis's speech, saying she was "out of order," the council would likely have turned down giving the property to GES for the pond.

"How the hell was that woman allowed to speak at all?" Burnside asked. "I thought the judge's order made that kind of crap illegal."

Mayenlyn had thought so, too, until he did some research into the legal concept of "privilege" which shielded people in courts – and sometimes public meetings – from being penalized for saying libelous things.

"I checked with our legal staff and because she was speaking in a legally called public meeting, it would be a real stretch to say the judge's order can shut her up there," Mayenlyn said. "We can see what we can do before next week. But if you are worried about Stafford and his column, if he found out we were involved in trying to muzzle McCallis again it would be like throwing fresh meat to the lions."

Mayenlyn immediately regretted using the word *lions* and hoped that Burnside didn't think he was somehow making a reference to the book by Charles Avery Sawmill.

If he did, Burnside let it slide.

"Rod. We have to get that brine pond property in GES's name. It was supposed to be signed over to us months ago. Hell, it's half excavated. We can't store propane in those caverns without using it. And we have six weeks before we promised to start taking shipments."

Before he hung up, Mayenlyn said he would call Pennisen – and go to Rockwell Valley himself if necessary to lobby the town council before the next meeting.

He scanned Stafford's column again, then checked to see if Sawmill's book *Cannibals and Christians: The Extractors vs. The Sustainers* had popped up on the Goodreads website yet.

It hadn't, but a quick search for the song "I Owe My Soul to the GES Store" brought up eight references, including a YouTube video of the group performing it live at a bar the night before.

Mayenlyn watched it. Then he frowned.

The video had already been viewed nearly 1,000 times in less than a day since it was posted.

But it is catchy, he thought, humming along.

And I owe my soul to the GES store.

Chapter 16

The *Horseheads Clarion* staff took a vote Monday morning to ban Halloween candy from the office at the end of the day.

The vote was taken while the staff sat in the conference room looking at a bowl of assorted sweets big enough to launch even an unenthusiastic dental hygienist into a lecture on what sugar does to teeth.

Because Halloween had been Friday – and Noah was really big into it, dressed as a cowboy – Jack had brought in most of what Noah had reaped.

"I can't have bowls of candy sitting around," Jill said. "But it's nice gesture, Jack."

Jack noted that even after the vote Eli and Keith kept snagging smaller pieces.

"And look at this guy," Jill said, pointing to Keith. "Even with his hand wrapped in that mini-cast he can't stop."

At Jill's insistence, they finally moved the candy bowl out to the front desk for customers.

"Now that we solved the Halloween Candy Crisis, can we keep going on the news budget?" Jack asked.

Eli tapped on computer keys, a smooth movement that always reminded Jack of a concert pianist. The screen on the wall popped up with Eli's story list for Tuesday and Friday, a mix of news stories ranging from crime to weather to the always-looming specter of what the gas industry was up to, locally and nationally.

"I want Keith to follow up on the brine pond business in Rockwell Valley," Eli said. "The council meeting is tomorrow night, so we could put a story on the website today and then for print tomorrow.

"And, of course, we need to staff the meeting, too."

Keith held up his cast and pointed to Rue.

"I'll help with research but my typing is a little slow right now," Keith said. "The doctor said this cast will be on for maybe just a week. But I can wiggle my fingers. I just keep whacking the keyboard with the edge of the cast."

The topic of staffing the Rockwell Valley meeting bounced around, eventually landing in Rue's lap.

Reporting on the Industrial Sedition Act had stalled, except for a brief piece on *Veritas For All* that claimed the drafters of the ISA were proposing a new federal agency: the Federal Eco-Terrorist Administration.

"No one – and I mean no one – has been able to confirm that," Eli said. "But there's been a lot of funny Internet chatter about the acronym it would make."

After the staff got done making their own cheese-related jibes at FETA, they worked at parceling out the rest of the stories while Jack reported his Friday column had drawn a stern response from Grand Energy Services.

"GES has been pretty quiet about my columns for a long time. But I got a beauty today from their vice president for PR.

"Can you put it on screen Eli? It came in as a letter to the editor to Eli."

```
Dear Editor:
    Friday`s   column   by   Jack
Stafford  in  which  he  maligned
the   oil   and   gas   industry
continued  a   long   string  of
unfair    and    unsubstantiated
charges.
    Grand    Energy    Services
condemns   violence,   supports
free   speech,   and   continues
to  do  its  best  to  serve GES
customers in the region.
    To say otherwise is an evil
canard.

Rod Mayenlyn, vice president
for information
Grand Energy Services
```

Flathead, Missouri

The staff was still laughing about the word *canard* when Jack's cell phone beeped with a text message from Professor Charles Avery Sawmill, home recovering from the attack.

> ```
> The police just called. They
> want me to come in to Rockwell
> Valley Police Dept. to reclaim
> my computer. When I asked why
> they wouldn`t just bring it
> by, they said it was evidence.
> But they wouldn`t say anything
> else. That sound odd to you?
> ```

Chapter 17

When Eli arrived at the *Clarion* office the following morning, Rue Malish was crying at her desk.

It was a gentle sob, but her red eyes gave away that she had been crying for some time. She turned her head to hide the tears as she offered a perfunctory greeting to Eli.

What now? Eli thought. *How many weeping women do I have to deal with?*

As Eli had been getting ready to leave for the newspaper, his wife Shania had a meltdown in their kitchen when he didn't want to eat the scrambled eggs she had fixed.

Uncharacteristically, she swore at Eli, a string of language that made Eli's jaw drop. Then she quickly apologized, plunking down in a chair at the breakfast table.

After a few minutes of across-the-table hugs and hand-holding, Shania admitted that she was frightened the closer it got to the time to deliver their baby – now only about six weeks away.

She was also having troubling managing Millie's Diner and wasn't pleased with the server she had hired to take her place.

"And poor little Noah, I want to watch him for Jack, but it's just too much right now," Shania said.

Sitting at his desk in the office, Eli remembered watching the day before when Cass had come into the office with another woman who looked a lot like her, just shorter. He found out later it was Jack's other sister-in law – Anne from Vashon Island. The three of them spent about a half-hour in a closed-door meeting with Jack that ended with Cass coming out of the office in tears and Anne in an angry scowl.

Shit, I suppose I have to ask, Eli thought. *God!*

Eli had learned from Jack that when people were upset, it was important to try to defuse whatever was bothering them, not make it worse. And so because Eli and Rue were the only people in the office, he sat down in the chair by her desk and simply waited for her to speak.

He figured correctly that she would be most at ease right there and likely to keep some level of professional composure. If she burst into tears like Shania had, he was pretty sure he might have to grab some tissues.

"It's that farmer, the environmentalist whose big into solar?" Rue said. "I found out last night that his wife Audrey is very sick. I mean, really sick. It started out with sores in her mouth that her dentist is stumped by. But then her hair started to fall out."

The front door to the *Clarion* swung open, letting in a blast of cool November air, reminding Eli to assign Jill or Stan to write a weather story. The first snow of the season was close, and while the newspaper had bigger fish to fry, readers wanted to know if it was time to pull up the covers.

"What's up guys?" Jack asked.

He looked a little rumpled, his hair not as neatly coiffed as normal. And if he had shaved, he had done so very quickly, Eli thought.

"Rue was just telling me that Lasse Espinola's wife is really sick," Eli said. "They're not really sure what it is, except she has sores in her mouth, feels like hell and her hair has started falling out. That right?"

Rue nodded her head, averting her eyes from Jack.

Jack nodded back and headed for his office, turning around in his doorway.

"I know you both already thought about this, but his well was contaminated from fracking, wasn't it? Are you looking into that?"

Eli held up his hands as if to say "yes" and watched while Jack went into his glassed-in office and sat down.

Then he turned to Rue, who had stopped crying completely, but looked like she could let go again easily.

"Rue, how did you even find out that Espinola's wife is sick?" Eli said.

She closed her eyes while the tears started again.

"He told me last night when he came to my house," she said. "And he's sick, too. Really sick."

Eli just stared at Rue, knowing she would answer the question he didn't want ask.

"We're just friends," Rue said, tears welling up again. "Honestly. But no one is going believe that."

Chapter 18

When Jack got home late that afternoon, his mind was reeling.

First, he had to deal with what Rue Malish called a *non-affair affair* with someone she had written a number of stories about, a pretty clear ethical violation. Then he found out that Lasse Espinola's illness – and the illness of his wife, Audrey – was likely related to the hydrofracking-related poisoning of their main water well that had made their animals sick.

It had been Espinola's veterinarian who made the connection when Lasse described the sores in his wife's mouth, similar to the sores that his cows had shown before they keeled over and died.

I feel old and tired, Jack thought as he walked through the door. *Maybe just tired.*

When his sister-in-law Anne had shown up unexpectedly at his office the day before, at first Jack was surprised, then angry.

Cass hadn't let him know Anne was coming. And Jack didn't like those kinds of surprises.

And then when Anne skipped normal niceties and started immediately talking about Noah and wanting Jack to let Noah go back to Vashon Island with her and Cass, he blew up.

"In my office, you waltz in and start saying you want to take my son away?" Jack said. "Christ, Anne. What the fuck are you thinking?"

Devon had called Anne the family accounting queen because of her skill with numbers and her cold analytical skills. Devon joked that when they were growing up, Devon, Cass and Anne started calling one another Science, Drama and Numbers, nicknames even their parents started using.

It had been Devon's love of science and writing that brought her together with Jack.

But Devon had eventually convinced Jack that Anne had a compassionate side too and that he should turn over fiscal responsibility for the publishing aspects of his book, *An Endless Quest for Hope and Solutions,* to her.

Anne was kind and generous when Jack and Noah had stayed at the Walsh family 10-acre estate on Vashon Island while Jack went through his brief hospital stay and rested up before returning to New York and the *Clarion*.

Anne and Cass argued several times on Vashon when they thought Jack couldn't hear about Jack and Noah simply staying on Vashon Island and not going back to New York and the newspaper. Cass thought Jack needed to get back into the saddle as publisher of the newspaper. Anne thought Noah would do better on Vashon and with access to medical specialists in Seattle.

As Jack walked into his home, he saw the dining room table was set with the good china his mother had loved and fancy wineglasses from his friend Oscar Wilson's Lakeside Winery. Noah and Belle the Labrador were on the floor and didn't take notice of Jack.

Jack heard Cass and Anne laughing in the kitchen.

Well, that's a good sign, Jack thought.

He had barely gotten his overcoat off when Noah spotted him and ran up to throw his arms around Jack's legs.

Then from the kitchen Anne came out, drying her hands on her apron. Her face broke into a smile as she got close and she offered both her hands to him, palms up.

"I am *so* sorry I came on so strong yesterday and again this morning," Anne said. "*Goddamn* those long air flights and layovers. Cass and I talked all day and decided a nice family dinner was in order. We are family, Jack. All four of us. And I blew it. Let's start over. Okay?"

Cass came out of kitchen and looked across the room at Jack and Anne still holding hands. Noah was still clasping Jack's legs and Belle was looking pensively at the humans, wondering where they were going to sit and what food she might get a shot at.

"We'll have a group hug later," Cass said, a big smile on her face. "But right now dinner's ready."

Jack realized that he had stopped breathing and that he didn't want to let go of Anne's hands or have Noah let go of his legs. And he was ready for that group hug right *then*.

"Cass, come over here, please. I want everyone in on this."

Family, Jack thought. *Family*.

Chapter 19

Rockwell Valley Police Chief Melvin "Bobo" Caprino and Lt. Del Dewitt watched out Bobo's office window as retired Professor Charles Avery Sawmill climbed into his car, carefully putting his laptop computer on the passenger's side seat.

Their interview with Sawmill had only taken about 20 minutes.

"That poor old guy might never sleep again after seeing those pictures," Dewitt said. "I don't think I'll get them out of my mind for a long time either."

When the professor's computer was brought into the station as evidence in the burglary/attack on Sawmill and reporter Keith Everlight from the *Horseheads Clarion,* the Rockwell Valley PD computer technician had snooped around – as he *always* did, even if he had strict orders against it.

He found a file innocuously titled "Vacation Photos" that had hundreds of photos of kiddie porn, some involving real – or staged – torture.

"Yeah. I was watching his face close when you turned the computer so he could see it," Bobo said. "That garbage was sure *not* his."

The photos put a new spin on the incident as soon as Bobo and Dewitt had seen them.

The computer had been left near the front door – one of the most valuable things in the entire house.

"Too fucking convenient for my taste, Del," Bobo said.

Lt. Del Dewitt put his coffee mug down for a moment, watching as Sawmill carefully negotiated the intersection as he pulled out of the police department parking lot.

"So the question is, who would want to set up an old guy like that?" Dewitt asked. "And why beat him up? He seems harmless."

Bobo's phone rang on his desk before he could answer, another out-of-town newspaper asking questions about Judge Owen T. Beigenlaw's court orders and martial law in Rockwell Valley.

"Del, do you remember what it was like here before GES came to town?" Bobo asked. "It was always quiet. I mean, no thefts, only bar fights between local drunks, kids stealing each other's bicycles. None of this out-of-town bad-guy shit we have to deal with. Including out of town media. Christ."

Dewitt stood up, looking towards the door, making Bobo think Dewitt suddenly needed to refill his coffee mug.

He was wrong.

"Chief. I want to go check the photos I took at Sawmill's the next day," Dewitt said. "I took some shots outside right where that reporter scuffled with whoever decked Sawmill and pounded on him. There was glass from the smashed headlights all over. And our guys trampled the driveway pretty good. But I don't know…"

Bobo looked puzzled for second.

"Footprints?" he asked.

Del grinned.

"Yeah. Maybe *big* footprints."

Chapter 20

The stiff wind off Rockwell Valley Lake was cold with occasional sheets of driving sleet as Alice McCallis climbed into a small aluminum rowboat loaded with protest signs tied to a half-dozen small floats she was going to attach to the newly installed warning buoys for the just-constructed natural gas pipeline installed by Grand Energy Services.

The pipeline sat on the bottom of the lake as deep as 50 feet in some spots, with floating signs saying "Keep Clear – No Anchoring" spaced at 300-foot intervals across the half-mile stretch of lake at the extreme south end.

The signs and pipeline were only a half-mile offshore of downtown Rockwell Valley, creating what the *Horseheads Clarion* – and most local residents – described as "a scenic industrial blight" for anyone on the waterfront, at the marina, or looking out the front of the historic hotel to the north.

For Rockwell Valley Mayor Will Pennisen, it *was* scenic because its completion two weeks before meant that he would likely get a big bonus – and maybe a promotion. At least he hoped a promotion was coming, as the natural gas had just started flowing from the hydrofracked wells to the west.

Plus, the completed underwater pipeline waved a nice political finger in the face of McCallis and her *No On Gas* protesters, who had argued unsuccessfully for nearly three years against both the pipeline for natural gas and the approved salt cavern storage of both that natural gas and liquid propane gas.

NOG had run out of money for legal challenges to the final leg of construction under the lake.

Even the pro-bono lawyers had packed it in, moving on to other environmental legal battles.

Pennisen sat in his GES truck watching McCallis struggling with the rowboat.

Freeze your ass off, you old bitch, he thought. *I don't think I'll even bother getting you arrested today. Put up your stupid signs.*

About 10 NOG protesters were cheering McCallis on as she rowed against the wind out towards the pipeline buoys. But the group stayed firmly on shore while the 79-year-old activist grimly pulled on the oars.

All of them had been arrested at least once in the last year and had been warned stiffly by Rockwell Valley Judge Owen T. Beigenlaw at their last court appearance that if he saw them in his court again for trespassing – or for violating any of a blizzard of his restraining orders and orders of protection for Grand Energy Services and its employees – they would spend serious time in the county lockup.

Beigenlaw had even started casually mentioning the shadowy Industrial Sedition Act and the Federal Eco-Terrorist Administration, neither of which actually were a reality. They remained speculative fodder for a few media outlets and fringe websites while Congressional leaders continued to deny there was any such legislation – or agency – up for discussion.

A White House spokesman had said the whole idea of ISA and FETA was simply "some paranoid whack-job's wet dream."

The spokesman made the comment *anonymously*, of course.

Rockwell Valley Police Chief Bobo Caprino was also watching the protesters and Alice McCallis's nautical adventure. But he was inside the warm hotel, sipping a cup of coffee with Lt. Del Dewitt, waiting to meet with the hotel manager about security for a big GES celebration.

"I'm am sooooo sick of these GES assholes," Bobo said. "Sick of them. Any minute now Pennisen is probably going to call Alicia and tell her that someone is bothering his precious pipeline. Jesus. ... Look at those warning buoys. They really *are* ugly."

Dewitt sipped his coffee, silently cheering McCallis as she made it to the first marker squarely off the small pier in front of the hotel, used by tour boats and historic sailboats in the summer.

"Shame we couldn't match those footprints for evidence," Dewitt said. "But now we know. That GES ape with the clown feet is bad news. How is Sawmill anyway?"

Bobo smiled and motioned to the shoreline where retired Professor Charles Avery Sawmill was holding a sign that said "GES Go Home" on one side. The other said "Caligula rules GES."

The two policemen heard a cheer go up from the NOG group as Alice McCallis pulled away from the first buoy, where she had attached her own float with a slender five-foot plastic rod sticking up with a white flag, its red letters waving gaily in the 10-mile-per-hour breeze.

How appropriate, Bobo thought.

The letters on the flag said *S.O.S.*

Remember Lot's Wife

Chapter 1

It was Billy Jack Bordin's fourth week on the job, and today he regretted how much he lied about his experience to get hired at the Grand Energy Services natural gas and liquid propane storage facility at the north end of Rockwell Valley Lake.

It was true he had worked for seven years for GES in the natural gas industry in Texas. But he never actually operated any equipment that controlled the flow of gas or used the sophisticated software that routed natural gas from storage area to storage area via a spider web of pipelines.

In truth, he was in the control area's office all the time – but mostly dealing with small computer issues and keeping the photocopiers and printers humming.

When the husband of a female GES co-worker threatened to remove his larynx with a hunting knife if he didn't stop flirting with his wife, Bordin hastily applied for a transfer to Pennsylvania that the Texas GES administration was very happy to approve.

Then when he arrived at Rockwell Valley, he used his Texas twang to sweet-talk his way into becoming one of a dozen operators of the newly installed computer system that controlled all the storage of natural gas in the salt caverns with a parallel set of controls for storage of liquid propane gas in other places on the same site.

When he first saw the control room atop a tower overlooking the 400-acre salt cavern property, which also had a stunning view of Rockwell Valley Lake, he whistled involuntarily.

Kee-rist. It looks like the bridge of a goddamned aircraft carrier, he thought. *What they had in Texas was a Model T compared to this.*

When Bordin arrived, the GES facility was almost done testing the new storage system, pushed hard by GES headquarters in Flathead, Missouri to get the equipment online and product in the caverns.

The LPG was being brought in by railcars on a new set of tracks and siding. The natural gas was flowing right from the wells through the new pipeline constructed to the west.

Today the system was up and running, only a week into moving the natural gas and LPG in and out of the salt caverns, ticking along automatically.

Bordin hadn't touched a button since arriving, leaving all that to his boss and the primary operator of the facility, Curtis Wildemon, a GES veteran of 30 years.

But on this early Saturday morning in December, Bordin found himself all alone in the control room when the two-man night shift left. Wildemon was late coming in, stuck in traffic backed up because of a propane truck and auto collision on Interstate 86 near Horseheads, NY.

"If I can get turned around and off this freaking parking lot of a highway, I'll be there in a half hour," Wildemon told Bordin via cell phone.

"If I'm going to be any later, I'll call. But right now check the roster. Call one of the other standby operators in until I get there."

Although one person *could* run the system easily, federal and state regulators had insisted that GES always have two trained workers in the control room. GES workers nicknamed it "The Heart Attack Rule."

Bordin hung up the phone, and instead of calling right away for backup, he turned on the satellite radio system, tuning to a comedy channel featuring a boisterous redneck comedian making crude jokes about his ex-wife. Bordin enjoyed being alone in the tower where he normally had Wildemon telling him so many GES and gas industry war stories that Bordin wanted to scream.

He stood up and looked down the hill at Rockwell Valley Lake, using the company's $2,500 nitrogen-filled field glasses to check out a flock of geese landing on the lake, a quarter-mile away.

The comedian's tirade and the audience laughter on the radio was loud enough that Bordin didn't hear the insistent beeping sound coming from the control panel.

And while he marveled at the gracefulness of the geese, he also missed seeing the red letters that had appeared on the control panel screen:

SYSTEM ERROR

Chapter 2

When the first snowball walloped Jack in the back of his head, he was doubly surprised.

The snowball itself was cold and wet. Some of the snow trickled down his collar.

But the real surprise was that Noah had pegged him so solidly, the nearly four-year-old's pitching arm far more developed than Jack thought it was.

"We've been working on his throwing," Jack's sister-in-law Anne said. "I'd say he's got it down pretty well."

The early Saturday morning sun was particularly bright after several days of snowfall that left a blanket of nearly two feet of snow on the ground. For Noah and Belle the Labrador, the snow was a great toy. And Anne and Cass had helped him build a small snow fort in the front yard, where Noah had amassed an arsenal of pre-made snowballs.

Cass was in the house making breakfast. And Oscar Wilson was due to eat with them.

Showing up on a Saturday was very unusual for Oscar, given his work schedule as owner of Lakeside Winery on the east shore of Seneca Lake. But Oscar and Jack had fallen back into their easy friendship now that nearly a year had passed since Devon's drowning.

It was an anniversary no one wanted to bring up.

"So how did a Seattle girl learn to make such good snowballs?" Jack asked Anne. "You don't get any snow at all out there, do you?"

Anne hefted a snowball, freshly made by Noah. He was industriously packing the snowballs and putting them up on the edge of the fort for Anne to throw.

"No, not right near us. But our parents used to take the three of us snow skiing every winter. We'd take snowballs up on the ski lift with us and throw them at the skiers below," Anne said.

Jack laughed, remembering how when he and Oscar were young teens they would stand on the highway overpass and drop snowballs onto passing cars.

"When Oscar gets here we should have a full-scale snowball fight," Jack said. "But I want you on my side."

Cass came out on the front porch, holding the telephone in her hand.

"Oscar's running late. He said to go ahead and eat and he'll eat whatever's left over," she said. "And Jack, he said you should check the news out of Washington."

A snowball whizzed by Jack's ear as he reached into his pocket.

Noah had a big grin on his face, until his Aunt Anne caught him with a solid snowball in the middle of his small chest.

"Crap," Jack said. "Seven text messages from Eli and Keith. I wish those guys would just make voice phone calls. I keep telling them."

He left the front yard snowball battleground and walked up the porch steps, stopping just long enough to give Cass a quick update as he read his messages.

"It's about that whole business of the Industrial Sedition Act. Apparently some sources are saying there's going to be an announcement next week, somehow connected to the trouble in the Mideast. It's not just the weird websites reporting this. It's some of the wire services, too."

Cass threw her arm around his shoulder and called to Anne and Noah.

"Well, the world can wait while we have pancakes and bacon," she said.

"And I made enough that even Oscar couldn't eat it all."

Chapter 3

The ballroom at the Rockwell Valley Lakeside Hotel was festooned with banners and gaily colored decorations, all of which Rod Mayenlyn hoped Grand Energy Services CEO Luther Burnside would appreciate.

The planned reception, dinner and party to celebrate the completion of the GES natural gas and liquid propane gas projects was also meant to draw attention to GES, which badly needed capital and investors for several other expansion projects in three western states.

The invitation list was a who's who of people in the natural gas industry, though many of the biggest hitters – and potential investors – had sent their regrets. They weren't interested in leaving their warm hideaway homes in Key West, Bonaire, Bequia and other tropical spots to come to freezing north-central Pennsylvania.

Still, it could generate a lot of favorable press – at least that was what Rod Mayenlyn was telling Burnside. Unfortunately the press RSVP list was pretty light, too. There wasn't that much of a story to tell about a big company getting its way and completing a project.

No matter what, Mayenlyn was sure that Burnside would still be glowing from his cover story in *BizzBuzz* magazine that had hit the stands two days before.

Burnside was featured in a photo on the cover, sitting in big chair and looking like the photographer was trying to imitate a photo once taken of late actor Marlon Brando, posed in character as Don Corleone in the movie *The Godfather*.

The headline on the cover said:

> "Luther Burnside: The New Don of Natural Gas"

Among the teaser boxes on the bottom of the magazine cover was also a headline about the Industrial Security Act:

> "The ISA: Urban myth or a good idea to protect U.S. resources?"

Mayenlyn wandered from the ballroom back into the kitchen area where, even though breakfast was still being served in the hotel dining room, the kitchen was buzzing with a dozen people, all baking and prepping the food for the night's festivities.

The head chef was shouting orders to his staff as he walked in and out of a shiny, new-looking 10' by 20' walk-in freezer that looked like a spaceship had been dropped in the middle of the huge kitchen area.

It had been designed and installed by a company in Big Flats, NY called Finger Lakes Engineering, a company known around the world for building extra-beefy cooling and refrigeration units – strong enough to withstand explosions from inside or outside the unit. It was overkill, but just the size needed now that the hotel was grabbing more and more business.

The chef nodded curtly to Mayenlyn, whose suit and tie – on a Saturday morning – were a dead giveaway he was probably a GES executive.

"We'll be ready," the chef said, anticipating Mayenlyn's question about how things were going.

"It strained our meat supplier to get that many filet mignons, but we have it covered. You should check with the bar guy. He had some issue with getting French champagne. I think he had to go with the some local sparkling wine instead."

Mayenlyn felt his heart drop slightly. The champagne was one of Luther Burnside's signature things at these dinners. Mayenlyn went back into the ballroom where the bartender was stacking bottles next to a 10-foot-long bar-on-wheels.

Out the front windows, Mayenlyn could see the buoys marking the underwater GES natural gas pipeline that was carrying natural gas at that very moment from the hydrofracked gas wells to the west to the storage in the salt caverns at the north end of the lake.

One sad-looking sign that said "S.O.S." was hanging crookedly off one of the markers, the last remnant of Alice McCallis's protest a month before.

"Please, please tell me you have the French champagne we ordered," Mayenlyn said. "Please."

The bartender stopped putting bottles on the shelf and stood to his full 6 foot, four-inch height, startling Mayenlyn slightly.

Remember Lot's Wife

"Couldn't get it. Just not available. I'm going to serve some really good local bubbly wine. It's from a Seneca Lake winery in New York. It actually tastes a lot better than that French champagne that was ordered."

Mayenlyn shook his head and stalked out, angry but quickly calculating how to sell the disappointment to Burnside as a positive.

Maybe I can sell it as a GES bone to throw to the locals, he thought. *Supporting the regional economy.*

The bartender went back to stocking his shelves, wondering if later he really *would* have the guts to slip a few drops of a clear liquid laxative into some of the drinks he served to the GES executives at tonight's party.

It sure sounded funny the day before when he joked about it with his grandmother, who had been regaling him with tales about a group called the Wolverines who had wreaked havoc with their pranks against GES and other gas companies several years ago.

"But don't get caught," Alice McCallis had said. "Times have changed."

Chapter 4

The staff of the *Horseheads Clarion* was divided on whether or not to attend the Grand Energy Services victory *soirée* at the Rockwell Valley Lakeside Hotel that night.

"I have better things to do on my Saturday night than watch those arrogant bastards gloat about ruining Rockwell Valley and putting a bomb in the salt caverns," Keith Everlight said.

The thought of going to the GES event had soured days of celebration in the wake of New York's sudden and unexpected ban on hydrofracking. The staff had been writing stories for days about what impact that would have, most of them positive. And the stories were full of hope that the fracking ban would somehow translate into shutting down the storage of fracked gas in New York state as well.

And then Keith, Jack, Eli and reporters Rue and Jill had ended up in the office to talk about the Industrial Sedition Act and if they needed to put something up on the *Horseheads Clarion* website right away.

They had barely shaken the snow off their shoes before Eli announced that the earlier reports from different wire services were most likely trial balloons put up by whoever it was in the federal government who thought the ISA and the proposal for the Federal Anti-Eco-terrorism Administration were good ideas.

"It turns out the wire services just pulled most of their information from *Veritas For All*," Eli said. "But they even didn't bother to attribute it."

He shook his head in disgust.

Jack felt his stomach growl – the pancakes and bacon from an hour before disagreeing with his digestive system.

"Well, I think it would be a gracious thing for us to attend the GES dinner, smile, and know that first thing Monday morning we will continue to hit these guys with everything we have," Jack said. "They won this round. That doesn't mean we give up. And keep an eye on this ISA thing, even as farfetched as it seems."

Jack watched Keith spinning a coin on his desk. Then he looked at the rest of the staff.

Remember Lot's Wife

"But I am asking one person here to stay put in Horseheads. That's you, Eli, for obvious reasons. When *is* the baby due, anyway? It's this week, isn't it?"

Eli for a moment looked like he had completely forgotten that his wife Shania could give birth at any moment to their son, the naming of whom was proving elusive.

Shania wanted to name the baby Elvis. But Eli said a more pedestrian first name was really needed, given that the baby's last name would be Gupta.

"Anyway, Eli, you're here. And whatever the rest of you guys decide is okay with me. But I'm going. Cass *might* go with me. Or Anne. Oscar's going for sure in my car. So I have room if somebody wants to carpool," Jack said.

"The weather is supposed to be crystal clear, in case you're worried about snow. And there's a full moon. Might be beautiful looking at the lake."

Keith's coin stopped spinning and fell over.

"Heads. Crap. Okay. I'm going," Keith said. "I can't wait to see that moon reflecting on the water – with those scenic gas pipeline markers."

Chapter 5

The phone rang six times in the control room of the Grand Energy Services salt cavern natural gas and liquid propane storage facility at the north end of Rockwell Valley Lake before Billy Jack Bordin heard it and picked it up.

The traffic on Interstate 86 had cleared enough that Curtis Wildemon was able to get rolling just a few minutes after he had told Bordin to call in a second operator to be in the control room with him.

On the other end of the phone line, Wildemon could hear the blaring radio in the background and was just about to blast Bordin for having it turned on at all when Bordin spoke over the noise.

"Chief. I was just about to call you," he said, seeing the flashing red **System Error** message on the screen for the first time.

"I think we just went offline or something. I think we need to reboot the computer."

Wildemon braked his car and jerked his steering wheel so hard to the right to get onto the shoulder of the freeway he nearly put the car into the ditch.

"What the hell are you talking about? Unless the power went down, we *can't* be offline, it's a closed system. And the back-up generators take over anyway. What's going on?"

Bordin looked at all the gauges and realized that while the control screen said **System Error**, all the various measurements of gas pressures, brine pond levels and gas flows were normal.

"Well, um. The main control screen says **System Error**, so I thought I should reboot the main computer. *Um.* That's what we did in Texas," Bordin said.

Wildemon's scream was so loud Bordin almost dropped the phone on the floor.

"*Jesus Christ!!!!!* Do not. I repeat do NOT reboot that computer. You could scram the whole goddam facility. Everything would stop cold," Wildemon said. "I thought I showed you what to do with that screen. Christ, don't do anything until I get there. Who did you call to come in? Are they on their way?"

Bordin scrambled over to the control room bulletin board where he found the list of names of other operators.

"Yeah, well, I, um. I got two busy signals. And, um, then I saw the screen flashing," Bordin said.

"But, um, do I need somebody still?"

Wildemon barked back.

"No. I'll be there in 15 to 20 minutes. But you watch the gauges, not the screen. If you see any dips or spikes, you call me right away. *Right away*, Bordin. And turn off that goddamn radio."

Wildemon hung up the phone and pulled out into the now-light traffic, giving his car a shot of gas that pushed his speed up to over 80 miles per hour as he approached the New York-Pennsylvania border.

"Goddamn know-nothing Texas *asshole*," he said aloud in his car.

He was so angry at Bordin and distracted by thinking about the **System Error** message that he blew right through a New York State Trooper radar trap.

He didn't make it to the Rockwell Valley Grand Energy Services salt cavern storage facility for nearly an hour.

Chapter 6

The consensus of Cass and Anne was that Jack should wear a bow tie to the Grand Energy Services banquet and reception that evening.

Jack's assessment was that he looked pretty silly in a bow tie.

But he knew better than to argue with the two sisters — at least at the outset of such conversations, which is why he found himself staring into a mirror, a floppy red bow tie glaring back at him against his cream yellow shirt.

"Really?" Jack said. "Really?"

Anne reached around in front of Jack, straightening the tie slightly, then stood off to one side.

"Jack? Yes. Really," she said. "It looks *so* stylish. Honest to God. You look handsome."

Jack fussed for moment with the tie, noticing that it was almost 4 p.m. and Oscar would be arriving soon to drive down to the festivities.

He decided that he would leave the bow tie on for the moment, knowing he could ditch it and slip on a regular tie with a tidy Windsor knot just before he left.

He looked in the mirror one more time.

You know, they might be right, he thought. *Looks very George Will, I suppose.*

He was looking intently at the tie when he noticed Cass and Noah slipping into the room from upstairs.

He let out a quick "Wow!" before he caught himself as he turned around.

Cass was wearing a black sleeveless cocktail dress with pearls. She had piled her hair up on top of her head and whatever makeup she had put on made her look like an actress ready for a red-carpet movie premiere.

And she is an actress, Jack thought. *A beautiful one.*

But then Jack looked at Noah, who was sporting a smile as big as Jack had ever seen — and wearing a child's suit, a cream yellow shirt and sporting a floppy red bow tie.

"Jesus. Noah! You look great too, buddy. Just great," Jack said, half-laughing and feeling some tears welling up.

"You know what, Noah. You look a lot better than I do. Maybe you should go to this thing tonight with your Aunt Cass instead of me."

Anne grabbed her cell phone and starting snapping photos of the three of them. First it was a nice formal shot, then bunched together in a hug. Jack picked up Noah and held him in his arms. The last shot featured Belle the Labrador in front.

"Okay," Anne said. "I'll go get dressed. I'd like to get in some of these photos before we all go."

She headed upstairs with Belle and Noah on her heels.

Jack looked confused when he realized Noah was going, too, and that the suit and bow tie were not just a joke on Jack.

"I should have warned you earlier," Cass said. "I am sorry. But we're *all* going. The whole family. Those GES people need to see *our* faces. Just like you say in your columns. The faces of the community? Plus it might be fun. Really. We're all getting cabin fever. Right?"

Cass gave Jack a friendly punch to his chest, the same kind of little tap Devon used to do.

The punch reminded Jack – again – how much Cass *was* like Devon: A walking surprise machine.

And then he thought about all the *behind-the-scenes* work it had taken for the women to get that suit of clothes for Noah – and even having Noah keep it a secret.

"I'm not so sure about taking Noah. But I can't wait to show off the two beautiful Walsh sisters in Rockwell Valley," Jack said.

Cass and Jack were still hugging when Oscar arrived – wearing a floppy red bow tie.

Chapter 7

Rockwell Valley Police Chief Melvin "Bobo" Caprino knew that if he made the arrest he wanted to make at the Grand Energy Services reception, it could be his last one.

And Lt. Del Dewitt – who had put together the evidence package linking Calvin Boviné to the assaults on Prof. Charles Avery Sawmill and Keith Everlight – was pretty sure he might be looking for new employment soon, too.

The two men were looking at the forensic evidence report spread out on Bobo's desk, waiting for the former Mrs. Melvin Caprino to get done with dressing and putting on her makeup in the ladies' room.

"I figured out how to jigger it so I can get my full retirement," Bobo said. "If they do try to fire me, I already found an attorney who specializes in wrongful terminations. And Del, with that education of yours, you can get a job anywhere."

Dewitt looked at the DNA evidence file again, hoping Bobo was right. He had taken some DNA samples from Keith Everlight's fingernails after Everlight told him that besides punching his assailant that night in Sawmill's driveway, he had raked his fingers across his eyes and scratched the man's skin under the ski mask.

Enough skin came off under his nails that the lab was able to make a positive I.D. when comparing it with a DNA sample Dewitt had gotten from a wine glass Boviné sipped from at a GES celebration months before. Dewitt took the sample, hoping to link Boviné to the vandalism at Lasse Espinola's farm and other supposed Wolverine activities, but that was before CEO Luther Burnside had sweet-talked the chief into ignoring that particular crime.

He was even reviewing the evidence from Tyrone Arthur Garber's fall from the railroad trestle.

"Why the change of heart, chief?" Dewitt asked. "I mean, why now?"

Bobo straightened his tie and sighed.

"Oh, I don't know. I guess I just missed her bitching at me all the time somehow," he said.

"No, no, chief," Dewitt said. "Not *Alicia*. I mean Boviné. I thought you had, um, an *arrangement* with GES not to go after him."

Dewitt squirmed uncomfortably in the chair, unsure if bringing up Caprino's willingness to bend the law for GES had been such a good idea.

Before he could answer, Alicia, Bobo Caprino's ex-wife and the incumbent lead dispatcher of the Rockwell Valley Police Department, breezed into Bobo's office, wearing a black sheath dress that made Bobo realize that in the roughly year and half since their divorce, Alicia had lost at least 25 pounds and been doing some serious working out.

He found himself sucking in his stomach.

"Hellooooooo, *there*," Dewitt said, immediately regretting the comment when Alicia shot him such a hostile look it almost made him spill his coffee.

"Whoa there! I'm just sayin' you look *nice*. Not your average dispatcher. You know."

Bobo nodded appreciatively, too, and smiled.

"Shut up, Del, before she decks you. And Alicia. You do look great. And you're packing, right?"

Alicia patted the inside of her thigh to indicate where she had strapped a slim .32 caliber pistol.

"We better all get going over to the hotel," Bobo said. "It was nice of them to provide us with a guest list that showed Boviné would be there.

"Oh, and Del? The short is answer is Alice McCallis."

Dewitt looked confused as he put down his coffee mug on the way out the door.

"That goddamn rowboat?" Bobo said. "Christ, she's 80 years old now, I think. We watched her paddling out there in the lake in a snowstorm to put out her protest signs while those GES jerks like Pennisen were laughing at her. Laughing! That bullshit ends tonight."

Alicia took Bobo's arm on one side and Dewitt's on the other as they strolled through the police squad room on their way out the front door of the Rockwell Valley Police Station.

The dispatcher on duty was so stunned she didn't see the light on the telephone panel blinking.

It was a call from Rockwell Valley Mayor Will Pennisen, who was already at the hotel sucking up to Grand Energy Services CEO Luther Burnside and wondered why Caprino wasn't there.

Chapter 8

The flu virus working its way through the Rockwell Valley community was wreaking havoc on Curtis Wildemon's scheduling of operators at the Grand Energy Systems salt cavern storage facility.

Remember Lot's Wife

He was down three operators already. And with the whole community somewhat spooked by the rumored arrival of a GES executive with the Ebola virus that night, any sniffle would cause the normally macho gas employees to call in sick.

And so at 6 p.m. Wildemon reluctantly called Billy Jack Bordin *back* into work as an operator until the two men on the 11 p.m. to 7 a.m. shift staff came on.

One of the normal 3 p.m. to 11 p.m. operators had called Wildemon and said he felt really sick and needed to leave. The other operator said he felt ill, too, but would be okay to finish.

"Billy Jack, you are going to have to step up here and be the lead dog even though you worked a shift already today," Wildemon said. "You'll have Hegas working with you, but he says he doesn't feel good either. So you'll be in charge. I'd do it myself but I have to go to this party thing at the hotel. But goddamn it ... if you have any issues, you *call* me. Hegas might not be a lot of help. Here's your chance to make up for this morning's fuckup."

Billy arrived at the storage facility as the worker he was replacing was driving out. He noticed that the supposedly sick operator was grinning like an idiot as he fishtailed his pickup truck past Billy's car, even sticking his arm out the window to give Billy a one-finger salute.

Sick, my ass, Billy thought. *Oh well, I need the overtime. And I bet Hegas isn't sick either.*

Hegas, like Billy, was a recent Rockwell Valley import, brought in a wave of new employees to run the gas storage facility. No one knew his full name except maybe Wildemon and the people in the GES payroll department.

But he liked to be called Hegas from Vegas, even though he was from Oklahoma when he had worked for GES. As far as Billy could tell, Hegas had never been near Nevada.

He was already a local legend for being a madman-party guy and had been thrown out of three Rockwell Valley bars for being too rowdy.

The door at the bottom of the tower leading to the stairwell was locked. And repeated banging on it by Billy didn't get a rise out of Hegas.

Billy called the control room on his cell phone, slightly worried that Hegas actually *was* sick. The phone rang a half-dozen times before Hegas finally picked it up.

"Yeah. Hey, Mr. Wildemon, nobody's here yet."

Billy quickly explained that he had been called in to work but had left his card for the key lock at home.

It was a full minute before Billy heard the door buzz, signaling it was unlocked.

He bounded up the stairs and waited at the control room entry door until Hegas buzzed him through the second security door into the tower control room.

The smell of the marijuana hit him immediately, even though a small fan on a desk was blowing out an open window.

"Hello there, Texas!" Hegas said. "It's Saturday night!"

Chapter 9

The ballroom at the Rockwell Valley Lakeside Hotel was jammed.

Jack, Cass and Oscar made their way back over to the bar after sending Anne and Noah back to Horseheads in

Jack's car when Anne pleaded she had a headache and didn't know anyone. And it was obvious the adult hubbub wasn't much fun for Noah.

As the room filled up and the conversations got louder, Noah had started holding his hands over his ears, making a scrunched up face – as if the noise hurt.

But thank God he can hear, Jack thought. *Thank God.*

Keith Everlight had arrived as Anne's headache was coming on and offered to drive Jack, Cass and Oscar back to Horseheads later.

"Not sure how long you want to stick around," Keith said. "But except for the GES big shots, the community people here are pretty cool."

Keith had become a local hero in the last year in Rockwell Valley for his coverage of GES, the Alice McCallis arrests and trials, and his dashboard cam incident story that had graphically demonstrated how GES was bullying the town.

When he had arrived at the GES party tonight, a lot of people had wanted to chat with him – even a couple of friendly members of the Rockwell Valley Town Council.

Cass and Oscar were at the bar waiting for the very tall bartender to give them a glass of wine when Cass felt a tap on her shoulder.

"Um, I don't know if you remember me or not," Bobo Caprino said. "We met at a GES party awhile back."

Cass took her drink from Alice McCallis's grandson and turned around to greet him.

"I sure do. And I have to say, what I remember most is you on your hands and knees looking through the crowd," Cass said, a big smile on her face. "You told me that night it was police business."

Caprino's face flushed while he quickly introduced his ex-wife Alicia to Cass, explaining that it really *was* police work that had him crawling around on the floor that night.

He had just enough to drink that he told Cass the case he had been working on *that* night was going to be closed very soon. Maybe even at tonight's party.

Alicia gave him such a shot in the ribs with her elbow that he spilled some of his drink.

"Sorry," Bobo said. "I talk too much sometimes."

Jack joined them just as the police chief was leaving and grabbed a glass of wine.

"Interesting that these guys are serving your signature Riesling with other New York wines," Jack said to Oscar. "I didn't think you had this much Oscar's Boot left over."

The grin on Oscar's face told Jack there was a longer story about the wine being served.

Outside of the floor-to-ceiling lakeside windows the moon was reflecting on the water, making for a postcard-perfect scene. At least it would have had it not been for the warning buoys bobbing on the surface above the natural gas pipeline sitting on the lake bottom.

Police Lt. Del Dewitt sipped his glass of wine while he looked out at the water, happy that the chief wasn't a real hard-ass about alcohol on the job at social functions, even when they expected action.

With the amount of coffee Dewitt swallowed most days, he could drink a bottle of wine and barely get his amped-up self back down to where most normal people operated.

Dewitt heard a booming voice in the crowd behind him he was pretty sure might be Grand Energy Services CEO Luther Burnside. Dewitt had just read an article that morning in a business magazine about Burnside being called the "The New Don of Natural Gas."

He turned around and saw Luther Burnside with a GES staff member he thought was a guy named Michael standing about 20 feet away.

Alworthy, Althouse? No, no, Ahlbright. Yes, Ahlbright.

Along with them was a new-to-the-community GES employee named Wildemon who was running the new gas storage facility.

But looming behind the trio was a big hulk of a man wearing an expensive but poorly fitting suit, his huge feet visible between the other men's legs.

And I can guess what that bulge is under his coat, Dewitt thought.

Dewitt shuffled across the room to find the police chief, who had just walked away from a tall woman who Dewitt was pretty sure was editor Jack Stafford's girlfriend or maybe one of his reporters.

"We're gonna need a bigger boat," Dewitt said.

Bobo looked puzzled, as he frequently did when Dewitt tried to be clever.

Alicia laughed, but let Dewitt explain.

"Chief, didn't you ever see the movie *Jaws*? Really? God …"

Chapter 10

Wilmot Carville got to his Rockwell Valley lakeshore house about 6:30 p.m. from his janitorial job at Rockwell Valley Hospital, totally spooked from watching the doctors and nurses spend hours doing the final preparations on the new isolation facilities attached to the intensive care unit.

He had heard that some big shot from Grand Energy Services who had contracted the Ebola virus in Nigeria was being flown in for treatment and to be nearer to his family with Christmas less than a week away.

Wilmot couldn't get out of the hospital fast enough when his boss sent him home after only working three hours instead of his usual eight.

The hospital administration seemed a little spooked and sent all non-essential staff home as people walked around in moon suits, practicing for when the GES executive arrived at 7 or 8 p.m.

Wilmot figured they didn't want extra witnesses for the arrival of their first-ever Ebola patient and the first time the isolation facilities had been used, just in case there was a screw-up.

Working swing shift was Wilmot's favorite because his wife, Amethyst, worked at the GES main office in downtown Rockwell Valley from 8 a.m. to 5 p.m., leaving him most days to do whatever he wanted without having to follow spousal commands.

And most nights she was snoring like a buffalo when he came home, though in the last few months her sister Alicia had been hanging out at their house quite late, with the women talking conspiratorially about Alicia's ex-husband, Police Chief Bobo Caprino.

"You're off way early," Amethyst barked at Wilmot as he walked in the front door. "You didn't get fired or something?" She gave a forced laugh and half-snorted.

Wilmot kept moving, giving his wife a quick hand wave of *hello,* making sure he slumped his shoulders to look tired as he whisked through the living room.

The television was blaring one of those amateur *make-yourself-a-star* talent contests.

As he went into the kitchen, Wilmot spotted an empty wine bottle on the table.

Oh shit, he thought. *I'm not ready for this.*

"There's wine open in the fridge," Amethyst yelled over the sound out of a slightly off-key teenage soprano girl trying valiantly to sing "The Impossible Dream," from *Man of La Mancha.*

He opened the refrigerator and saw that a *second* wine bottle in there was half-empty.

I am out of here, Wilmot thought.

"Thanks. But I'm going to grab a beer and check out the boat," he shouted from the kitchen. "Might be a good night to fish. Full moon."

When she didn't respond, Wilmot peeked warily around the corner.

Amethyst's mouth was hanging open, her eyes closed.

Run Forrest Run! Wilmot thought.

He moved deftly through the house to the closed-in front porch where his heavy winter coats, boots, hat and most important – his fishing gear and stocked beer cooler – were always ready for winter fishing forays.

It was a mild, clear December night with a light breeze out of the north. The temperature was hovering just at freezing. And as Wilmot gently opened the door that led to the lake and his small cabin-cruiser-style fishing boat, he could see it would be a perfect night on the water.

The Rockwell Valley Lakeside Hotel lights five miles away were illuminating the water where he was pretty sure the fish would be congregating.

All around that gas pipe, Wilmot thought. *Easy-peasy.*

Chapter 11

The open window, the electric fan and most of a can of aerosol air freshener had done a good job of getting the pot smell out of the control room.

Plus Billy Jack Bordin had called Curtis Wildemon's cell phone to tell him he had arrived and Hegas was actually feeling better.

"Enjoy the party, boss, everything is totally copacetic here. Totally."

Bordin could tell that Wildemon really hated it when someone used words like *copacetic*. He often made snide references to "college boys" when people did.

But the phone call plus Wildemon's likely imbibing plenty of GES-paid-for booze would keep him far away from the control tower tonight.

And everything runs itself here, so what the hell? Bordin thought.

The GES plans called for cutting back to a single operator within a few months anyway. The two-man crews were only a sop to the federal and state regulators who insisted on the redundancy.

And in addition to that, there was the red *panic button.*

Bordin looked at the three-inch bright red button on the wall by the door that had the word **STOP** in white letters printed on it.

Above it a small sign, also red with white letters that said: **EMERGENCY ONLY**.

It reminded him of a similar-looking button on a web printing press his father had operated at a small Texas newspaper. When you pushed that button to do an emergency stop, the press rollers braked immediately, usually shredding the web of newsprint and requiring hours of work to get the press printing newspapers again.

Bordin had been warned by Wildemon that the same thing would happen here. The button would send out an electronic signal to shut down all operations – the natural gas flowing into the caverns, propane being put in or removed and all the other automatic systems that controlled the entire plant.

It would even send a signal to the railroad to halt shipments of LPG and throw a switch to keep trains from bringing LPG tankers into the newly constructed railroad car siding.

"To be honest, Bordin, we don't know *completely* what would happen if you push that button," Wildemon had said during Bordin's training. "But we are sure it would stop the flow of gas and LPG. And it would be a fucking mess to get everything going again."

Bordin looked at the clock and realized it was just past 7 p.m. and that he was suddenly starving.

Probably a contact high from the pot, he thought.

He suggested to Hegas that they order a pizza delivered to the control room – even though the rules expressly said no food or drink was allowed around the controls.

"We better get *two*, man," Hegas said. "I got a serious case of the munchies. Ho-ho!"

He laughed so hard he nearly slid off his chair onto the floor.

Chapter 12

Jack Stafford and Grand Energy Systems CEO Luther Burnside were sizing each other up from across the crowded ballroom, each stealing glances at the other while trying not to be too obvious.

Jack wanted to let him know – in a polite, cocktail-party sort of way – that while GES had gotten to build what Jack believed was a dangerous and detrimental gas storage project and pipelines, the *Horseheads Clarion* was going to keep hammering away at the corruption that had allowed its approval, the likelihood of an incident and any violations of environmental laws.

Burnside wanted to tell Jack in a considerably *less polite* manner that the newspaper had lost its crusade, GES was planning on a big expansion of its company in New York soon and that there wasn't a goddamn thing Jack or the *Horseheads Clarion* could do about it.

Michael Ahlbright had cautioned Burnside earlier in the day against gloating too much and confronting Stafford. He even reminded Burnside of Mark Twain's old saw, "Never pick a fight with people who buy ink by the barrel."

Burnside brushed aside the caution.

"Actually, Michael, you gave me an idea," Burnside said. "The *Clarion* doesn't print its own paper, right? Let's buy the company where he gets it printed. We can jack his rates up and make his life miserable. I like that idea. Do it."

While the two men considered the right moment to approach each other, Police Chief Bobo Caprino, Lt. Del Dewitt and police dispatcher and spouse Alicia Caprino were all circling the room, watching an increasingly nervous Calvin Boviné.

Boviné had moved into the middle of the ballroom, where he continually rotated his position, aware of the police chief and his lieutenant. He could tell there was something odd about Alicia, but the room was so full of half-drunk people he wasn't sure what it was about her that bothered him.

The room had three exits leading into the main hotel and large doors leading to the lakeside patio which had bright red *EXIT* signs above them. The patio was empty. All the tables and chairs that normally sat out there during the summer had been stored away. Snow was heaped up in two-foot mounds.

Boviné caught Caprino looking directly at him from the hotel side of the room. Dewitt was only 30 feet to Caprino's left. And the woman had disappeared.

He started staring across the room towards CEO Luther Burnside, putting a concerned look on his face, as if something was wrong, while still watching Caprino and Dewitt out of the corner of his eye.

It worked.

Suckers, Boviné thought.

Caprino and Dewitt swiveled their attention to Burnside for a moment while Boviné backed up slowly towards the lakeside doors.

He spun around and broke out of the crowd, heading quickly for the patio doors and the outside.

His hand was on the door handle when he heard a male voice behind him.

"Hey *Bo-vine*, I think you forgot to put on your ski mask. It's cold out."

Chapter 13

The satellite radio in Jack's car went in and out of service as Anne drove herself and Noah home to Horseheads.

Noah had calmed down immediately when they got out of the noisy ballroom. He fussed just a little in the car.

Poor little guy is probably tired and missing Jack and Cass, Anne thought.

But the food Noah had managed to shovel in during his short time at the GES reception had filled his belly sufficiently that he had finally dozed off halfway home.

Anne left the radio on a station that played a lot of child-friendly music, light tunes and some recordings from Public Broadcasting children's television programs.

As they drove along, an announcer was talking to a children's book author about nursery rhymes, reciting a few favorites that Jack, Cass and Anne would read to Noah at night when he went to bed.

The tunes brought back memories for Anne, thinking about how she and Cass and their late sister Devon sat in the backseat of the Walsh station wagon on Vashon Island, listening to many of these same songs.

When the television was on at Jack's house – *and not tuned to some damned news program,* Anne thought – she and Cass would try to find PBS children's programming for Noah to watch.

He loved it.

For Anne, it brought back of a flood of memories of Devon. When Devon had died, Anne had blamed Jack for taking her to Tonga and the drowning accident. It was irrational to blame Jack. She understood that intellectually. But she still felt it sometimes and struggled when Jack came to Vashon Island and stayed with her and Cass while he recuperated from his near breakdown.

In the month or so since coming to New York to try to get Jack to let Noah be raised by her and Cass, she had *slowly* changed her mind. Jack *was* a good man. She understood the goodness that Devon had seen and what had drawn her to him. Now Anne was coming to believe it might take all three of them to be parents to Noah to give him the family he needs.

The idea made her smile, though *that* thought faded as the car skidded on some black ice.

I just cannot live here in the winter, she thought. *This is all crazy.*

Noah was awake as they pulled into the driveway, rubbing the sleep from his eyes.

As Anne got out of the car, she thought she could still hear the radio.

Didn't I turn the car off?, she thought.

She turned back and reached for the steering column.

Oh my God, she thought. Oh my God.

A smiling, alert, wide-awake little Noah Walter Stafford was swaying his head back and forth as he sat still buckled in his seatbelt, reciting what he had just heard on the radio.

> "An itsy, bitsy spider went up the water spout,
>   Down came the rain and washed the spider out."

Anne dropped her cell phone in the snow twice as she fumbled to call Jack and Cass to tell them.

"This is Jack Stafford, leave a message."

Shit, Anne thought. *Shit! Please pick up, please.*

When he didn't she left a message.

"Jack, I, I, I. Jack, my God, Noah was talking in the car. Talking! He can talk again!"

She ended the call and turned back to the car where Noah was still sitting, looking at her curiously.

"Where's my da?" he asked. "I'm hungry."

Chapter 14

Marijuana was not Billy Jack Bordin's drug of choice. He was a beer and whiskey kind of guy, though he had found that the younger women he dated really like pot better for the most part.

After spending a half-hour getting the smell of the pot out of the control room, he told Hegas that pot was off their menu for the night. Bordin didn't want to get fired in case Wildemon decided to make a surprise visit.

Bordin's edict didn't bother Hegas much. He had smoked enough that he was starting to doze off.

"Man, where's the pizzas?" Hegas said. "I am *sooooo* hungry."

Bordin picked up the field glasses and scanned the property, well lit with floodlights and illuminated by the new 60-foot-tall flare stack that seemed to be burning non-stop to get rid of excess gas from the natural gas and propane grid that criss-crossed the lakeside facility.

Out on the lake, he could see a light – maybe a small boat – heading towards the Rockwell Valley Lakeside Hotel, visible tonight in the crisp air.

Goddamn cold night to be on a boat, Bordin thought. *Damn cold.*

Bordin checked his watch and saw it had been more than a half-hour since they called for the two pizzas. The girl who took the order had promised they would be there in 30 minutes.

He turned around to ask Hegas if he had any money to help pay the pizza delivery person when they arrived. But Hegas was sound asleep, his feet up on the control console, his mouth wide open.

Bordin didn't really want to reach into Hegas' pocket. Instead he rifled through his own wallet, pulling out the two $20 bills he kept in the back of his billfold for emergencies.

Fifteen minutes he later wished he hadn't been so squeamish about reaching into another man's pocket.

If he gone searching for Hegas's cash, Bordin probably would have found Hegas's key card for the downstairs door to let himself back in after he paid a pimply faced teenager for the two pizzas.

Instead, Billy Jack Bordin, dressed only in a t-shirt, jeans and work boots, was standing outside holding two steaming-hot large pepperoni and mushroom pizzas.

And he was screaming at the top of his lungs for Hegas to open the door and let him back into where his fleece jacket, cell phone and car keys were stacked neatly on the counter next to the company field glasses, right where he put them.

Wake up, you stoned freak, Bordin thought. *Wake up!*

He screamed one more time, looking up at the windows.

Then he noticed that the flare stack wasn't burning.

And most of the lights above the propane storage caverns had gone black.

Chapter 15

His hair-trigger temper had gotten Calvin Boviné in trouble many times in his life. But his fists – and people's fear at his size and fierce scowl – always saved him.

Still, he *knew* it was a mistake to stop at the hotel patio doors and turn around to see who had called his name, especially mispronouncing it.

Keith Everlight didn't realize that as Boviné stopped and turned, Rockwell Valley Police Chief Bobo Caprino and Lt. Del Dewitt were frantically trying to get through the close-packed crowd. All Keith could see in front of him was what looked like 300-plus pounds of solid muscle with fists the size of canned hams.

He looks like a rhino, Keith thought. *And a pretty pissed-off one, too.*

Boviné closed the 15-foot distance between the men so fast that Keith was nearly caught off guard, backing up quickly to avoid what he was sure would be a blow that could crack his skull.

But just as Boviné got close, he froze and stood up straight, a surprised look on his face.

Alicia Caprino, in her cocktail dress and heels, looking for all the world like one of those sexy women in a James Bond movie, had the barrel of her .32 caliber automatic pressed against a spot just under Boviné's left ear, pushing hard enough that he was up on his toes slightly.

"Police, sweetheart," Alicia said. "Don't move a muscle or you'll be in a wheelchair eating mush for the rest of your life."

The up-on-the-toes stance proved to be more strategy than fear.

Boviné tipped his head to the right and pivoted away from Alicia, knocking her down while she fired her gun into the air, hitting an antique glass chandelier that would later cost the Town of Rockwell Valley $3,600 to repair.

"Boviné," Keith shouted. "Boviné."

Boviné whirled to take a quick bone-crushing swing at Keith Everlight, only to see that Keith had disappeared. Boviné turned, kicked Alicia's gun away from her hand and headed for the door. But Keith was standing between Boviné and the door.

How do you stop a charging rhino? Keith thought.

Chapter 16

The surface of Rockwell Valley Lake was so smooth that it almost lulled Wilmot to sleep as he motored slowly south towards the Rockwell Valley Lakeside Hotel.

Even with his engine running, he could occasionally hear snatches of music being played as people opened doors to the outside from the ballroom where he knew Grand Energy Services had some kind of big party going on.

He munched on day-old pizza he had grabbed from the refrigerator – a leftover from the night before when he had come home after 11 p.m.

The hospital was about a half mile directly south from the hotel, and he could see its upper floors and the helicopter pad on the roof. Wilmot had snuck up there a few times to see the spectacular view of the lake, all the way north to the new GES gas storage facility.

Wilmot could see the hospital roof was all lit up. The doctors were probably waiting for the expected Ebola patient to arrive by chopper.

A gentle north wind had come up, barely 5 mph, as Wilmot turned off his outboard engine 100 yards from the GES buoys marking the no-anchoring zone over the gas pipeline.

As he dropped his anchor, he could see a few small knots of people outside smoking cigarettes on the hotel patio.

If this wind kicks up at all, they'll be back inside quick, he thought.

He set two long fishing lines, baited and with heavy sinkers, in the water, letting out plenty of line so it would drift closer to the buoys. Since the construction of the pipeline, the fishing had actually improved at that end of the lake, people said.

Wilmot thought he could make out the steady *whump-whump* sound of an approaching helicopter far in the distance.

Glad I'm not at the hospital, he thought. *I might even take a sick day tomorrow, too.*

He was huddling under the boat's canopy, staying out of the breeze and dozing off from the effects of his third beer and four slices of pizza when both his fishing lines started to move.

He was groggy when he started to reel in the first line. It didn't feel like there was a fish on, he noticed. But it definitely felt like something was tugging on both lines.

In the few minutes it took Wilmot to find his handheld spotlight, he felt his boat swing on its anchor, shifting around slowly so that the bow headed south and not north.

Now that's really weird, he thought. *The wind is still out of the north. I feel it. And it's goddamn cold.*

When the spotlight hit where his bait had been near the buoys marking the natural gas pipeline, Wilmot could see large bubbles popping on the surface here and there.

The bubbles were creating a small current pushing slowly in his direction.

Chapter 17

Jack and Cass waited in the parking lot while Keith Everlight gave his statement to Rockwell Valley Police Lt. Del Dewitt.

His hand still hurt, but the ice bag provided by the bartender was easing the swelling.

As Calvin Boviné had charged towards Keith standing in front of the hotel patio doors, Alicia Caprino, still laying on the floor after being knocked down, managed to slip her foot between his legs just as he started to move forward.

His huge bulk gave him too much forward momentum and he went down hard onto the wood floor.

As Boviné tried to push himself up on his hands and knees, Keith stepped in and threw three punches as hard as he could muster: Two to the side of Boviné's head, the third an uppercut to the forehead that snapped Boviné's head back with a cracking sound.

By the time Dewitt and Police Chief Melvin "Bobo" Caprino got across the room, Boviné was on the floor groaning, Keith was holding his quickly swelling hand and Oscar Wilson, winery owner and probably the *only* man in the room who came close in size to Calvin Boviné, was sitting on Boviné's back, holding him down.

Oscar had a huge smile on his face.

"Keith should be done in a few minutes," Jack said. "The police wanted him to go the station, but I explained that we needed to get back to Horseheads. And I see the state police just arrived. Quite a story, this will be."

Inside the hotel there was near pandemonium among the community members, the GES executives and employees and particularly in a small knot of men including CEO Luther Burnside, his aides Michael Ahlbright and Rod Mayenlyn, Rockwell Valley Mayor Will Pennisen and Rockwell Valley Judge Owen T. Beigenlaw.

And as the police chief and Lt. Dewitt led Boviné through the crowd to the state police cruiser outside, Caprino stopped where the men were chatting.

"The state police will be taking this suspect into custody outside, right now," Caprino said.

"And gentlemen, I would like to officially request *none* of you leave Rockwell Valley until we get a chance to sort some things out about Mr. Boviné's recent activities on behalf of GES."

Caprino walked about 10 steps, stopped and turned around to face the men.

"You, too, judge. There's a federal marshal on his way here right now who has asked to talk to you personally."

Chapter 18

The pot-induced dream that held Hegas's attention ended suddenly from a combination of acute hunger and a cracking sound a few feet from his head.

He shook himself to wake up, disoriented by the sleep and the pot.

He tried to focus on a nearby window that appeared to have a crack in it. And outside where there should be *so* many lights that it looked like a city, there were just scattered pinpricks around the property.

The control room lights were on, but Hegas thought he could hear the sound of a generator humming in the lower floors of the building.

He remembered the pizza and then realized that Billy Jack Bordin was missing.

Damn, he thought. *Did he leave me here alone?*

Then a rock bounced off the already cracked window.

Oh shit, Hegas thought. *Bordin!*

He tried to focus his eyes to find the button to open the doors down below, remembering faintly that Bordin didn't have his key card to get back in.

As he buzzed, he heard the downstairs door open and slam shut, added to the thumping of Bordin's boots coming up the stairs. Hegas was still puzzled by the lack of lights outside as he buzzed Bordin into the upstairs door.

Bordin burst into the room, tinged blue from the cold and shaking.

"Check the fucking gauges, Hegas. Jesus Christ, something's going down," he yelled.

Hegas glanced at the dials, but was much more interested in the pizza.

I wonder how we can reheat that, he thought.

"Oh God, we have to call Wildemon. *Now*. I don't know what to do," Bordin said. "Look at the gauges."

Most of the needle gauges for the system controlling the liquid propane gas salt cavern storage were fluctuating back and forth, like the tachometer of a revving automobile engine. The digital gauges had numbers on them that didn't make much sense to Bordin.

The only steady needle gauge indicated that brine water was flowing at a fast clip into the largest of the LPG storage caverns where the pressure of brine was used to push the propane up and out to load it into waiting tanker trucks.

Except there were *no* LPG tanker trucks being loaded.

Bordin shifted over to look at the gauges for the system controlling the natural gas salt cavern storage. They were all steady except for the three that showed the pressure in the pipeline that brought natural gas from the hydrofracked wells from the west to the storage facility.

Bordin wasn't sure, but it looked like the gauges were showing pressures half of what they had been earlier in the day when he was working with Wildemon.

"We are soooo fucked," Bordin said. "I think I need to just push the panic button and just shut it all down. Shit!!!!!!"

Hegas chewed thoughtfully on a piece of half-frozen pizza.

"Um, whatever, dude. You're the guy with *all* the experience."

Chapter 19

Anne tried to get Noah to go to bed, but he was having no part of it.

"Noooooooo.... Aunt Annie," he said. "Nooooooo.... I want Da first."

After not speaking a word for nearly a year, Noah had become a chatterbox, which had Anne alternately laughing, crying and wondering *again* about the future.

She and Cass and Jack had worked into a domestic routine that had become unnervingly comfortable for her. She missed the Walsh family home and land on Vashon Island, especially as winter grabbed New York by the throat. A few days before, when the sun came out for a half-hour between snow squalls, the clerk at the local supermarket told Anne to enjoy it.

"Last winter the sun stopped showing itself right about now and didn't come back until April," she said.

But now that Noah suddenly was speaking again and his hearing had come back, she was even more torn about whether to leave or stay.

And so is Cass, she thought. *Damn.*

The house phone rang just as she got Noah set up watching an old Sesame Street video. She expected it to be a call from Jack, but saw that it was Jack's editor Eli.

"Eli! Is the baby here?" Anne asked. "Jack told me Shania was due anytime."

"No," Eli said, sounding impatient. "Um, but thanks for asking," he quickly added. "But where's Jack? I tried his cell phone and he's not answering."

Anne watched Noah swaying to the music as the Sesame Street characters danced across the screen. She thought she heard him singing again, too.

"As far as I know, he and Cass are still at the Rockwell Valley party," Anne said. "One of your reporters, Keith, I think, is going to bring them home. With Oscar."

The phone went quiet for moment.

"Can you give me the cell phone for Cass?" Eli said. "I tried Keith, too, and he's not picking up. I need to warn them."

Anne stepped into the kitchen with the phone.

"Warn them about what?" she said.

"The gas storage," Eli said. "I got a call from someone who lives on the hill across the lake from the salt caverns. She said there's something going on with the lights and she thinks she can hear some kind of alarm. I don't think Keith should drive near it coming home."

Chapter 20

Retired professor Charles Avery Sawmill thought the barely visible mist creeping southward in uneven ripples, just inches above the surface of the lake was fog.

Coming on little cat's feet, he thought, smiling. *Just like Carl Sandburg said.*

The evening was so crisp and clear that he had moved from his warm living room out onto his enclosed lakeside porch a few miles north of Rockwell Valley. He marveled at the calmness of the water and the incredible sky with a full moon.

And there's enough bright stars to make the ancients happy, he thought.

He was wrapped tight in a wool blanket, sipping a Bombay gin martini and enjoying the silence, punctuated only by occasional blips of noise that had come from the Rockwell Valley Lakeside Hotel south of him, where he knew there was a big celebration. It was being put on by Grand Energy Services to commemorate the opening a few weeks before of its natural gas and liquid propane gas storage facility at the northern end of the lake.

Sawmill had opposed its approval, but like most of Rockwell Valley, he was resigned to the fact that they would have GES as a neighbor.

He did take some solace from a phone call earlier that day from Police Chief Melvin Caprino. The chief had called him to say that his officers would be arresting the man they thought had assaulted him at his home and most likely was also responsible for putting the kiddie porn on Sawmill's computer to try to ruin his reputation.

I am so tired, Sawmill thought. *Maybe it's time for bed.*

He stood to go inside and saw a boat headed up the lake running very fast, most likely the same small cabin cruiser he had seen heading south less than an hour before.

It sounded like the outboard belonging to a neighbor across the lake that he saw out fishing many mornings and with whom he occasionally chatted when the fellow ran his trolling lines near Sawmill's dock.

Wilbur? William? Sawmill thought.

He was near the doorway, heading into the house, when heard the sudden wail of a siren to the north shatter the night just as the fog came abreast of Sawmill's dock and just as the cabin cruiser and fog collided mid-lake.

Sawmill had his back to the water but saw a flash of light reflected in his porch windows, followed by a blast of searing heat on the back of his neck. A moment later a shockwave propelled him through the open doorway and into his house with such force it blew him through a partition wall between the living room and bedroom, depositing him onto the floor in a heap, as flames erupted all around.

Wilmot, Charles Avery Sawmill thought. *His name is Wilmot.*

Chapter 21

Every bone in Jack Stafford's newsman's body told him they should turn the car around and drive back into Rockwell Valley when they saw the brilliant flash of light coming from the direction of Rockwell Valley Lake several miles to the east.

The sound – like a distant peal of thunder – came a few seconds later.

But Cass – who was the most sober person in Keith Everlight's car and driving – simply said "No."

"Your son is speaking again, Jack. After a *year*. Noah is *talking*. Anne says he won't shut up. I will not let *you* get in harm's way, even if I have to get Oscar and Keith put you in the trunk of this car. We are going *home*."

The drove on in silence, working their way along a circuitous route through the Pennsylvania mountains that

Eli had suggested. It would keep them well away from the natural gas and LPG storage facility at the north end of the lake.

Eli said that a dozen different Rockwell Valley area volunteer fire departments were being called out, with a request for mutual aid out nearly 100 miles. A spokesman told Eli there had been an explosion but not at the gas storage facility itself. Dozens of cottages were burning along the lakeshore, and there were some small fires burning at the facility itself.

The state fire marshal had been consulted and was telling firemen to stay well back from the salt cavern storage until a special Grand Energy Services team from Texas could be flown in – 8 to 10 hours at least.

"Your only piece of equipment to fight this kind of fire is a good pair of binoculars," he told Eli.

It had been about the only light moment since the blast.

"Look, Cass. I understand what you're saying," Jack said. "But I have to go back there. I'm a newsman. This is the story we've been warning about ever since these assholes said they wanted to do this. It's happened. We can't just sit this out. Keith? A little help here?"

Keith just shook his head in the back seat without speaking. He was feeling so adrenalin-depleted from his encounter with Calvin Boviné he was nearly asleep.

Cass suddenly jerked the steering wheel to the right, pulling into a turnout off the highway.

Her face was covered in tears as she pounded the steering wheel hard several times.

"Damn you, Jack. Damn you. Damn you. *Damn you.*

"My sister Devon loved you so much she would have done anything for you. She gave her life protecting Noah. She gave her life protecting *your* son. And now you want to go charging into a burning building for what? For what? Eli is already handling this. That precious little boy loves you so much."

Cass plucked a handkerchief out of Jack's pocket and dried her tears.

"Remember the old Bible story about Lot's wife?" Cass said. "Well, we're not looking back – or going back."

She had barely finished her sentence when the second flash of light filled the sky from the same direction.

Chapter 22

The flash of the first explosion up the lake lit up the windows of the Rockwell Valley Lakeside Hotel with a blinding light, prompting screams from the crowded ballroom.

Some people moved towards the hotel exits. Most were stunned and just watched in awe as flames erupted along the shoreline.

The executive staff from Grand Energy Services stood speechless near the patio doors, all clustered around CEO Luther Burnside.

Burnside was still in shock from the arrest of Calvin Boviné and the police chief's warning.

Police Lt. Del Dewitt stood in the kitchen on the other side of the ballroom, remembering his boot camp instructor's words about explosions.

"If you *see* the flash and you're still *standing*, get your ass to *cover*."

And so by the time the actual shockwave rolled down the lake and hit, Dewitt, Police Chief Melvin Caprino, Alicia Caprino and a dozen guests who had been standing near the kitchen were huddled inside the walk-in refrigerator-freezer. Crammed in there too were the kitchen staff and the bartender, who had already been in the freezer, replenishing his ice supply.

Even with the heavy door closed tight, the sound of shattering glass was deafening. The electricity went out, plunging the freezer into complete darkness.

Several people fumbled with their telephones to light the inside of the freezer.

One woman was just getting her flashlight app on her phone working when a second, even louder explosion rocked the freezer, knocking a few people off their feet.

The people inside the freezer wouldn't know until the next morning that the second explosion was from the ignition of leaking natural gas bubbling up from the underwater pipeline right in front of the hotel.

Chapter 23

11 dead, 300 hurt in Rockwell Valley gas blasts – sabotage suspected

United News Service staff report

Fracking Justice

ROCKWELL VALLEY, Penn. – The twin blasts that took the lives of 11 people and injured as many as 300 others Saturday night might have been caused by saboteurs, Grand Energy Services officials claimed today.

In addition to the police and fire department investigation, GES, owner and operator of the newly built salt cavern gas storage facility at the north end of Rockwell Valley Lake, is conducting an internal probe into why several million gallons of liquid propane gas flowed out of caverns and down on to the lake surface. They are also investigating the cause of the natural gas pipeline leak in front of the Rockwell Valley Lakeside Hotel.

"The fail-safe systems of the facility were designed with the absolute highest state-of-the-art safety engineering protocols to prevent anything like this," Ida Merganser, acting president of Grand Energy Services told UNS. "We are looking into every possibility, including that these tragic explosions were the work of eco-terrorists who deliberately caused this. We've asked for federal help in our probe, too."

Merganser was named acting president in an emergency meeting of the board of directors of Grand Energy Services this morning in Flathead, Missouri.

Ms. Merganser is executive assistant and personal secretary to CEO Luther Burnside. Burnside is listed in critical condition at Rockwell Valley Hospital from injuries he sustained in the blast that nearly leveled the Rockwell Valley Lakeside Hotel.

Hospital officials said the majority of Burnside's injuries came from flying glass. A hospital source, who requested she remain anonymous, said Burnside had suffered as many as a thousand cuts from slivers of glass and is not expected to recover.

Seven other members of the executive staff were also critically injured in the blast. Three are missing, Merganser said.

Police also announced this morning that they had positively identified the remains of Rockwell Valley

> Mayor Will Pennisen, whose body was found crushed under a collapsed wall. Pennisen had been the administrative manager of the GES facility and oversaw construction of the salt cavern storage project.
>
> "As tragic as this event was, GES promises to rebuild and regain the confidence of the Rockwell Valley community," Merganser said. "It`s a matter of national security that we maintain our energy independence and not be defeated by setbacks like this."

Chapter 24

Cell phones with both still photos and video captured the horrors of the explosions in such graphic detail that Eli Gupta was having to edit almost all of them before publishing.

The photos and videos had flowed in to the *Horseheads Clarion*'s email like a tsunami after the explosions as Rockwell Valley citizens documented the fires and destruction in the wake of the two blasts.

A heavy December snowfall on Sunday made the scene even more eerie.

Eli had spent most of Sunday posting stories, pictures and videos on the *Clarion*'s website, generating so much Internet traffic it overwhelmed the newspaper's server twice.

Alice McCallis, who had been at Rockwell Valley Hospital when the blasts hit, had acted like a media photo department dispatcher, asking her fellow protesters to rush to the scene to chronicle what had happened.

"How much more video do you have, Eli?" Jack said. "And the stills. I hardly know what to put on the front page of Tuesday's paper."

The whole staff had come in Sunday to sort through the mountain of information coming in from Rockwell Valley.

As he had promised Cass, Jack stayed home in Horseheads but dispatched reporters to Rockwell Valley.

By Monday morning the news services were clamoring for more photos and videos from Saturday night.

Eli let out a loud whooping sound, a sound Jack knew signaled something significant.

"Let's watch this on the big screen in the conference room," he said. "The small computers can't do it justice."

Jack, Eli and Keith propped themselves up in the conference room while Eli showed video footage he had just received from a friend who had been the co-pilot in the helicopter hovering near the Rockwell Valley Hospital Saturday night.

"We did a feature on his air-ambulance service two years ago," Eli said.

The nose-mounted helicopter video camera had captured the eerie-looking fog floating on Rockwell Valley Lake and the sudden ignition of the liquid propane gas as it was ghosting southward on the surface.

The voices of the pilot, the co-pilot and two medical crewmen tending to the Ebola patient in the back were difficult to hear over the sound of the chopper's rotors, except for the string of epithets when the LPG ignited the firestorm that swept the lake and set cottages and trees on fire.

"Watch this as they drop onto the roof. You can see the fire has started. If they hadn't gotten down, they would have been knocked out of the sky," Eli said.

As it was, it was clear from the shaky image the shockwave did buffet the landed helicopter.

"Here's the miracle in all this, if you are looking for one," Eli said.

"That Ebola patient? They had just gotten him out of the chopper and inside the hospital when the second blast lit off. He and the crew could've been blown off the roof. The chopper slid right to the edge but didn't topple."

The helicopter's camera had captured the flames of the second blast, too.

"Let's get that video up on our website right away," Jack said. "And send the link out to our media friends. That's even more graphic than any of the other stuff we have."

Jack's cell phone beeped – a text from Rue Malish.

```
Sorry, but the FD says Prof.
Sawmill was killed in a fire at
his house. They found his body
this morning.
```

Chapter 25

```
From the Horseheads Clarion

Column One
Horseheads Clarion
```

Time for real apologies, reparations and community healing

By Jack Stafford

The name Rockwell Valley will now be remembered alongside San Bruno, Calif., Lac-Megantic, Quebec, Canada and perhaps even Bhopal, India.

What they all have in common is the terrible industrial-related disasters that killed people, injured many others and caused nearly unbelievable destruction of property.

And in each case, it was caused by a combination of corporate greed, sloppiness in applying safety standards and a business culture completely devoid of any concern for the health and welfare of workers and the communities in which the tragedies occurred.

In the case of Rockwell Valley, this newspaper had been asking questions - and demanding answers - ever since Grand Energy Services of Flathead, Missouri first proposed using the salt caverns to store natural gas and liquid propane gas.

The most charitable assessment by safety and gas storage experts – other than those on the GES payroll – was that this project was far too dangerous to operate safely and would be a ticking time bomb.

As you have probably read and seen on the *Clarion*'s website, in newspapers and national news reports, that bomb went off Saturday night, with a death toll of 11 persons at the moment. Many more people are in critical condition in hospitals stretching from Rockwell Valley to New York City to Cleveland and Pittsburgh. Many are not expected to survive.

One of those persons is Luther Burnside, CEO of GES and hailed just this month on the cover of a national business magazine as "The New Don of Natural Gas."

We take no pleasure in Burnside's horrible injuries. But it was his company's bypassing of safety regulations – and his refusal to install even the lowest of low-level industry standard safety monitors – that contributed greatly to this disaster.

He also used every chance to bypass expert inspections, follow long-established regulations or heed the constant warnings from citizens and noted scientists about the likelihood of what happened.

The explosions, the fires, the deaths, the injuries. They are all bad enough, each and of themselves.

But Grand Energy Services, in a breathtakingly craven display of greed, announced that it plans to rebuild its facility and reopen the salt caverns for natural gas and LPG storage.

That announcement came before all the corpses had even been removed from burned-out homes and businesses – and even as GES blast victims were still being shuffled from hospital to hospital to get the best life-saving treatments.

On its face, most rational people would think that given the nature of this tragedy – and the clear recklessness of GES that caused all this – that the thought of rebuilding would be so absurd, federal and state regulators would keel over laughing.

But they are silent because GES immediately waved the national security and "energy independence" flag.

And, perhaps not too surprisingly, the company is trying to shift the blame for the two explosions away from itself to unknown eco-terrorists.

The mood in the nation`s capitol unfortunately swings so much in favor of energy companies there is a small chance GES might get away it.

Might.

The *Horseheads Clarion* is going to do its best to ensure that the people of Rockwell Valley are not brushed aside after making such a huge sacrifice.

We will be watching very closely and we will continue to publish stories, photos and videos every step of the way.

It is reprehensible that even in the face of a tragedy of this magnitude, the company won`t admit its failings. This was a complete collapse of responsible action on the part of GES.

The Rockwell Valley community is owed sincere apologies, assurances of true safety (not something ginned up by the GES public relations machine), and most important, economic reparations for the loss of life and property.

What was once a thriving tourist community with a jewel of a lake for recreation is today a burned-out hulk that will require untold millions of dollars to rebuild.

Those untold millions should come directly from GES coffers – and quickly – not taxpayers.

Saddest of all, this entire disaster was completely avoidable.

Completely.

Jack Stafford is the publisher of the Horseheads Clarion *and publishes Column One every Friday. He can be reached at JJStafford@HorseheadsClarion.com.*

Chapter 26

Three months after the explosions that rocked Rockwell Valley, two large white tents – the kind most often seen at weddings – were filled with Rockwell Valley citizens and media, waiting for the start of a special Rockwell Valley Town Council meeting, held on the former site of Grand Energy Services salt cavern liquid propane gas and natural gas storage facility, down on the shore of the lake.

Several hundred people who couldn't get inside the tents crowded around the edges, straining to hear.

Newly elected Rockwell Valley Mayor Melvin "Bobo" Caprino sat at the council table from which he shot a quick wink at his ex-wife Alicia, who was sitting in the front row of the Rockwell Valley Town Council meeting, right next to Acting Police Chief Del Dewitt.

At the far end of the council table, newly elected council member Alice McCallis had a stack of papers and file folders ready for her presentation about a proposed ethics council – one of a series of good government initiatives McCallis and Caprino had teamed up on to present since being named to office in a special election held in the month after the explosions.

The first order of business, however, was agreeing to accept the deed to the land and salt caverns at the north end of Rockwell Valley Lake owned by Grand Energy Services.

GES had offered the land to the town, hoping to curry favor with the judge hearing its bankruptcy proceedings as well as the multi-billion dollar's worth of negligence claims filed against the company and its board of directors.

"Our acceptance of the property on which we are meeting is in no way even a partial *settlement* of our claim against GES for its gross negligence," Caprino said. "But taking it means no one – and I mean *no one* - is going to try to pull another gas storage stunt here. Ever."

Caprino's statement brought the crowd to its feet and it took a solid five minutes of clapping, cheering and whistling before it was quiet enough for Caprino to continue.

Initially Caprino and the newly elected members of the board considered accepting the property and selling all the valuable lakeside acreage to a developer.

But McCallis suggested that the upper reaches be set aside for affordable homes and possibly a senior housing project, with the shoreline reserved for a town park, a nature center and new public marina.

"Mr. Mayor, I'd like to make the motion to accept this land in the memory of all those who died last December," McCallis said.

The crowd broke into applause again with cheers, tears and whistling.

"Further, I would like add to the motion that the council name this park *Sawmill Shores*, in honor of our fallen friend."

The council vote was unanimous, and this time the cheering went on long enough that Mayor Melvin "Bobo" Caprino simply gaveled the meeting to a close.

"This meeting is adjourned, but the party to celebrate should begin," Bobo shouted, trying to get the crowd's attention.

Epilog

Eli Gupta sat on the huge veranda overlooking the sound between Seattle and Vashon Island.

He bounced his six-month-old daughter Nikki on one knee, simultaneously working his laptop computer keyboard one-handed on the other.

A warm, early June breeze was coming across the water to the Walsh property Jack Stafford had nicknamed "Tara" after the Southern plantation in *Gone With the Wind*.

Two months after the twin liquid propane and natural gas explosions in Rockwell Valley, Jack, Noah, Cass and Anne had packed up their Horseheads belongings and left in a caravan for Anne and Cass's 10-acre property on Vashon Island for an extended trip west to sort things out.

"When I took a leave of absence from this newspaper a few years ago, it was in the wake of a terrible gas-industry tragedy, too," Jack said in a speech at a packed going-away party at Oscar Wilson's Lakeside Winery on the east side of Seneca Lake in the Town of Hector.

"Maybe the severity of this disaster will cause states and the federal government to realize how out of control these corporations are. Maybe not. But the *Horseheads Clarion* isn't going to let GES or any other of these goddamned greedy companies get away with this kind of negligence. Not now. Not *ever*. Not as long as we have a dollar to print and get the stories out. We need to ask what kind of energy we want in our state. We need to demand it and that it be provided safely. It's time for leadership and forward thinking."

A week later, two cars and a 40-foot RV expertly piloted by Oscar Wilson headed cross-country, caravanning in a southerly route to avoid any spring snowstorms in the Midwest and the Rockies.

Oscar's RV was still in the driveway at Tara. After staying for a month and earning the nickname "Uncle O" from an adoring Noah, Oscar flew back to New York to run his winery.

Eli finished his email to Keith Everlight, asking him to assign a follow-up story on a federal investigation into Grand Energy Services' bribing of state inspectors in Texas, Oklahoma, Ohio and Pennsylvania.

The company's bankruptcy proceedings were running into trouble in the courts. The judges were feeling the heat of raging public opinion that GES shouldn't be allowed to simply hide behind the courts, as most of these accident-prone energy corporations had in the past.

A U.S. attorney in Ohio – where a GES gas pipeline exploded, killing two people in a public park barely a month after the Rockwell Valley disaster – was threatening to go after the entire board of directors of GES on federal charges of racketeering.

After rereading his email, Eli changed the salutation from "Keith" to a more formal greeting of "Keith Everlight, managing editor, the *Horseheads Clarion*." Then instead of

Epilog

using his normal signature of "Eli," he changed it to "Eli Gupta, Associate Publisher, the *Horseheads Clarion.*"

Eli's daughter Nikki had been born just two days after the explosions. Shania was already talking about a brother for Nikki.

Nikki had her father's same smooth brown skin but looked like she would have the shocking blonde hair Shania had sported since she was a baby.

Eli watched Jack and Noah walking up from the shoreline trailed by two dogs: Belle the Labrador and the Australian-Shepherd mix named Tokanga who had lived on Tonga with Jack, Devon and Noah. As soon as the caravan arrived at Vashon Island, Jack sent for Tokanga, prompting a memorable yipping, licking, frolicking airport reunion between the dog and Noah.

"Are you working, Eli?" Jack said. "Better not let Shania catch you. She said this is a vacation and you are *definitely* off duty."

Eli closed the laptop and shifted Nikki to his other knee.

"Off-duty with a six-month-old is an oxymoron, Jack. And as if *you* ever take any vacation time," Eli said. "Cass told me last night you have been working every day on your new book since we got here, even on Sundays."

Within weeks of the explosions in Rockwell Valley – and the unexpected announcement of the ban on hydrofracking in New York – Jack's book publisher asked him to write a book tentatively titled *Saving Pennsylvania: An Environmental and Economic Manual.*

"The book's going great, Eli. I thought I would need much longer to write it, but I should have a rough draft almost ready for the editor in a few weeks. The New York fracking ban is giving a lot of people hope in Pennsylvania. And a lot of ideas."

Eli bounced Nikki for a moment before speaking.

"So you will be back to the *Clarion* sooner maybe than you thought?"

This time Jack paused while he picked up a stick off the ground. He threw it towards the water, sparking a three-way race between Noah, Belle and Tokanga to fetch it, though the two dogs outpaced Noah quickly.

"Yes. Maybe in two months or so, though it won't affect our deal for you to handle the majority of the publishing chores. I'm thinking we should open a satellite office in Rockwell Valley. We can help rebuild the community. An office would show our commitment. We'll both be plenty busy."

Eli stared out at the water for a moment.

"I like the idea, Jack. But what about Noah? Will Cass or Anne come back with you to New York to help take care of him?"

Jack laughed. "Spoken like a true parent, Eli, especially with a newborn. I don't know right now. Honestly. Noah is really getting to be a handful. A four-year-old dynamo."

At the water's edge, Tokanga and Belle pounced on the stick Jack had thrown. But when Noah caught up he dove into the mix, grabbing the stick along with the two dogs and crashing to the ground in a three-way wrestling match.

"This place is really good for him," Jack said. "It's healthy. Safe. Lots of room to run. And it's been good for me, too. Particularly as a quiet place to write. We're still working out this family thing. Living with two sisters-in-law

Epilog

who have become surrogate mothers to your child is, well, *challenging*. But it sure helps to have all this space and three houses. Cass and Anne are great. I'm a lucky man."

Eli, Shania and Nikki were staying in the second largest of the three houses, a nicely appointed three-bedroom, two-bath unit dubbed "Devon" because it had been her favorite place growing up. Cass and her sister Anne lived in the large main house, nicknamed "The Manse." Jack and Noah had their bachelor quarters in a two-bedroom house that included a small, enclosed porch office where Jack set up a writing space with a Seattle skyline view.

Cass and Anne called Jack and Noah's place "Boys Town."

Jack had just thrown another stick down towards Belle, Tokanga and Noah when Cass, Anne and Shania came out onto the porch with platters loaded with pancakes, sausages, crescent rolls, fruit and steaming vegetables, a late/breakfast/early lunch mélange of food for everyone.

They sat down, Jack sitting at the head of the long table between Cass and Anne while Noah chased the dogs around the yard.

Anne and Cass had big smiles watching the boy-chase-dogs, dogs-chase-boy routine on the lawn.

Eli put Nikki into a high chair between himself and Shania. Then he stood and raised his orange juice glass.

"Um, this is a *happy* toast, not a sad one, okay?" Eli said. He received a huge groan in reply.

"No, no. I mean it. A happy toast. Really.

"It's to Devon. She was your sister. She was Jack's wife. And she was also *our* friend. She was a great friend to Shania and me. I know she's smiling, seeing all of us around this table at this place she loved, with all the people she loved. So, um, here's to Devon," he said raising his glass.

Anyone watching without hearing might have thought Eli had just delivered some *awful* news, based on the expressions and sudden welling up of tears from everyone around the table.

Then Jack stood up to offer his own toast as Noah jumped into his chair next to Jack.

"I second that toast and want to raise it a notch. Maybe several notches," Jack said.

"When I lost Devon, I thought my life was over. Done. Devon had come in to my life when I was still grieving for my first wife. Devon saved me with her love and by giving us this little guy."

Jack paused for a second to ruffle Noah's hair.

"Then I got saved again. This time by all of you, after Cass dragged me back here. I don't know what the future holds, really. We have the newspaper in New York and this great life here, too. Really, the older I get, the less I'm sure of sometimes. But I do know with such good friends and such good family that things are going to be okay. That sounds pretty inadequate for what I'm feeling right now."

The sound of Tokanga barking loudly at the water's edge interrupted Jack's toast, drawing everyone's attention to the sound.

Close to shore a pod of a dozen black-and-white killer whales was cavorting, leaping into the air, a sight Jack has seen several times from his writing porch office in the last few months.

"Devon and Noah and I used to watch the whales right off our shore in Tonga almost every day," Jack said. "They

Epilog

were humpbacks in Tonga. Much bigger. But it was kind of, well, life affirming to see them. Magnificent, just like these creatures. Noah always wanted to swim out to them, even as a toddler. He would have, if Tokanga hadn't always grabbed him by the diaper to pull him back."

The pod had just started moving off when the spell was broken by the sound of a spoon banging loudly on the table.

Everyone turned and saw Noah looking impatiently at his plate, the platters of food out of his reach.

"Da. I'm hungry," Noah said, pointing his spoon at the platter of pancakes. He rapped the spoon on the table a few more times.

Cass reached for the platter and held it in the air next to Noah's plate, waiting.

After a moment of staring down at the table, Noah finally whispered "please," followed by another pause while Cass held two child-size pancakes on a serving fork above his plate.

"Please. Please *Aunt Cassie*," Noah finally said loudly, earning not only the pancakes but a solid kiss on his cheek from Cass.

Cass put the platter down and looked at Jack.

"Did you want to finish that toast now that the whale show is over?" she asked.

Jack smiled.

"I think you and Noah just did it for me," Jack said.

#####

A NOTE ABOUT THE AUTHOR

Michael J. Fitzgerald is a daily newspaper columnist who has been writing about politics and the environment for decades. He first learned about hydrofracking when he retired to New York and saw *No Fracking* signs posted in yards around the county, erroneously assuming the signs were a reference to the television program *Battlestar Gallactica*. Since then he's become an expert eco-political reporter, writing about how decisions are being made in regards to science and energy. Four years after his return to his New York roots, hydrofracking was banned in New York State.

Fitzgerald worked as a writer and editor for six daily newspapers in California and is now a columnist for the daily *Finger Lakes Times* newspaper in Geneva, New York. He has published hundreds articles and photos in regional and national magazines.

He is a professor emeritus of Journalism at California State University, Sacramento. He grew up on the shores of Lake Chautauqua in New York and is married to journalist Sylvia Fox.

Michael J. Fitzgerald is available for selected readings and lectures. To inquire about a possible appearance or speaking engagement, please contact him through his website at authormichaeljfitzgerald.com.

If you are interested in new releases or speaking engagements or bonus material provided by the author, please visit the author's website at authormichaeljfitzgerald.com and sign up for his newsletter.

Also by Michael J. Fitzgerald

The Fracking War (Mill City Press, 2014)

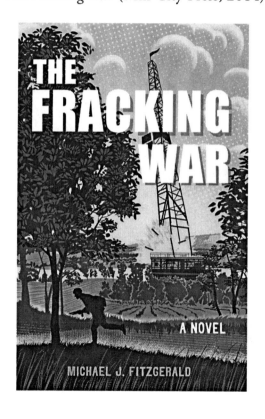

Praise for *The Fracking War,*
the first book in the series by Michael J. Fitzgerald.

"It was Uncle Tom's Cabin, not economic data, that turned the page on slavery. It was *The Grapes of Wrath*, not demographic reports, that opened a nation's eyes to Dust Bowl dislocation. Out of that tradition comes Michael J. Fitzgerald's *The Fracking War*. Here within a smoldering crucible of social crisis is a tale of power, money, fateful choice and consciences aroused. If you like your drill rigs served up within the context of a fast-moving plot line, you've got what you want right in your hands."

Sandra Steingraber, biologist, environmental activist and author of *Living Downstream* and *Raising Elijah*.

"If you thought the debate over energy policy was a tad dry, this novel might change more mind. God hope it never comes to this!"

Bill McKibben, founder, 350.org and author of *Eaarth: Making a Life on a Tough New Planet.*

CPSIA information can be obtained
at www.ICGtesting.com
Printed in the USA
FFOW05n1059280515